Frat House Secrets

Guilty Pleasures Editions, Volume 5

Romeo Preminger

Published by Romeo Preminger, 2022.

FRAT HOUSE SECRETS

First edition. December 5, 2022.

Copyright © 2022 Romeo Preminger.

ISBN: 978-1737878070

Written by Romeo Preminger.

Chapter One

WHEN I STARTED freshman year at New Jersey State University, I hadn't planned to end up in the middle of a sex and murder scandal. So like sure, nobody plans for that to happen, but my point is, back in high school, I was a really, *really* boring person. If they had the category in the yearbook, I probably would've been voted Least Likely to Get into a Sex and Murder Scandal.

I was a straight B student. I drove my dad's Hyundai Elantra, and it was so old, it didn't even have Bluetooth or a phone charger. I never went over the speed limit, I stopped for yellow lights, and I always let drivers make a left turn in front of me. I basically hung out with my friend, Gary, who lived across the street and was the only boy who dreaded gym class as much as I did, and Kathleen, who sat next to me in band. She played first piccolo, and I played second. My social life consisted of band practice, Friday study night at Denny's with Gary and Kathleen, and playing *Guild Wars* with my online friends. I didn't drink, smoke, vape or do weed, and I was a virgin. When I came out as gay to Gary and Kathleen, two days after graduation, Gary told me, "Y'know, that's probably the only interesting thing about you. Congrats." I was basically invisible, and I'm not even exaggerating. Sometimes my teachers would look at me funny and ask if I was new to class. It was *that* bad.

Everything was going to change when I went away to college. I was going to reinvent myself and stop being the guy who sat on the sidelines watching everyone else have a life. My mom and dad thought I should consider a small, private college, but I was dead set on New Jersey State. Besides the fact it was the only school that accepted me into a health sciences program, they had 70,000 frickin' students! That had to give me the best odds of meeting people with whom I had things in common and to make a ton of friends. I was ready to be myself around kids who didn't know me from high school. I was *so* ready to find a boyfriend, I'd run probability calculations on it. Thirty-two thousand students at the university were men, and going conservatively, if five percent of them were gay, that was sixteen hundred potential guys to date. There were less students in my hometown's two high schools combined. My new college life was going to be epic.

But it totally didn't start that way.

As soon as my parents drove off and left me alone on campus, I started feeling like I was having a heart attack. Stepping off the sidelines and meeting people sounded great in theory, but now that I actually had to do it, I couldn't get air into my lungs and my legs were giving out. Kids in the dorm were going room to room to introduce themselves and make plans to meet up for dinner and go to parties. I just wanted to hide. I had no idea how to act around people. I was sure everyone was going to think I was stupid. The university had a huge list of activities for orientation week, but I couldn't leave my room. I was spiraling big time with anxiety. Every time I tried to work up the courage to venture out and talk to people, I stopped myself because I thought everyone was going to laugh at me. I was the lame-ass kid who hadn't made any friends.

In my head, I'd pictured becoming insta-besties with my roommate, and we'd do the orientation thing together. Well, I got Shawn Hurley. He was six foot two, blond-haired, blue-eyed, at least two hundred pounds, and from some town in Indiana I'd never heard of. It didn't seem possible we were the same age and gender. His first question to me was: "What sports do you play?"

I play ping-pong occasionally. My grandparents have a table in their basement. And one of my Sims' ex-boyfriends is a European soccer player. He kind of lost interest after a while, but my Sim put up a soccer net in the backyard in case he comes back.

I had the sense to not say any of that out loud. Instead, I smoothly mumbled I'd been so busy with school, I hadn't gotten around to sports. Shawn got the picture and found some brahs down the hall to hang out with. He must've started sleeping in someone else's room because I rarely saw him, which in a way was a huge relief. Later that week, we crossed paths in the dorm. He was swaggering down the hall with four dudes who were just as big and built, and they smirked at each other as they passed by. I was sure Shawn told them what a hopeless wuss I was.

Classes hadn't even started, and I was ready to call my parents and beg them to let me come home. I didn't fit in. I'd never fit in. What kind of loser spends orientation week locked up in his dorm room? My social failure at high school was happening all over again. At least I'd tried. Some people aren't cut out to go away to school. I'd be fine taking classes at the community college in town, and maybe I'd get through life with a job that wasn't public-facing, like a lab technician or a billing clerk at a hospital, though I sucked at math. As for finding a boyfriend, that seemed pretty hopeless, but I could try to cultivate a relationship with someone on Twitter so long as we never had to actually meet. Kathleen said I was good with emojis.

This was all seriously depressing.

I gave myself a twenty-four hour waiting period before making the call to my mom, and the next morning I noticed an email in my inbox from the LGBTQ Alliance. I'd forgotten that before I moved to campus, back when I had a shred of self-belief, I filled out a sign-up form to get their announcements. The email was a reminder for their welcome meet-up that night. I read it three times and paced around my dorm room. Then, I told myself: *Ethan, grow some balls and go to the damn meeting.*

My balls didn't cooperate, still burrowing inside my body for dear life, but I pushed myself to head over to the student union that Friday night. It was terrifying. I never went to anything alone. I'd only come out to Gary, Kathleen, my mom and dad, and my older brother, Tim. And as for meet-ups, I was horrible at unstructured activities. Introducing myself to strangers? Truly, I wasn't sure if I could do it without fainting or possibly vomiting on someone. But that email felt like a lifeline I needed to grab. Worst case scenario, I'd get my parents to drive up that weekend, move back home, and I'd never have to show my face to anyone at New Jersey State again. I found the stairwell to the second floor of the student union, and I stumbled into the meeting room.

Thirty, maybe forty people were chatting in noisy clusters. Vertigo gripped me, but I managed to take three deep breaths, step over to a welcome table, and write my name on a name tag. My hand was trembling so bad, it looked like it had been written by a five-year-old. A pair of young women at the table nodded to me encouragingly, and I turned around to face the room.

The room blurred and started spinning. Little by little, I made my way back toward the door. I was thinking if I did things very *slowly*, like those gecko lizards you see on nature shows, sneaking up on prey, people wouldn't notice I was running away like a coward.

I don't know how long I'd been inching in that direction when I noticed an Asian kid who appeared to be doing the same thing. Our eyes met. He smiled, and then screwed his face up with concern.

"Do I look as nervous as you? Because the veins in your face are showing. You okay?"

I glanced at him twice but said nothing.

He looked at my name tag. "*Ne-Va-Mm-I-E*. Is that Nevil? Or Numanji?"

I realized I'd slapped my name tag on upside down. I couldn't form words.

"I'm Jayson," he said. "That's short for Juan-Fernandez Jayson de la Cruz Ramirez. My parents wanted to make my life as complicated as possible. It's a Filipino thing."

I peeled off my name tag. "I'm Ethan." I balled up the sticker in my fist and kind of rocked in place. I really, really didn't want to be a spaz, but obvs, I wasn't doing so well.

"Are you a freshman?"

"Uh-huh."

Jayson's face lit up. "Me too. It's kind of mortifying, right? Like I thought it was a good idea to sign up for a quadruple suite on North Campus. Y'know, it increases the likelihood you'll actually make some friends." He wrung his hands. "Not for me. Two of the guys did pre-freshman summer together, and they're inseparable. All they do is play ultimate Frisbee and talk about their Dream League football teams. The kid I share a room with told me he never met anyone Chinese. When I said I was Filipino, he looked at me like I was lying to him. I think he's scared of catching the 'China Virus.' He sprays down the bathroom with sanitizer every time I use it, and he puts his name on all his dishes, cups and silverware with a Sharpie."

I guffawed. We didn't have many Asian students in my high school, but even I knew the difference between China and the Philippines. I found myself loosening up, and I told him about Shawn Hurley.

"Straight guys are the worst, right?" he said. "Oh, no offense. I shouldn't have assumed. The meeting invite said the group is open to allies."

I'm pretty sure Jayson was being P.C. while having little doubt I fit somewhere under the rainbow umbrella.

"I'm gay," I told him. My face burned up, but that felt surprisingly good to say. "I've never met anyone else who is. Unless you count some YouTubers I follow. Which totally doesn't count, and I don't even know why I said that."

"YouTubers kind of count," Jayson said. "Who do you follow?"

"Connor Pyke. Raymond and Armando."

"Travel vloggers. Are you like into traveling?"

I snorted and blushed. Connor posted videos hiking shirtless through national parks, and Raymond and Armando were this beautiful couple who vlogged while globe-trekking to places like Thailand and Nepal. "I just think they're cute."

"That's totes legit," Jayson said. "I fan-gurl a dozen guys on Instagram. And I basically have to lock myself in my room and close the drapes to open up my Twitter feed. It's *that* gay. Once I tapped it on by accident while I was in line at 7-Eleven, and the woman behind me literally covered her daughter's eyes and rushed her out of the store." He looked at me sidelong. "Is this your first time coming out?"

"No. Well sorta. Here at college. I came out to my friends and family this summer. I thought it would be easier being away from home, but it's not." I peeked at him to see if he was ready to move along to talk to someone less pathetic. He didn't budge. "How about you?"

Jayson blushed, adorably. "I bet you wouldn't know from looking at me, but yeah, this is my first time coming out to a group of people. But I was in drama club so everyone kind of knew. I used to break out in numbers from *Hamilton* in the middle of the cafeteria, and I had an autographed photo of Lea Michele in my locker. But I told my parents the girls I was hanging out with were my girlfriends. If they knew I was gay, they'd probably ship me off to live with my mom's family in Manila to straighten me out. Anyway, I never said anything to my friends at school, and I guess no one had the guts to ask."

That sounded kind of serious. I told him, "I had a fake girlfriend in eleventh grade."

"Is she your bestie now?"

"Yeah." Everyone at school assumed Kathleen and I were in a relationship. We'd gone to prom together, but we'd always been platonic friends.

"I think that's how it works. I had this *thing* with Kenya Reynolds when we were in the cast of *Mamma Mia*, but it just morphed into a friendship. She helped me with my makeup when I dressed up as Elsa for the Halloween dance."

I stared at him for a moment, trying to picture it. Jayson had high cheekbones and probably the prettiest face I'd ever seen on a guy. I could imagine him pulling off Elsa from *Frozen* really well. "Where are you from?"

"California. A little town called Encinitas. That's near San Diego. What about you?"

"Lancaster, Pennsylvania."

Jayson clasped his mouth dramatically. "Are you Amish?"

"No."

"I watched every season of *Return to Amish*. I'm kind of obsessed."

"I'm not Amish."

"And I once just *randomly* found this Amish porn channel on XTube. You know about it? Well, it didn't look all that authentic, actually. They probably film it in the San Fernando Valley." He studied me. "You know, you kind of look like one of the actors. Are you, like, excommunicated?"

I snort-laughed. "I'm *not* Amish." I could've told him he was being as presumptuous as his roommate. Lancaster is a small city, but it's really diverse and pretty much like any modern town in America. It's not like everyone has a horse-led wagon to get around. But I had the feeling Jayson was going to tease me about being Amish one way or another, and I totally didn't mind. He didn't mean it in a bad way, and he was really funny.

"All right. So, what do you do for fun in Lancaster, Pennsylvania?"

"Not much." I grinned nervously. "I'm probably the most boring person you ever met. I played the piccolo in band and spent a lot of time gaming."

"What's your favorite game?"

"*Sims 4.*"

Jayson got that excited look on his face again. "Mine too. Tell me about your Sims' husband."

I hadn't even told Gary and Kathleen about that, but I found myself spilling everything that night. "His name's Alexander. He's a landscape architect. I figured, like that's kind of practical. We've got a koi lily pond and one of those garden mazes in the front lawn."

"Hawt."

"What about yours?"

"He's in a throuple. It was a quad for a while, but James, he's a backup dancer on a show in Vegas, and he ran off with an acrobat from Cirque de Soleil, so it's just the three of us, for now. Viggo and Dmitri. Viggo's into extreme sports, and Dmitri flips houses and has a personal training gig on the side." He smiled to himself. "My virtual reality is a lot better than my reality. Here I am on a Friday night, with the timer on my phone, recording how long I can take it until I bail on being around LGBTQ people in real life. I have to report back to my therapist."

I gaped at him. It was a combination shock and admiration gape. I wished I'd thought about setting the timer on my phone.

"I have complex trauma from minority stress and social anxiety. What about you?" Jayson said.

"I don't have a therapist. But I think I definitely have social anxiety."

Jayson scanned the meeting room. "So, what're we going to do? Hang out here like wallflowers or take the plunge and start meeting people? Just so you know, I'm totes chill with either."

I glanced at the crowd in the middle of the room. Everyone looked friendly, but my vertigo was coming back again.

"How about this?" Jayson said. "We'll work the room together. And if either one of us feels like he's having a panic attack, we'll use a safe word." He bounced in excitement. "Listen, this is my favorite one." He put on his acting charms. "Hey, Ethan. We better FaceTime with Aunty Elphaba before she turns in for the night." He beamed at me like it was genius. "What do you think?"

I chuckled. "We're not related. Why would we both have to FaceTime with Aunty Elphaba? Why Elphaba? Is that even a name?"

Jayson stared at me wide-eyed. "You never saw *Wicked*?"

I slowly shook my head.

"Idina Menzel? Kristen Chenoweth?" He pouted. "We'll have to do something about that. Anyway, it's the perfect signal. C'mon."

Jayson led me over to the other students, and we totally, actually talked to people. The two of us became BFFs after that night.

We didn't have any classes together. I was in the health sciences program, and he was a business major. Jayson had wanted to do theatre arts, but his parents were really strict. They gave him a choice of either majoring in pre-med or business, and he thought he might be able to at least do something creative in the advertising side of his degree. I told him I wanted to get into the physician assistant program after my sophomore year.

So, even though we were studying completely different things, every day after classes, we met up for dinner at the dining hall. On weekends, we studied at the library and at night, we caught the bus to go downtown to get bubble tea and walk around the outdoor mall. When we got back to campus, we staked out a spot in the quad and told each other stories about growing up, our biggest hopes, and our deepest fears. Pretty soon, it was like we'd known each other forever.

Sometimes Jayson busted out with show tunes, which was kind of awkward at first, but he's got a great voice. He didn't turn me into a 'Broadway Baby' as he called it, yet. But I do know *Wicked* now, and *Hamilton*, and *Frozen*, and *Dear Evan Hanson*, and *Come From Away*, and *Rent*, and yup, he made me watch a lot of musicals on his laptop. We always had a blast hanging out.

Jayson wasn't like any friend I ever had. Part of that was because he's gay like me, and maybe a little part was the fact I never had an Asian friend. But it's not like he was *so* different from me in most ways. We both played *Sims 4*, and we grew up watching all the same TV shows, and we both had the biggest crush on the same actor in *Riverdale*. I could talk to Jayson about anything. He was just super cool and super funny, and I was kind of in awe of him because Jayson was so *Jayson*, and he didn't care what other people thought of him.

There were some things we didn't have in common, actually. His dad owned a dry cleaning franchise, and his mom was the director of a nursing unit at a hospital. He went to Catholic schools, and he'd been to New York City a half dozen times and the Philippines and London. My dad drove a truck for a lumber company, and my mom worked in customer service at a health insurance company. They never had money to take me and my older brother anywhere besides the amusement park forty-five miles from town, and two summers, we took day trips to the Jersey Shore.

Jayson was also a total fashionista. He wore designer brands I never heard of. I did my once a year back-to-school shopping at Old Navy and Target. But Jayson wasn't snobby. He told me he liked my camo jacket and my striped socks. He also said I could borrow anything from his closet. I had my eye on one of his oversized print cardigans. I was two inches taller, two inches wider in the waist, and wider in the shoulders and longer in the arms, but I still thought I could pull off his sweater.

Now, in case you're getting the wrong idea about where this story is headed, Jayson's totally adorable with his sculpted, brush-up hair, his dimpled smile, and his crazy way of saying whatever's on his mind. But we're strictly friends. *All right*. We tried making out once, and let's just say it confirmed what both of us were feeling. We're gay besties, or sisters, as Jayson calls it. That's actually what I needed more than anything.

As the semester moved along, we went to weekly LGBTQ Alliance meetings, but other than that, we weren't doing so well at making other friends. Together, we were less shy around people, but we were still shy, and both of us were kind of feeling things out at school. Since Jayson didn't get along with his suitemates, we ended up in my dorm room most nights. Shawn was always somewhere with his jock friends. It worked out perfectly. Jayson and I got a lot of studying done without any interruptions. My health sciences courses were pretty serious, and I had Bio 101 and English Lit in my first semester.

One night, after we knocked off from studying, Jayson climbed up with me to my loft bed to look at videos of the YouTubers I follow. Not long into it, I could tell his attention was slipping away.

"So, you never did anything with a guy before?" Jayson asked.

"I told you that." Then I remembered something I hadn't told him. It was really lame, but I'd already shared just about every lame story about me, including when I was a sophomore and had a crush on a senior Jamie Kilpatrick. We walked the same route home after school, and I was so scared he'd be grossed out by me, I started taking the long way home.

"Last year, Kathleen hosted the band party after the Christmas concert. A group of us stayed late in her basement, and we played truth or dare. I got dared to kiss this kid, Perry Struebel, and we had to do it in front of everybody for like one full minute."

Jayson nudged closer. His eyes were twinkling. "How was it?"

Just thinking about it had me feeling warm inside. "Really good. But Perry is totally straight. He just went along with it to be funny. For me, when we did it, I knew *that* was what I wanted." I wriggled my toes, remembering. I turned to Jayson. "What about you?"

Now he was the one getting red in the face. "I never told anyone about it, but I kinda had this thing with a boy from Drama Club. Gil

Veracruz. We used to sneak off at cast parties and make out in the closet." He laughed. "Like literally in the closet."

He was making me giggle. "Like just make out? Or more?"

"I never had his penis in my mouth, if that's what you're wondering." He hid his face. It was killing me how cute he was when he got all discombobulated. To torture him some more, I kept staring at him.

"Okay, so there were some hands below the waist. *Over the clothes*. And once we parked behind a movie theater, and we went a little farther, and we both came in our underwear."

We burst out laughing like fools. I know it sounds totally juvenile, but that's just how we were together.

Jayson went on. "Gil said he was straight, and it was just something we were doing now and then. The summer after junior year, he started dating Monica Benedetti, and he wasn't interested in hooking up in closets anymore."

I felt for him, though I was kind of jealous. At least Jayson had done things with another boy.

I bumped my shoulder against his. "How 'bout this? We both find boyfriends this year. But we swear we'll stay friends no matter what. No ghosting each other." I thought of something else important. "And we always tell each other who we're interested in so we'll never break up as friends over some guy."

Jayson smiled. But as he thought things over, that smile faded. "You'll have no problem. I don't know about me."

That was totally weird because I was thinking the exact opposite thing. "Why would you say that?"

"You're the type guys go for. I might as well be invisible."

"That's so not true." My voice was squeaking. "I've never even been with a boy. How am *I* the kind of person they go for?"

"Ethan, at least two guys at the Alliance are crushing on you."

"Who?"

"Abe and Rashid. Tell me you didn't notice."

I hadn't. Actually, my mind was blown. Abe was this artsy kid who silk screened his own T-shirts. Rashid was a dancer in the fine arts program and also the secretary in the Alliance. I didn't think I'd talked to either of them for more than two minutes.

"You totally didn't notice," Jayson said with a laugh. "You're too much, Ethan. Or maybe that's the best way to play the game. Get guys interested by acting like you don't notice they're interested."

"I don't have a strategy. Believe me. I have absolutely no idea how to be around gay guys. Like, how do you even become boyfriends in the first place?"

Jayson grabbed my laptop. "We'll ask Reddit."

I stopped him. "Wait. You never explained why you think you'll have a harder time finding a boyfriend."

He looked at me crookedly. "I'm a Gaysian twink. Besides old white guys, there's not much of a market for us."

I didn't know what to say to that. I mean, *I* thought a lot of guys would probably find Jayson attractive. But if that was his experience, I didn't want to negate it. "Abe kind of scares me. He's so quiet. And Rashid's nice. He's just a bit too femme for me."

Jayson scowled. "You're femme-shaming him?"

"No. I don't think so. Was I? I mean, there's nothing wrong with being femme."

He laughed. "I'm just teasing you. But that's what I'm talking about. For guys like me and Rashid who are a little extra, it's harder dating. The gay community is really masc-oriented."

I got what he was saying, though I'd never felt all that masculine myself. That had been my hang-up all my life. I felt like boys didn't like me because I'm too girly. I can't throw any kind of ball, I hate sweating, and I'm completely awkward and self-conscious around guys. But I could see, compared to Jayson, I looked more masculine on the outside even if I was an insecure mess on the inside. For the first time, we reached a subject I wasn't quite comfortable talking about with Jayson. I don't know why. I changed the subject.

"I bet there's guys in the Alliance who want to date you." I remembered something. "What about Joon?"

Jayson rolled his eyes. "Why? Because we're both Asian?"

I burned up in the face. I was putting my foot in my mouth left and right. "I didn't mean it like that. The two of you talked after the meeting last week. I think he's good-looking. And he seems really nice."

"We talked because we've both got a paper due in Western Civ."

We were silent for a while. I felt like a total jerk.

"I'm sorry. It came out of my mouth without thinking. That was totally uncool. Can you forgive me?"

Jayson nodded. "Yeah. It's not a big deal. But for the record, I've never been attracted to Asian guys. My therapist says it's some kind of deep-seated, self-hating thing. But I think it's just how I'm wired. I grew up around all you white boys, so who else am I supposed to be attracted to?"

"So, is there anyone you're interested in?"

He hesitated for a couple beats, but then he couldn't hold back. "There's this boy in my communications class. Trevor Aberdale."

I could see the stars in his eyes.

"We're paired up for an interviewing assignment. He's this gorgeous, preppy kid from Connecticut, and I have to stop myself from staring at him."

I smiled because I could picture it.

"But I'm, like, ninety-nine percent sure he's straight. I think I weirded him out talking about Broadway shows."

"Maybe he's just shy. You could ask him if he wants to do something after class."

Jayson sighed. "I guess."

"If he turns you down, it's his loss." I peeked at him. "Jayson, you're the coolest, *hawtest* person I know. Did I ever tell you that before?"

He smiled and laughed. I smiled and laughed. We spent the rest of the night talking about boys and googling kids we're into.

Chapter Two

GOING AWAY TO college was turning out to be awesome. I made a great friend, and I was doing things besides going to classes and hiding in my room to play video games. I'm not talking about big, impressive things. Jayson and I didn't get invited to any parties, and we always grabbed the same two-person table in the dining hall, near the door to the kitchen. We talked about boys who caught our eyes, but neither one of us had the guts to talk to them. For me, though, just having a friend to hang out with was a huge deal. We texted each other all day long. Whenever one of us was freaking out about our classes, we talked the other down from the ledge.

Unfortunately, the LGBTQ Alliance imploded that semester. We were planning an event for National Coming Out Day, and a tense conversation blew up when some of the students wanted to use the word "womyn" on the flyers and others insisted it erased the identities of non-binary individuals. Other people objected to overshadowing Indigenous People's Day and Hispanic Heritage Month. Jayson and I stayed out of the fray like we always did, but half the people stormed out of the meeting, calling the executive board a bunch of transphobic, cultural imperialists. I was learning that the LGBTQ community was complicated. The group suspended meetings while the board worked on a new mission statement and bylaws.

One Wednesday when Jayson and I both had a midday break between classes, we met for lunch at the dining hall. Lunchtime was crazy in the student union. I usually avoided it and got a bagel at the coffeeshop in the basement of the sciences building or skipped lunch completely. But that day, I convinced Jayson to brave the crowds and use our meal plans since money was tight until I got my first work-study check from the bookstore. Leaving the dining hall, we had to walk through the student union mezzanine, which was filled with tables for Greek Week.

Greek Week is when fraternities and sororities try to recruit freshmen. The floor was packed with brahs in baseball caps and girls with blond highlights and lots of eye makeup. It was totally not our scene, and we were having trouble weaving through the masses just to get out of the student union. I spotted Shawn with his jock friends chatting up the Zeta Kappa Epsilon table, aka 'Zeke,' which I'd heard was the football frat. I looked in the other direction, and my gaze landed on a guy with thick, sandy hair, and a face and a body that made me part my lips in a full jaw drop.

He was one of the frat people behind a table. I pulled my eyes away. The guy was seriously hawt as Jayson liked to say, but there was so much testosterone in that crowded hall, I was fearful I'd get caught looking and a mob of brahs would beat the living shit out of me.

Disastrously, we had to sidestep a little closer to the table to get by a knot of people in the middle of the hall. Then even more disastrously, I couldn't help myself from giving the frat guy a second look. He caught it, smiled, and waved me over. Or did he? I glanced around, thinking he had to be looking at someone else. While I idled in terror, Jayson took account of things, and the frat guy called out: "Hey, whassup?" Jayson turned to me curiously. No part of my body was working, including my brain, so I wasn't much help.

Jayson pulled me along by the arm, and I was face-to-face with the gorgeous dude in his lettered jersey. I was sure he was only being friendly so he could turn around and make fun of me.

He reached out his hand. "How's it going? I'm Oliver." I managed a firm bro handshake. "You guys looking to rush? Or have you already decided on your top choices?"

I don't know what he saw when he looked at me, but I thought it was pretty obvious I was the kind of person who cowered from the sight of Greek letters. Meanwhile, I'd never touched the hand of anyone that attractive, and I was worried anything that came out of my mouth would be three octaves too high. Jayson filled in.

"We were just passing through." He coughed out an awkward chuckle. "We're not exactly fraternity types."

Oliver nodded. "I see you, man. You've got lots of options for student life. The Greek community's not for everyone. But have you heard about Tau Alpha Theta?" He introduced two dudes who were standing with him. "This is Dom and Luis. They rushed last year."

I'd been so painfully aware of Oliver, I hadn't even noticed the other people behind his table. Jayson introduced himself and shook hands with the guys. I followed along, mumbling my name. All three of them were super friendly and encouraging. We'd either gone through a wormhole and entered some bizarro dimension, or the guys were playing an elaborate joke.

"Tau is the bomb, dudes," Dom said.

"It's a life-changer, for real," Luis added.

I noticed something that sent things even farther into cray-cray territory. Luis was wearing a little rainbow pin below the collar of his Greek letter T-shirt.

"So, tell us about yourselves," Oliver said. "What are you guys into?"

I let Jayson field that one. He twisted up his mouth. "Well, we met at the LGBTQ Alliance during orientation week." He squirmed and wrung his hands. "We game. I was big into drama club in high school. I've got a tiny obsession with Broadway. I've seen *Wicked* eighteen times. Three in New York, ten in Los Angeles, and all five nights when the traveling company came to San Diego."

I was beet red for both of us. Oliver and his friends didn't look like gamers or Broadway fans. They were seriously cut-up like they had to be in training year-round for some sport or the other. But nobody laughed or rolled their eyes. In fact, they smiled.

"I used to be obsessed with *Final Fantasy*," Dom said. "I'm a computer science major, which keeps me pretty busy nowadays. But we've got all the systems at the house: XBox, Playstation, Nintendo Switch."

Oliver gave Luis a playful squeeze on the shoulder. "Luis here steals the show on Karaoke night." He chuckled. "And every time he takes a shower."

That was suggestive enough to get me breaking out with a cold sweat. Vertigo had started creeping up on me again, but from the look on Jayson's face, we weren't going anywhere.

"If you were stranded on a desert island with just one Broadway soundtrack, what would it be?" he asked.

"Oh, that's easy," Luis said. "*In The Heights*, hands down."

Jayson's eyes popped. Then he quietly glanced around. "You guys aren't your typical fraternity, are you?"

Oliver beamed. "That's what I've been trying to tell you, Jayson. We welcome all kinds of quality men. Our mission is to build a more inclusive society." He glanced at me. "We've done a lot of work with the LGBTQ Alliance to raise awareness. We actually were the first fraternity in North America to prohibit anti-gay discrimination. And TAT was raising money for Marriage Equality-New Jersey years before the Supreme Court decision."

Jayson scrunched up his brow. "So, you're a *gay* fraternity?"

"We're gay and straight." Oliver smiled. "And everything in-between."

I watched Jayson's face lift and fall. "Is there a height requirement?"

The guys laughed in a good-natured way. "No height requirement. We've got brothers of all body types."

Dom smiled at us. "Oliver intimidated the fuck out of me when I first met him last year. Some of us are into physical fitness as a lifestyle thing, but you can bet by five o'clock Friday, even Oliver ditches his alcohol and sugar-free diet."

"And we've got the best live-in cook on campus," Luis said. "You can say goodbye to shitty dining hall food for the rest of your life."

This was all sounding so compelling, but I was wondering if it was too good to be true. Sharing a house with gay men who looked like fitness models and didn't care I was a dweeb? Like, there had to be a catch. And possibly a hidden camera.

Oliver handed us a pair of glossy postcards. "Come by our party this Friday. You'll meet the other brothers. No pressure. You can decide for yourself if we're the kind of organization you want to be a part of."

The postcard was emblazoned in rainbow colors: "Tau Retro Rave." I wasn't even sure what a rave was, but it looked really exciting. The invite had an image of a shirtless guy with an amazing torso, and he was wearing sunglasses and a visor.

"Thanks." Jayson gave me a quick glance. "We'll just have to discuss and like, make sure we're free."

I smiled and wanted to say thank you too, but I still couldn't get words out of my damn mouth.

"Hey, Ethan," Oliver said. "I like your nine moods of a ninja tee."

That was totally random, hard to believe, and extremely flattering all at once. We did a round of handshakes, and then Jayson and I stumbled away like zombies.

When we'd put some distance between us and the student union, I turned to Jayson. "What just happened?"

"*Oh. My. God.* We just had hand-to-hand contact with the three hawtest guys on campus." He squealed, and then he looked at me very seriously. "You think we should go back? Maybe they need help handing out flyers or straightening up the table."

I wrangled him by the shoulder. "I'm serious. What the fuck *was* that?"

"Calm down." Jayson grinned mischievously, and then he told me in a sing-song voice, "I think Oliver likes you."

I scoffed.

"'I like your tee?'" he said. "He was totally flirting with you."

"No, he wasn't. He's probably just into ninjas or something."

"He's *hawt*," Jayson shrieked. He also started jumping up and down.

Now I was worried we were drawing stares. I yanked him over to a bench where there were fewer people around. We needed to have a sensible conversation. "This could be like one of those horror movies, where they lure people to an abandoned building to harvest their body parts."

Jayson scowled. "That only happens in Slovenia. And maybe Brazil."

"Then they're probably gay-baiting us. They want to get us over to their house to pistol-whip us to death."

Jayson held the glossy party invite in front of my face. "They're handing *these* out at the table. With their address. If they're planning on murdering us, they're not doing a very good job covering their tracks."

I got his point. But the situation still had me paranoid.

Jayson fixed on me in terror. "What are we going to wear? I don't own anything for a rave. You kind of do. You've got that cat T-shirt with Day Glo eyes."

I faced him firmly. "We're not going."

"Honey, we're going. We've got invites to a party with upperclassmen, all of whom have sick bodies, and they're either gay or heteroflexible. This might never happen again in either of our lifetimes. I'll take my chances on getting murdered."

"What if we get raped?"

Jayson quirked an eyebrow at me. "Your mind can go to really dark places. You know that?"

I curled into myself, covering my face. I felt like I was going to break into tears, my go-to for handling pressure.

Jayson clasped my shoulder. "Hey. Listen. I know you're scared shitless, but we'll be together. No unattended drinks. We can even use our safe phrase if one of us freaks out."

I glanced at him. "That's exactly why we can't go. Normal people don't use safe phrases so they can get out of awkward social situations." I heaved a breath. "What if they're like a cult, trying to recruit us? I wrote a paper about cults in tenth grade social studies. We're like the perfect targets. Eighteen years old. College students. Non-religious affiliated. White."

Jayson narrowed his eyes at me.

"I'm sorry. Oh my god, I'm sorry. I just don't—"

"See me as Asian?"

I gawped at him. "No. I was going to say, I just don't know how to stop putting my foot in my mouth."

"Right."

"Jayson, you're a Jaysian Gaysian."

He laughed. That worked whenever I said it.

"Ethan, you're a Mennonite Sodomite."

I laughed too. Jayson pulled out his phone and did a search on his browser. Tau Alpha Theta had a Wikipedia article, and it seemed to check out. The first fraternity in the country to initiate openly gay students. They had twenty-one chapters across the US. Their Insta was pretty normal. No ritual human sacrifices, just shots of guys horsing around, mostly shirtless, some with body paint. It was getting my underwear feeling tight, and then Jayson proudly brandished a photo of Oliver nearly losing his swim trunks while getting tackled with a nerf football. I told him to fuck off and swipe it away, while thinking about when I'd have a chance to look at it in private.

Jayson went through two pages of search returns. It was all the usual stuff. Facebook pages. Twitter accounts. The only mildly negative thing we saw was a local newspaper article from fifteen years back that said an alumnus, Luke Renfield, had unsuccessfully challenged the chapter's policy of initiating gay students, and that the frat had lost some donors due to their progressive politics. That actually sounded like a point in TAT's favor. We even looked at a thread about the fraternity on Reddit, where everything and every person in the world gets torn apart. TAT either had an amazing media manager, or they were squeaky clean. People just posted about how great the fraternity was.

Jayson set down his phone and gave me a triumphant smile. "Totes legit."

I felt a little better, but the prospect of walking into that party still scared me. "You really want to rush? What if we get rejected? Or what if *one* of us gets rejected?"

"Ethan, chill. We'll just go to the party. Oliver said we can decide for ourselves."

"What if we really like it? And then we decide to rush? You know, they probably invite a ton of guys so they can be selective. Can you even see yourself being part of a fraternity like that?"

Jayson sighed impatiently. "Ethan, you think way too far ahead in the future. You can find something to worry about twenty-four seven. Don't add a week or a month from now to worry about."

"The party's in two days."

"And we're going, and it's going to be amazing."

I thought about that for a moment. I knew I worried way too much, but I couldn't help it. I drew a breath. "Yesterday is history. Tomorrow is a mystery. But today is a gift. That's why it's called the present."

Jayson looked at me funny.

"That's a poem my English teacher had posted in her office."

"All right, Rando." He grinned. "How 'bout: Everyone deserves a chance to fly? That's from *Wicked*."

I cracked a smile. Then I shivered. I was going to a fraternity party.

Jayson glanced at his phone, and his face paled. "Holy fuck. One thirty classes started ten minutes ago."

We both shot up from the bench and went barreling to our classes.

Chapter Three

THURSDAY AFTER DINNER, we took the bus downtown to buy something to wear to the party. I told Jayson I couldn't afford a new outfit, but he insisted he'd put everything on his credit card, and I could pay him back later. I was getting my first paycheck the following Friday, so I figured that wasn't so lame. I'd just have to be really good about using my meal plan instead of buying coffee and bagels. Did I mention Jayson is *the best* best friend in the world? We got off the bus at the downtown mall stop and ran over to Hot Topic before they closed.

I only wanted a cool but moderately priced T-shirt. Jayson had done research, though. He said we needed tank tops, UFO pants, backpacks, caps, and glitter paint. I found a *Dragon Ball Z* tank that I really liked, and Jayson made me get a size small, though I always wore mediums. He picked out a girl's size *Sailor Moon* tank in pink, and we found baggy pants with lots of zippers, neon mini backpacks, and baseball caps with some kind of alien iron-on. On the checkout line, Jayson grabbed candy bracelets, sparkle Chapstick, and guyliner. I winced when I saw the total price come up on the cash register.

We hauled two giant bags out of the store and walked back to the bus stop.

"What're the backpacks for?" I asked Jayson.

"Bottled water."

My nose twitched. "You don't think they'll have water at the party?"

"You always bring bottled water to a rave. That's what the internet said. You have to keep hydrated. It has something to do with the drugs."

I stopped in my tracks. "Drugs?"

Jayson shrugged.

"What kind of drugs?"

"Hallucinogens. Mollies. Weed."

My blood pressure spiked. "They're going to make us take drugs?"

Jayson laughed. "No one's going to *make* you take drugs. But from what I read, there's a good chance they'll have drugs there."

"I don't want to do drugs," I told him. "You shouldn't do them either. You can get addicted and end up dropping out of school."

"Chill, Ethan. I'm not going to do drugs." He wriggled his eyebrows. "But I bet they'll have alcohol."

"The drinking age is twenty-one. We could get in a lot of trouble."

"I drank at a party after prom."

I gave him a double take. "What did you drink?"

"White Claw Hard Seltzer." He got goofy-faced. "I drank like two, and I was totally wasted."

"We shouldn't drink. You said yourself, we're going to look out for each other. Besides, we don't want to make a bad impression."

He batted his eyes at me. "I know you want to make a good impression for Oliver."

I lumbered away from him.

"You're so uptight," Jayson squealed. He caught up to me, looking serious. "If he asked you to give him a blow job, would you do it?"

I'd thought about that. Many times in the past twenty-four hours. I lied. "We barely know each other."

"What if he wanted to kiss?"

My face burned up. "He's, like, older. He's not going to want to kiss me." I looked at him. "What if someone wants to kiss you? Like Dom?"

"He's really cute. I think I'd do it. And I'd give him a blow job."

I gawped at him. "Don't you think you should wait to get to know him first?" My brain knotted up and terror set in. "You think people will be doing blow jobs? I don't even know how to do a blow job."

Jayson brushed my back. "Breathe, Ethan. I was kidding. Sorta. If you want to have a boyfriend, you're going to have to do blow jobs at some point. But it doesn't have to happen tomorrow night. I mean, unless you really want to."

My head was scrambled. I'd pictured doing lots of things with guys, but it was scary that those things might actually happen. In my head, I had like zero sex appeal. I was awkward. My skin was really pale, I was scrawny, and my dick was nowhere as big as the guys I'd seen on porn sites.

I barely slept that night, worrying. I tried catching up on readings for my Bio 101 class, but I mainly googled blow jobs and rave parties and drugs. It was getting me feeling more and more insecure. People died from drug overdoses at raves. I'd imagined blow jobs thousands of times, but the articles I found made them sound really complicated.

On Friday, Jayson came over to my dorm room at five so we could get dressed together. I pulled on my crazy zipper pants and my skintight tank top, and Jayson told me I looked good. And when I looked at myself in the mirror, I kinda sorta felt good. He looked awesome. He'd dyed a streak of his hair electric pink, and his shirt and pants fit his trim body perfectly. Jayson outlined his eyes with mascara, and then he did mine and showed me how to apply glitter gel to my face and arms. We looked amazing. Then Shawn showed up with two of his buddies.

I guess he'd come by to grab some of his clothes. He glanced at Jayson and me while he was going through his dresser, and an evil grin curled up on his face.

"Where the two of you headed tonight? An Ariana Grande concert?"

I could see Jayson getting uncomfortable. It emboldened me.

"We're going to the Retro Rave at Tau Alpha Theta."

One of Shawn's friends snorted. "The fag fraternity."

I didn't know I had it in me, but I kind of grew two sizes that night. I stared flames at the idiot.

"You don't call gay men fags. That's really offensive and immature."

He held up his hands. "Whatever, dude."

"You know the only thing that's missing from Tau Alpha Theta?" Shawn's other buddy said. "A 'w.'"

Shawn smirked. "That's right. 'Cause with a w it spells: TWAT."

The three idiots stared at us and chortled. Shawn went back to rustling through his dresser cabinets to pull out clothes. I watched him look back at his friends with a humorous gleam.

"This is why I'm asking the director of Res Life to give me a new dorm assignment. I didn't sign up to live with a circus freak."

"That's fine with me," I told him. "I didn't sign up to live with a dumb-ass homophobe."

Shawn glared at me. I gave it straight back to him. I thought he might come at me, but he just rolled his eyes and packed his clothes in a duffel. "You and Pikachu have a real good night."

"That's racist. He's Filipino. And he has a name."

Shawn shrugged and swaggered out of the room with his friends. Jayson gazed at me like I was a superhero.

"When'd you get so ballsy?"

I couldn't explain it. Stupidity just got me so angry sometimes, I forgot about being a wimp.

MY INNER WIMPY child came back in a hurry, however, when we rolled up on the Tau frat house. Music and lights pulsed from the windows of a humongous Victorian mansion. A crowd of kids pooled by the front door, waiting to get in. They looked like underclassmen. It was dark at nine thirty, but people were dressed pretty normal as best as I could see. Meanwhile, I was wearing makeup for the first time in my life, and my shirt was so tight, you could see my nipples through the fabric. I kinda liked dressing up, but not so much being in public. Jayson, on the other hand, strutted on with more confidence than I'd ever seen. He'd put on a pair of women's platform boots that gave him more height than me, and he had one heck of a swish in his walk all of the sudden. We caught a lot of looks working our way up to the big guy at the front door.

We showed our invites, and the bouncer gave us a glance. "IDs?"

We scrounged our school ID cards out of our pockets. The guy looked at them and blinked. "Like a driver's license?"

Thank god I'd brought mine in case they needed a copy for my rush application. But Jayson had left his back at his dorm.

"I swear he's old enough to drive a car. We're freshmen. He'd have to have graduated high school really early."

"Please," Jayson begged.

Something we said was amusing. The bouncer dude shook his head. He asked us to show him the back of our hands, and he stamped us with a joker. "Nice outfits." He looked at me firmly. "Try sneaking beer, and you'll get your ass thrown out like this." He snapped his fingers. Then he opened the door and nudged us along.

I bit down on my lip and veered away from looking at Jayson. If I did, we were both certain to jump around like little kids.

Inside, it was almost as dark as outside. They had black lights in the hall and strobes and lasers flashing from one of the rooms inside. I peeked in that direction. That room looked like it had been cleared out of furniture, and it stretched all the way to the back of the house where a deejay was set up on a platform. A hundred or more people were dancing, chatting in groups and drinking from red Solo cups. It smelled like beer-soaked rotting wood with a hint of vomit. *The scent of college popularity.* My face was plastered with a grin.

Jayson and I were stuck in the middle of the hall on sensory overload, not knowing where to go. Then a big guy wearing feathery angel wings and platinum lycra gym shorts stalked toward us, squinting.

"Ethan and Jayson?"

I hadn't recognized Oliver at first. Besides his angel costume, he was wearing black eyeliner and silver eyeshadow, and his hair was dyed silver and super sculpted. *Wow.* His hairless pecs and biceps literally sparkled.

"You guys look incredible." He pulled each of us in for a firm handshake and a pat on the back. *Wow 2.0.* His body was warm, and he was fragrant with body spray.

"Welcome to Tau." Oliver looked around. "You want something to drink?"

I proudly pulled a water bottle out of my backpack. "We brought our own."

"Cool. Cool. Well, let me introduce you to some of the brothers." He led us down the hall, past a staircase to the second floor. "You met Roberto. He's working the door tonight. And you remember Luis." He pointed him out. Luis was talking to a dude in a crop top with kaleidoscope tattoos all over his thick arms. Luis was tricked out with fluorescent spikes of hair, a chest-hugging tank and sparkle paint. We briefly said hello, and then Oliver nudged us along.

As we got deeper into the house, things got louder and more crowded. I had to lean in close to hear Oliver, which wasn't bad at all, though I started feeling meek and shy. "Dom's working the bar on this side." Oliver pointed in that direction. He stopped to talk to two guys who were passing around a vape pen. "Guys, this is Ethan and Jayson. They're thinking about rushing this year." Oliver turned back to us to make introductions. "This is Daryl, and this is Jacob. They room in the annex behind the house."

The two looked Jayson and me up and down and smirked to each other. They were both really cute, but they seemed cliquish. Daryl was a short black kid wearing a rainbow choker. Jacob was what you'd call a twink, if I'm getting that right. Skinny, pretty, with slight hips. And a nipple ring. It was nice to see not everyone in the fraternity was built like they competed in triathlons.

We shook hands and moved along. Oliver introduced us to a dozen other guys around the dance floor. Everybody was friendly, but it was loud and I was forgetting names no sooner than they were out of people's mouths. There was also a *lot* to look at. Shirtless kids thrashing around. Boys in drag. Boys kissing boys. Boys kissing girls. Boys sandwiched between two boys. Girls grinding against boys and grinding against each other. It really was gay and straight and everything in between like Oliver had said.

Oliver drew us over to a far spot on the floor where it was quieter. He was leading us toward a group of older-looking guys in muscle tees and board shorts. They were passing around a bottle of champagne, drinking straight from it.

"And these are Tau's big dogs," Oliver said. "Guys, this is Ethan and Jayson. They're considering rushing. This is our President Peter, VP Jamal, and Treasurer Tomas."

I couldn't believe we were getting the royal treatment. I'd never met the president of anything. Jayson and I politely shook everyone's hand.

"You two are adorable," Peter said. He glanced at his friends. "Is it just me or do the freshmen get younger every year?"

He was kind of fascinating. Even though he was wearing shorts and flip-flops, there was something classy about him. Maybe it was his neat crown of wavy hair and clean-shaven face. He had

Mediterranean features. Sharp, dark eyes with handsome, neat brows. I really was trying not to stare at him, and then I saw he had a gay pride tattoo on his upper arm.

"Where are you from?" Jamal asked.

"I'm from Encinitas, California," Jayson said, coyly shifting his weight like a streetwalker. "You wouldn't have heard of it. I'm a small-town girl."

I don't know where that came from. Dressing up had brought out a different side of him, but the three guys seemed to like it. Particularly Jamal.

"I grew up in Long Beach," he said, excitedly. They got to talking about California things.

"I'm from Lancaster. Pennsylvania," I told the others.

"Nice. Amish country, right?" Tomas asked.

I nodded. I wished I wasn't so painfully shy. I couldn't come up with anything to say, and I was facing people who would decide whether to accept me into the frat *if* Jayson and I chose to rush. He was rattling away in conversation with Jamal and making him laugh. It sounded like they knew some of the same places and people.

I felt a warm hand on the crook of my neck. Oliver's hand. Massaging me. "I practically had to throw out a hook to bring this guy over to the table at the student union." He gave me a warm smile. "Ethan's a little shy. And he's not sure if the fraternity scene is for him."

I didn't mind Oliver speaking up on my behalf. I basically didn't mind anything he wanted to do or say. But I hoped Peter and Tomas didn't think it made me look pathetic.

"Well, Ethan," Peter said. "I bet you can tell by now, Tau Alpha Theta isn't your average fraternity." He scratched behind his ear. "And a lot of us were just as scared about fitting in. I had a traumatic experience in high school, which made me afraid of guys." He glanced at Oliver. "Oliver did too, but you'd never know it by looking at him, right?" He gazed at me deeply. "He's a good friend to have. Whether or not you decide to rush."

That was like the kindest thing an older person had ever said to me. Besides my parents, who don't really count.

Tomas grinned at me. "I don't know, Ethan. The way you're rocking that outfit, I'd say I'm pretty sure you belong at TAT."

I blushed. "Thanks. It's mostly Jayson. I mean, he coordinated our outfits."

"He's totally lying," Jayson broke in. "Ethan has a great sense of style."

"What's your major?" Peter asked me.

We talked a little about that, and then Peter changed the subject. "Well, on to more serious matters, we do have rules for pledges. No drinking or using drugs at any Tau event. We could get our charter terminated by national and thrown out by the university."

Jayson and I both nodded soberly.

"And no sex with any other pledges or the brothers. That's really serious, too." He smirked. "When initiation is over, it's a different story. But you get caught this semester." He made the knife across the throat gesture.

Wow 3.0. He thought I could potentially be having sex with one of the fraternity brothers? I was happy just to be given the credit.

"Okay. Enough about the rules," Peter said. "You guys should have some fun on the dance floor and meet some of the other guys who are thinking about rushing."

Jayson glanced at me hopefully. I thanked Peter for letting us come to the party. Then Oliver drew us away. He said he was going to introduce us to some other freshmen.

While we walked behind Oliver, Jayson quietly spoke in my ear. "I wanna dance. Do you?"

I glared at him. I know it was ridiculous. It was a dance party. But I didn't want to look like a fool.

I whispered back. "You should dance. I'll watch."

Jayson gave me a beleaguered frown. Then we met four boys who were anxiously idling around. This time Jayson initiated introductions. We'd seen one of the kids at the Alliance a few times. Tyler. He was artsy and kind of extra, like Jayson, and they got screechy complimenting each other about their outfits. Then, an upbeat House track thundered from the speakers, and everybody wanted to hit the dance floor. Jayson eyed me pleadingly one last time. I shook my head, and then I watched them all run off and bounce around in a sea of people.

I drifted to the side of the room. I'd made it into the coolest party on campus, but it was feeling like that first meeting at the LGBTQ Alliance all over again. Jayson fit in, but I didn't. I couldn't be myself, even surrounded by other gay men. I was constantly imprisoned by my fear that people were going to think I was a dork, and I couldn't act all crazy and femme like Jayson and the kids we'd met. Was there something wrong with me?

I was so caught in my thoughts, I didn't realize Oliver was standing next to me. "You're really gonna be that guy who watches everyone else dance?" he said.

I scowled at myself.

"It's all right," he said. "But why?"

"I can't dance. I look like I have a brain injury."

Oliver scoffed. "I'm sure it's not so bad."

"No. It really is. Some kid recorded me at last year's Homecoming dance and put it on his Insta. You can google it. 'Biggest Loser, High School Dance Edition.'"

After I said it, I wished I hadn't. Now Oliver was going to see that humiliating video with all the nasty comments.

"What do you say to a tour of the house instead?"

He was being super nice, but it was making me feel guilty. "You don't have to hang out with me because I'm too lame to dance. I'm cool. I mean, you've got to have other things to do with your friends or potential pledges."

"Ethan, I think joining Tau could be really great for you. And great for us."

I looked at him like he was putting me on. "How?"

"We're a really accepting community. And I don't just mean in terms of being gay. For some of us, it's the first time being in a place with other guys where you feel you really belong."

It didn't feel that way to me. Besides being queer, it was like I had nothing in common with the other people at the party. I envied Jayson and his new friends. They were so easily able to be themselves and get all sexy with each other and probably they'd start hanging out, and I'd end up the dweeb who never got the joke, and they'd get bored of me.

Oliver looked me in the eyes. "It can take some time. We've all got our personal battles to work through." He curled up one side of his mouth. "It took some time for me, too. But you'll get there."

He was the only person at the party I related to, and I don't know if one thing has to do with the other, but I was seriously attracted to him, both physically and emotionally. I remembered something Peter had said. I was almost too shy to mention it, but then I asked: "You had a traumatic high school experience?"

He nodded. Then he brought out his phone from the back of his shorts. He tapped and swiped a few times, and then he showed the screen to me.

It was a photo of a kid, maybe fourteen, fifteen years old. He was really big. Had unkempt hair, and he was wearing a wrinkled polo shirt that was stretched tight over his big belly. I looked at Oliver, confused.

"That's me. Five foot nine and two hundred and twenty pounds, in tenth grade."

My eyes bugged. I could just make out the resemblance in the face.

"I felt awkward around boys as far back as I can remember. In third grade, I hated gym class so much, I rode my bike into a dumpster to deliberately hurt myself. That got me excused for a few months, and then I faked fainting and having convulsions. The doctors couldn't come up with a diagnosis, but they gave me a medical excuse. Then the emotional eating started. Kids made fun of me a lot, and I didn't have any friends. They called me Fudgie the Whale. My last name's Whaley. You heard of that Carvel ice cream cake?"

I nodded.

"Anyway, back then I was so embarrassed of myself, I thought I'd never find people who wanted to be my friend and not care who what I was hiding on the inside."

I could relate to that, big time. But Oliver was also built and gorgeous, and he fit in at that party one hundred percent. I blurted out, "How did you change so much?"

"There was this older kid who lived up the street from me. He'd dropped out of school and worked at a gym. He'd had his own problems at home and in school. He's gay. Used to get in a lot of fights. I grew up in a small city like you. Columbia, South Carolina. If you don't play sports or aren't into cars and guns, you're basically a freak. Anyway, Bradley, he just stopped me on the street one day, and we got to talking. He said he could help me out if I wanted to lose weight. He got me jogging and using weights in his garage and eventually into martial arts. It basically saved my life, and I don't mean in a superficial way. It built my confidence on the inside. So when I went away to college, I told myself: this is going to be different from high school. One day, I stopped by the Tau table just like you did, and I met this awesome group of guys who just accepted me. They weren't caught up on having to be a certain way in order to be a man. I had my insecurities to work through, but after a few weeks of rush, I opened up and put that shit in the past."

He put away his phone, and we exchanged a grin. I'd never have guessed he'd had that history or that we'd have anything in common. I told him about how I'd nearly bailed on college, and that I hated how awkward I was and had lots of problems with my body.

Oliver led me through a tour of the house. They had a huge kitchen, a dining room for like fifty or more people, a finished basement with a pool table, bar, and a gaming lounge, and nine bedrooms on the second floor, with another four in the attic. The house was really old. Oliver said it had been built in the 1920s, so it required a lot of upkeep. They had to be gentle with the doors, and somebody was always breaking an old knob and lock, particularly with one of the second floor bathrooms.

"How many people live here?" I asked him.

"Twenty-six. Fourteen of us have rooms in the main house, and there's an old servant's house in the back with twelve guys packed in there. We call it the annex."

My eyes widened.

"But we currently have sixty-seven members. A lot of the brothers live off-campus or the dorms."

A funny thought occurred to me. "I kinda assumed you were the head of everything. Because you were at the table."

Oliver smiled. "No. I'm just the Rush Chair this year." He glanced at me. "How you think I'm doing so far?"

I burned up in the face. We'd ended up in a quiet spot on the second floor hallway. I was dying for him to touch or kiss me, and if he wanted a blow job, I was totally down with that. Then I remembered what Peter had said about not having sex, and I tried to reset myself. "I think you're doing a great job. I have to talk to Jayson, but I'm pretty sure we're interested in pledging."

He raised his hand to slap me five. Then he crushed my hand in his with a big smile. That was the closest thing to a sexual experience I'd ever had. I won't get into details, but I was glad I was wearing baggy pants.

"I'm at the gym every morning at six thirty, Monday through Thursday. Meet me Monday, and I'll show you some of the equipment." He glanced over me. "You've got a great frame. I could help you bulk up if you wanted to."

That was the first time I'd heard that I had a great frame. And I'd never considered that it was possible I could 'bulk up.' I hated the gym, but it was sounding like a great idea. I wanted to be built like Oliver, so that maybe he'd think I was attractive. I started feeling shy again, and a little bit defensive. "Why are you being so nice to me?"

"Because someone helped me out when I was younger. I'm paying it forward."

A group of his friends stumbled along our way, and we all went out to the fire escape in the back of the house. They drank beer, vaped, and goofed around, and I just watched and listened to everybody, sitting next to Oliver, who I decided must be the coolest person in the universe. It was basically the best night of my entire life.

Chapter Four

AROUND FOUR O'CLOCK in the morning, I found Jayson, and we tramped back to my dorm room because it was closer than his north campus dorm. I felt kinda bad-ass, walking the streets in the middle of the night. Jayson looked wrecked from the rave. His makeup was melting, and his pink-streaked brush up hairstyle had deflated, but he had a big grin on his face.

"Best night ever?" I said.

Jayson wrangled me into a hug, and we jumped up and down. "Best night *ever*."

"You deserve the credit. It was the outfits that got us in," I told him.

Jayson scoffed. Then he smiled. "Yeah. It kinda was."

"Tell me everything that happened. I mean *everything*."

He got a little shy, scuffing his sneaker on the sidewalk. "You mean with Tyler and them?"

"Duh. Yeah."

He fidgeted with his hands. "Well. We danced. All night long. And we went out back to cool off. And I met this boy. Andrew." He broke out in a nervous grin. "He's a freshman. From Ohio. A music major. He got somebody to get somebody to get us a beer from the bar, and we drank it together." He hesitated. His face was really burning up. "And we made out in the bushes, and we touched each other's penises, *over our pants*."

My brain exploded. "Oh my God. You broke all the rules in one night."

He looked at me sidelong. "How?"

"One, we're not supposed to drink alcohol. Two, pledges can't have sex with each other. Three, pledges can't drink or use drugs."

"Isn't that just two rules?"

"No."

"Well, one and three are the same thing."

"They're not. One is about the drinking age. Three is about your conduct as a pledge."

"Maybe I won't pledge. *You* can pledge." He grinned at me. "And get me into parties."

I stopped in my tracks. I couldn't believe what he was saying. "We said we were going to pledge together." I cooled down some. "Listen, I'm not going to tell anyone you broke the rules. I just think you need to be more careful moving forward."

Jayson looked at me funny. "Y'know, we're not in high school anymore."

"Like, yeah. I'm aware of that."

"I mean, if I want to drink and fool around with a guy, I can do it. You don't have to Mommy me."

"I'm sorry—"

"I thought, as my best friend, you'd be happy for me." Jayson plodded ahead.

I caught up to him. "I *am* happy for you. I'm sorry, Jayson. Just forget I said anything."

He didn't speak for a while. Then, "I guess I forgive you. Just don't get judgy, okay?"

I nodded vigorously.

"Where'd you run off to all night?"

I told him about hanging out with Oliver and his friends. Jayson got that mischievous gleam in his eyes. "You like him."

"As a friend."

Jayson snickered. "As in you want his penis in your va-jay-jay."

My face shrank up. "I don't have a va-jay-jay."

He hid a smile, and then he glanced at my butt.

"Oh. My. God. You're talking about anal intercourse? With the Rush Chair?" My voice was cracking really bad.

Jayson calmed me down. "Relax. But did you kiss him? Or do anything else?"

"No. I don't even like him that way." It was a total lie. I don't know why I couldn't tell the truth about my feelings for Oliver. I guess it seemed like this sacred thing that would burn to ashes if I said it out loud. "Besides, and I'm not being judgy, but if we want to pledge, we can't fool around with anyone affiliated with the fraternity."

"Until rush is over." Jayson quirked an eyebrow at me.

"Is Andrew rushing?"

"Probably not. So there. I only broke one rule."

"I wasn't really angry about that. I was just freaking out." I glanced at him while we walked side-by-side. "Why isn't Andrew rushing?"

"He's mad busy. He's got orchestra rehearsals. Plus, he's auditioning for the men's choir. And he's going to be taking on students for violin lessons."

"Are you two, like, dating now?"

"I don't know." He looked at me, confused. "Do people even date anymore?"

"You're asking the wrong person."

"I guess I can ask Andrew tomorrow what our status is." He pulled out his phone, tapped it open, and grinned. "He put his number in my phone. How long do you think I should wait before I text him. Or should I FaceTime?"

An evil grin pinched up on my face. "Text him now."

Jayson looked at me like I was crazy.

"Seriously. It'll be super cute. I mean, if you really like him."

"I don't want him to think I'm a stalker."

"You made out in the bushes. He obviously likes you." Jayson looked petrified. "If I made out with someone in the bushes, I'd want him to text me. Unless like it was just a hookup thing."

"I don't even know," Jayson shouted in frustration. "How do you tell with guys? He told me I was cute. He wanted to hold my hand after we made out. We told each other what we're into." He glanced at me. "I said I was vers because that's what everyone says on the internet. But it really means you're a bottom, which I *think* I am? Andrew said he's vers too. You think that means we're not sexually compatible?"

My heart dropped a little. Oliver didn't ask me what I was into. Not that I'd have known what to say, but it would have shown he was interested in me. Or maybe I should have asked him to let him know I was interested?

"What do you think?" Jayson repeated.

"I so completely, totally have no idea. Does a bottom mean you only get blow jobs or you only *give* blow jobs?"

"Oh, I think everyone's vers about that." His phone dinged. We both froze and stared at it. Jayson showed me the screen like it was evidence in a murder investigation.

Andrew: I had a really great time. Let's meet up soon!

I screamed and hugged Jayson. Jayson shrugged away and tapped at his phone. His text whooshed out, sent.

"What did you tell him?"

"I asked if he wanted to meet up for coffee or for blow jobs."

"Wha?"

A text dinged back. I watched Jayson stare at it in horror. In slow motion, he showed it to me. A coffee cup and an eggplant emoji. We danced around and laughed like idiots.

"What do you wear to a blow job?" Jayson asked.

My eyes bugged. Jayson googled it.

THE FOLLOWING MONDAY, I started meeting Oliver at the athletic center at six thirty every morning. I know. I wasn't fooling anybody saying I just wanted to be friends. The only thing that could get me out of bed that early would be an earthquake or a guy I was seriously crushing on. Honestly, in any other circumstance, I'd choose riding out an earthquake over going to the gym.

But I was crushing on Oliver more than I'd ever crushed on anyone. I understood for the first time why they called it crushing because I truly felt like my heart was in a trash compactor. It hurt when I didn't see him, and it hurt when we got together at the gym. I loved everything about him—his gentle smile, his sandy hair, the golden undertones of his skin, his voice, his laugh, his kindness, and most definitely the way he looked in his sleeveless Tau T-shirt and his cotton gym trunks.

He was also incredibly patient, which he needed to be to get me started at the gym. I'd never used free weights or Nautilus equipment. I started on ten pound weights, which was super embarrassing while everyone around us was curling and squatting with multiple barbells. It was motivating, though, getting to spend time with Oliver. He was also in the health sciences program, doing the physical therapy track, so he told me which professors to look out for in the core science classes. It was especially motivating when he patted my back and said I was doing a good job. That was the most body contact I'd had with a fully grown man. Well, Oliver was twenty, but he sure looked fully grown. He had big hands, a furry stomach, and thick, powerful, hairy legs. When he stripped down in the locker room, I always booked over to a shower stall to get undressed behind a curtain. I had to wait it out until my boner went down.

That's how I can describe it. My entire body was a throbbing, aching boner when we were together, erect and alert, silently screaming for him to touch me. It was bad, but in just two weeks, I had some muscle definition. Oliver also gave me tips on my diet to build muscle. It was working. That was pretty cool. Right in time for the first official pledge meeting.

Of course, Jayson and I were going together. They said it was semi-formal, and Jayson helped me pick out a shirt and tie. His "thing" with Andrew was still kind of undefined, but I was starting to feel like he was growing up while I was still this virgin wuss. They got together for blow jobs in the basement of the music building two to three times a week. I told Jayson how I was feeling while we were getting ready.

"You should go on Grindr," he said.

I scowled at him. He knew how I felt about dating apps.

"Just for the fall semester. Think about it. All through rush, you're going to be around good-looking guys who you can't have sex with. You could find some rando kid and swap blow jobs so you won't be horny."

"I can't see myself doing that."

"Fine. Then don't complain."

"Is that what you're doing with Andrew? Just swapping blow jobs?"

Jayson sat down on the bed. He looked really sad all of the sudden. "Probably? He says he doesn't like texting or talking on the phone. And we're always on a timeline when we sneak into one of the practice rooms. You're only supposed to sign them out for a half hour."

"That's worse than an hourly hotel." It just flew out of my mouth. I felt really terrible saying that.

"I don't need to be slut-shamed."

"I didn't mean to slut-shame you." I sat down next to him. "You're not a slut."

"Aren't I, though?"

"Jayson, there's thirteen-year-old Amish girls who are more sexually experienced than me. I'm completely sexually repressed. So, don't take anything I say as judgy. I've got issues. Not you."

We were quiet for a while. I reached out to set my hand on his, and he let me.

"I just don't think Andrew has time for me. Or I annoy him. He never likes the gifs I send him."

"You send awesome gifs. If he doesn't like them, he's the one who's annoying. I mean, if you want my opinion."

Jayson grinned at me. I grinned back.

At the frat house, we joined twenty-two freshmen and sophomore pledges in the living room. We'd hung out with a few of them since the rave party. Tyler. This kid Vinnie who was loud and funny as hell, and his friend Scott, who didn't talk as much, but he had a great smile and seemed nice. They were friends from high school and commuter students.

We sat with them in one of the rows of ballroom chairs. I think everyone was nervous. It was really quiet, and none of us knew what to expect. I mean, Oliver told me the meeting was to explain what pledge training was going to entail, but we'd all heard rumors about secret rituals and hazing activities. Oliver said Tau didn't do those things. Still, a little part of me worried he might not be telling me everything because he was sworn to silence.

Oliver started by welcoming everyone and introducing the executive council. He looked so handsome and polished in a suit jacket and shirt and tie. Then, Peter spoke about the history of Tau Alpha Theta, which was really interesting. The founding member, Douglas Gideon, was a law student at University of Michigan in the 1970s. He wanted to create a multi-racial and multi-ethnic fraternity at a time when Greek society was largely segregated and socially conservative. Six other chapters across the country got their start in the first ten years, including New Jersey State. But the fraternity faced resistance on campuses and from the North American Interfraternity Council. It almost disbanded in the 1980s. In 1991, a Tau chapter at Northwestern University voted to broaden their mission and initiate gay students. Their membership grew, the idea caught on with other chapters, and TAT had a resurgence, establishing ten new chapters in the 1990s and four more in the 2000s.

"In joining Tau Alpha Theta, you're entering a brotherhood that's making history and creating positive change, not just here at New Jersey State, but across the country," Peter said. "We were one of the earliest fraternities to take a hard line against hazing and sexual assault on campuses. You're looking at the first president of a fraternity who's openly gay and of Middle Eastern descent. And our vice president, Jamal Fredricks. is the first transgender man to be initiated at a fraternity in New Jersey State's history, and we'll have many more. So thank you for pledging. Our diversity is our strength."

We applauded him. I was really liking how things were going so far. Then Oliver told us our first task as pledges was to pair up with someone we didn't know and talk about ourselves. Then, we had to introduce our partner to everyone. Oliver said there'd be a "pledge advantage" for whoever could say the most about their partner.

Talking about myself with a stranger wasn't something I looked forward to, but as people milled around, picking out their partners, an Indian kid named Ashok shyly came over to me and asked if I wanted to pair up. I said sure, and we wandered over to a quiet corner of the room.

"You want to go first?" he said. "Or we could flip a coin?"

I liked the idea of flipping a coin. We were both really nervous to go first. He had a quarter in his pocket, and it landed on heads, which was his call.

"So, I'm Ashok." He blushed and grinned. "Um...I'm from Smithtown. That's on Long Island. I'm majoring in engineering. I live in Jefferson Hall. North Campus." He got a helpless look on his face, which was really cute. "What else should I say?"

"Do you have brothers and sisters?"

He nodded. "I have two older sisters, Natalie and Rani. My mom's Indian, and my dad's Irish. They're divorced. They split up a long time ago. When I was in sixth grade. My dad lives in Queens." He peeked at me. "Is that too much information?"

"No. I mean, I don't have to mention that if you don't want."

"I don't mind. It's not a big deal."

Neither one of us said anything for a moment. I really liked Ashok already. He seemed like a nice guy, and I could relate to being shy.

"Why'd you decide to pledge?" I asked him.

"Well, I haven't told many people, but I'm gay." He was really blushing now.

"I'm gay too."

"That's a relief. I was hoping you were. Not that it matters. But it kind of does, don't you think?"

We looked squarely at each other for a blink and glanced away. He had really pretty hazel eyes.

"One hundred percent, I agree," I said. "I only came out to two friends and my family after graduation. But I've come out to like a hundred people in the past six weeks. It gets easier."

"I have an older cousin who went here. He's gay, and he told me about Tau. That's how I ended up pledging."

I wanted to ask more about his family, but it was time for us to switch. It was really easy talking to Ashok. I mean, it's not like my life story is so interesting, but I ended up telling him a lot.

"I was at the rave party too," he said. "I met Jayson. That's weird we didn't run into each other."

I shrugged. I didn't want to say I spent most of the night upstairs with Oliver and have to get into that embarrassing situation.

Time was up. We went back to join the others. Every pair introduced each other, and Vinnie was hilarious when it was his turn to go. He'd paired up with a pledge named Joseph who grew up in Philadelphia and had two moms. Joseph was straight, but he was more comfortable in a queer environment since he'd grown up around queer people. Vinnie was a natural with public speaking, almost like a stand-up comic. Oliver decided he was the winner. That meant he'd get a special advantage at our next pledge challenge. Then Oliver passed around a cell phone and told us to put our numbers and names in it.

"Keep your phones on at all times. When you get a text with the Swedish flag, your next assignment begins. When you receive it, you have fifteen minutes to report to the parking lot behind the Environmental Sciences building. If you're late, your pledge journey ends."

A nervous murmur passed through the room. Meanwhile, I couldn't stop sneaking looks at Oliver. He was the boss. So freakin' sexy. It was a Friday night, and I wouldn't see him again until Monday morning. I wondered if he thought about me like I thought about him. The meeting had ended, and people were exchanging numbers and talking about their plans for the weekend, but all I could do was watch Oliver chatting with Peter and the other members of the Executive Council.

Oliver glanced at me, and I burned up in the face. He waved me over. I was really wishing he hadn't. He was standing with Peter, Jamal, and Tomas, and I was sure to make an ass out of myself. I put one foot in front of the other and stepped over to him.

"How'd the first meeting go for you?" he asked.

"Good. Really good." All four of the guys were looking at me. I reached for something to make conversation, and I turned to Peter. "I really liked your speech. About the frat's history."

"Thanks," he said. "I don't get told that very often. Most of the pledges come here for the parties, not a lecture. And we'll have plenty of parties, but knowing the history of the organization you're joining is important."

I remembered that article Jayson and I had read online about alumni reacting negatively to Tau for being inclusive of gay pledges. Before I could get too nervous to mention it, I asked him a question. "Do you still have problems with alumni? My friend and I saw an old article about some people who weren't happy about the frat being gay-friendly."

The four guys passed glances at each other. I wondered if I'd made a big mistake, bringing up a sore subject or just being too nosy.

"You're smart to do your research," Peter said. "But that ugliness is pretty much in the past. The older alumni who don't like our policies have moved on, and we say good riddance."

Jamal jumped in. "Well, most of them."

"You're right," Peter said. "We've still got good ol' Luke Renfield. He comes to every annual alumni meeting to rant about us 'promoting' homosexuality."

I remembered that name from the article. "Why?" I asked.

"I guess he's made it his mission in life. He was a brother back in the early 90s. Y'know, before gay people existed."

The others smiled and laughed lightly. Peter fixed on me. "Luke's an army of one. The vast majority of our alumni support our mission and practices. It's nothing to be worried about."

He, Jamal, and Tomas had some other business to attend to, leaving me alone with Oliver.

"Was it wrong to ask about that?" I said.

"Not at all. It's good to show an interest in the organizational side of things. Who knows? You could run for a leadership position in the future."

I blushed at that. Oliver squeezed my shoulder.

"You're doing great, Ethan. Really."

I was a puddle of goo when he said things like that. Almost everyone had headed out the door, so I told him thanks and that I'd see him Monday morning at the athletic center.

AS JAYSON AND I walked back to the dorms, we were untypically quiet. I had a lot of things on my mind, and I guess he did too. I was really excited about being part of a fraternity with so many queer people, but in waves of trepidation, it hit me that I'd be even more "out" around campus. I was also going to have to tell my parents. They'd been accepting when I told them I was gay, but it still felt weird and kind of embarrassing talking to them about it. And someday, maybe, I'd have a boyfriend, and I'd want him to meet my family. That thought made me warm and happy again, and then I imagined that boyfriend being Oliver, who my parents would totally love. He was so well put together, and he had a great personality.

Finally, along the way, Jayson broke the silence.

"I'm going to tell Andrew how I feel. And I think you should tell Oliver too."

I glanced at him. "What do you mean?"

He rolled his eyes. "You obviously have feelings for him."

A rash of defenses rose up in me. "I told you, we're just friends."

We strolled along in silence.

"What do you mean, it's obvious?" I said.

"You look at him a lot. Every time we're at the house, you're right by his side."

"That's not true." My lungs constricted. "I look at him a lot?"

"You do." Jayson smiled grimly at me. "If you like him that way, you should tell him, don't you think? Instead of torturing yourself."

Everything he said made sense. But I was terrified. I lowered my voice.

"Okay. I do have *feelings* for him. I didn't want to tell you because it's hopeless. He's the Rush Chair." I peeked at Jayson. It actually felt good telling him the truth. "We've never done anything. I mean, he wouldn't. He's in charge of all the rules. And he's probably not interested. All we do is go to the gym and talk."

Jayson snorted. "You've got a boyfriend who only wants to talk, and I've got a boyfriend who only wants to have sex. We should combine them in a lab to make the perfect man."

"Oliver's not my boyfriend."

"Maybe, like you said, he's not making a move because of rush."

I'd thought about that. Every hour. I mean, Oliver was a lot more mature than me. Maybe he was just playing things cool. Two months wasn't so long to wait. I glanced at Jayson. His expression had changed, like he had something difficult to say.

"What?"

"I'm only telling you this because I'd want to know if the circumstances were flipped." He scratched his brow. "Don't hate me for it."

I nodded solemnly.

"The other night when we were over at the house, I saw Oliver talking to some guy."

I waited for more.

"I didn't see them like making out, but they were really close to each other. And the guy, he was touching Oliver. And Oliver didn't seem to mind."

I slowed my pace and dropped my head. Oliver liked someone else. I'd been a fool. He was never going to want to be with me. I didn't want to believe it. Jayson had to have misunderstood.

"Where were they?"

"In the hallway upstairs. I really had to pee, and someone was taking forever in the downstairs bathroom, so I went to use the upstairs one. I was desperate. I hate that bathroom. The doorknob is always falling off, and I always feel like I'm going to get locked inside or someone's going to walk in on me if I don't close the door all the way."

"Who was the guy?"

"Just some guy who came over that night. Remember, the older brothers were playing poker in the basement? I figured he was one of their friends."

"He wasn't a brother?"

"I don't think so. We've met all of them, I think. He wasn't at the meeting tonight."

"So, maybe he was just a friend. Did you hear what they were talking about?"

Jayson sighed. "I probably shouldn't have told you. You're not going to be able to stop thinking about it, are you?"

"Just tell me what they were talking about."

"I didn't listen. I was just walking past them."

"And they were touching? Like how?"

"Like the guy was really into Oliver. Feeling his arms. His chest." Jayson looked away for a moment. "And he put his hand on Oliver's butt."

I felt like I'd been stabbed in the gut. The corners of my eyes burned.

"Don't get that way. Ethan, seriously. I shouldn't have mentioned it. It was just something I saw. It doesn't mean they're together. Some guys are touchy-feely."

"Oliver didn't stop him. I guess he didn't mind," I said bitterly.

"It looked like he didn't mind." Jayson heaved a breath. "But the reason I'm telling you is, you should talk to Oliver. Let him know how you feel. 'Cause in the meantime, he might start seeing someone else."

I thought on that. It made a lot of sense. "Thanks for letting me know."

Chapter Five

I CHICKENED OUT. On Monday, when I met up with Oliver at the athletic center, I couldn't find the courage to tell him how I felt. I was too scared he'd say he didn't feel the same way about me. Even worse, he might think it was best for us to not hang out anymore, and then there'd be this weirdness between us whenever we saw each other at frat activities. I confessed my lameness to Jayson when we were at the dining hall that night.

Jayson had a thoughtful expression on his face. "You guys have never talked about sex or dating?"

I shook my head. I had no idea what he was getting at. "What?"

"It's just kinda strange. Isn't it? For the past three weeks, you've basically spent every morning with him."

I watched him finish a french fry. I had a feeling he had something on his mind I wasn't going to like hearing.

"If you're just friends, why wouldn't he talk about guys or ask about your love life?"

"I don't know. Like boundaries, maybe?"

"I guess. If he takes them super seriously. The other brothers talk to pledges about dates and hookups. I mean, if you're both gay and single, it kinda seems like a topic you'd have to make an effort *not to* talk about."

Now he was getting me worried. "I don't talk about it because he's the only person I'm interested in. You think he doesn't talk about it because he knows I'm croo'ing on him, and he doesn't want to hurt my feelings?"

"Could be. Though if he knows and he's not interested, the easiest thing for him to do would be to mention he has a boyfriend."

My heart lifted. "You think that means he *could be* interested in me?"

Jayson knit his brow. "Well, maybe. But he'd probably want to feel you out. If he was into you, he'd want to know if you were interested in other guys, don't you think?"

I was mad confused. Meanwhile, Jayson went on.

"Or, I guess he could just not be interested in anyone. Like sexually."

My eyes bugged. "You think he's ace?" We'd just attended a pledge workshop on sexuality and gender expression where they talked about asexuality.

Jayson gave me a sly glance. "How about this? Next time we're at the house, I'll ask him if he's dating anyone."

"No. You can't." My heart raced. "He knows we're best friends. He'll think I put you up to it."

Jayson waved me off. "I won't straight up ask him. I'll say...how come he never brings his boyfriend around?"

I looked at him squarely. "That's pretty much the same thing."

"How about I ask him for dating advice and work it into conversation?" His phone groaned, and he picked it up and glanced at the screen. "I chickened out too, by the way. Andrew and I are doing blow jobs at seven. Do you know how weird it is giving a blow job while someone is playing the French horn on the other side of the wall?"

I giggled. Then I told Jayson to please not talk to Oliver. It's not that I didn't trust him. I loved him dearly. But I could see him unintentionally turning that conversation into a disaster. He had no impulse control with what came out of his mouth.

I went to bed at eleven thirty that night. Then I jerked awake at midnight. My cell phone was dinging.

One Swedish flag emoji from Tau. One "WTF" from Jayson. I threw on a pair of jeans and a pullover, and I got into my sneakers and hauled ass to the parking lot behind the Environmental Sciences building.

EVERY ONE OF the pledges showed up, which we were really proud of. A few of the guys only had time to grab jackets, and they were shivering in pajama bottoms, T-shirts, and flip-flops. It was late October and maybe forty degrees. We laughed at each other's outfits while we were all nervous and wondering what the heck was going to happen.

A minivan zipped into the parking lot and screeched to a halt where we were gathered. Two guys stepped out of the front doors. They were dressed identically in black trench coats and work boots, and they had black wool masks covering their faces. I was shook. It was like a scene from an action movie, but happening in real time. The masked men shouted at us.

"Let's go, pledge dorks."

"Move."

All twenty-two of us had to get into their eight seat minivan, and the brothers yelled like military sergeants that we only had sixty seconds to do it. Anyone who didn't make it inside would be left behind.

It was actually hysterical. Really, we only had the six back seats and the room between. We got the bigger guys in first, then the medium ones like me, and finally the smaller guys like Jayson and Ashok. Sitting on laps didn't really work. We were jammed in all directions with lots of complaints about butts being shoved in faces, though everyone was cracking up. I don't even know whose behind and legs ended up on top of me. But we all made it in. The brothers closed the sliding door, and the van reeled away.

They'd covered the windows, so even those of us who weren't completely buried couldn't see where we were going. Meanwhile it was really noisy while everyone was laughing and joking around. Maybe fifteen, twenty minutes passed until the van slowed down and came to a halt. We then had to untangle ourselves to get out the door.

When I twisted and squeezed my way out to the chilly night, I saw we were in some kind of highway underpass, fifty yards long or more. It was pretty grimy, strewn with trash, discarded cans, and cigarette butts.

The brothers hollered for us to assemble by a street lamp.

"This is your second pledge challenge. Random acts of kindness. You're going to clean this tunnel spick and span." The other brother brought out rolls of garbage bags and boxes of vinyl gloves.

"You've got one hour for the challenge. If it meets our expectations, we'll drive you home to get cleaned up and grab some sleep before classes tomorrow. If it doesn't, all your garbage bags will be dumped, and you'll do it again until you get it right."

"Fontanelli. Get over here."

Vinnie stumbled to the front of the group.

"You won a pledge advantage, so you get to call." The other brother brought another big cardboard box out of the van and poured its contents on the sidewalk. "Half of you will be doing it in your underwear and wearing these. Around your head."

Slowly, I put together what I was looking at on the ground. Strap-on dildoes. In every color of the rainbow. Vinnie cracked up, but most of us kept it together to show we were serious about the task.

"Everyone except Fontanelli count off." We got into two lines to do so. "Fontanelli, what's it going to be? Odds or Evens?"

Vinnie took a glance around, and a smile lit up on his face. "Only because he's number four, and my ride-or-die to the end. And he can rock a pair of black boxer briefs. It's gonna be the evens, boys." He was talking about his best friend, Scott.

I was number six.

"All right. Evens, strip down." The brother turned to Vinnie. "You too. Evens need an extra man, genius."

I burst out with laughter along with everyone else. Then I started taking off my clothes for what was turning into the most fun night of my life.

THE FOLLOWING WEEK, at five a.m. on a Saturday, we got Swedish flagged for a challenge they called: Lend a Brother a Hand. As a group, we had to raise one thousand dollars for Tau's scholarship fund. We couldn't use our own money or ask our parents, and we couldn't do anything illegal. We only had until eight o'clock that night.

We all met up outside the student union since it was a central location, and we could grab something to eat when the dining hall opened at seven. Vinnie, who'd become the unspoken leader of our pledge class, suggested we work in task groups. That way, we could cover more territory, whether we were asking for donations on campus or trying to get a really quick GoFundMe campaign going. I got into a group with Jayson, Tyler and Ashok, and we brainstormed ideas.

"Well, it's like forty-five dollars per person, if you look at it that way," I said. "Or about two hundred for us to raise as a group."

"I don't think we'll get there through online donations," Jayson said.

"We could set up a table at the downtown mall," Tyler suggested.

Ashok joined in. "You need a permit. I volunteered for the Make-a-Wish Foundation in ninth grade. We needed permits just to ask for money outside grocery stores."

"Bake sale?"

I looked at Jayson funny. "You know how to bake? Where are we going to get access to an oven?"

"This is impossible," Tyler said. "We don't have a car, which pretty much limits us to asking for money on campus or in town.

And according to Ashok, we can't even do it in town unless we get a permit. So, we're basically stuck asking other students to give us money for a fraternity scholarship they don't care about. On a Saturday when there aren't many people on campus."

"What if we ask for money in exchange for something people want?" Jayson said.

Tyler smirked. "They said we can't do anything illegal."

Jayson swatted him. "I meant, like a five-minute massage."

"Don't you have to be licensed to do that?" I asked.

"We don't have to say we're professionals," Jayson said. "Everyone knows how to give a massage, right?"

"How much would we charge?" Tyler said. "No one's going to pay more than a few dollars for an amateur massage. And massages take time. How many are we going to be able to do in like twelve hours? Ten hours, basically. No one's going to show up to campus till ten o'clock or so."

"We could charge two dollars for a five-minute massage," Jayson said.

"We'd have to do a hundred to make our quota," Tyler retorted. "You really think we're going to find a hundred people on campus who want a massage?"

"Maybe if we say it's for charity?" I said. "And set up in a place where people are stressed out?"

Everyone was quiet for a while. We weren't making much progress.

"Ashok, what do you think?" Jayson asked.

"I think I might have an idea that kind of puts all of yours together. Offering a service in exchange for a donation is smart, Jayson. But like Tyler said, a massage might not be the right way to go. It's actually a lot of work for a small return. If our hands get tired, we might not even get through a hundred massages." He turned to me, and he stretched his hand over to lightly scratch my upper back.

"What about back scratches? They're really relaxing, and like Ethan said, if we stake out a spot with a lot of traffic, I think we'll get people. We can charge a dollar per minute. That gives people options, and hopefully they'll go for two or three minutes apiece. Maybe even five. And when they make payment, we can include a leave a tip option."

I thought it was a brilliant idea. The back scratch he was giving me was amazing. Tyler was a little negative about it, but when Jayson said he liked the idea, we were all-in.

We decided we'd set up on the lawn in front of the library to catch students who wanted to take a break from studying. People had midterms in a week or so. I was feeling pretty hopeful about our plan. Jayson and Tyler ran off to text all their friends and post about it on social media. Ashok and I looked up computer labs on campus and found one that opened up at seven o'clock. Then we went to his dorm room where we talked about ideas for posters and flyers, and he got them into his tablet.

We used up both of our printing budgets for the semester churning out flyers in the computer lab. Then, when the bookstore opened at nine o'clock, we were the first customers in the store. I talked to one of the student workers I knew to find marked-down poster board and Sharpies. We hauled everything to the library, where we found Jayson and Tyler sitting on blankets in a sunny spot. Thank god we had good weather.

Our teammates had changed clothes, and both of them looked fabulous. Jayson had sculpted his brush up and dressed in his favorite crop-top with "Princess" in sparkly letters. Tyler wore a tucked-in, vintage girl's blouse, tuxedo pants, and his combat boots. They both had put on matte, pale pink lipstick. We worked out a game plan while Ashok and I made the signs. Well, really, Tyler and Jayson told us the game plan.

"We think you guys should be the main back scratchers," Tyler said. "Because, Ashok, you have experience, and you two look cute together. Jayson and me will do promotion since we're like extra and that gets people's attention. And we're really going to need to round up people to make this work."

"And we're going to livestream on Insta," Jayson added.

I shrugged. "That's fine." I turned to Ashok. "Is it okay with you?"

"Sure."

They each grabbed a stack of flyers and headed off to catch people having breakfast at the dining hall.

It was slow in the morning. Ashok and I were getting worried. Not many people went to the library early on Saturday, and the few people who passed by us looked like they just wanted to get straight to work. Meanwhile, whatever Jayson and Tyler were doing wasn't helping. At least, so far.

I looked at Ashok glumly. "What do you think happens if we don't raise enough money?"

"I don't know." He picked at the grass.

"Or what if every other group raises their two hundred dollars, and we fall short?" I caught myself. I hadn't exposed Ashok to my obsessive side. "I'm sorry. I worry a lot."

"It's okay. I'm worried too. I came up with the back scratch idea, so you're all going to hate me if it's a disaster. But I don't think they'll kick us out as pledges just because we couldn't raise enough money." He looked at me with a little blush. "On the other hand, I'm secretly extremely competitive. It comes from having two older sisters. So, just so you know, I'm going to be super sulky and bitter if we don't make our quota."

I smiled. "No one's going to hate you if it doesn't work out. This is a group effort. Whether we succeed or fail."

Just then, we spotted four people on their way to the entrance of the library.

Ashok leaned over and spoke quietly. "I've got an idea. I'm going to scratch your back like you're a customer. Just close your eyes and look like you're enjoying it."

We shuffled around so I was sitting in front of him. I didn't have to act like I was enjoying it. I would've let him scratch my back all day long.

I listened as the little group drew nearer. It sounded like they were talking about us.

A girl asked, "What's this for?"

"Tau Alpha Theta," Ashok said. "We're raising money for students who can't afford tuition." He added, "Back scratching is a natural stress reliever and builds social bonds. It's just a dollar a minute. You want to give it a try?"

I peeked for a second or two. They were chatting among themselves, and then they headed toward us. Three girls and a boy. They looked like underclassmen.

"We'll take a minute for each of us," she said.

That was really encouraging for five minutes or so, but then campus was deserted again. Ashok checked his phone, and I checked mine. I texted Jayson to tell him we'd made our first four dollars and asked how things were going.

He wrote back: *Not great. Campus is dead. But there's a campus tour headed your way in about an hour.*

I told Ashok, and we came up with an idea. We needed to have a bunch of people waiting for back scratches when that tour came around. We texted everyone we knew on campus, which wasn't a lot between the two of us, since most of our friends were pledges anyway. But we begged the people we knew to come over to the library for a good cause.

An hour later, just in time for the procession of prospective students and their parents, we had Ashok's roommate Zi, his girlfriend Ashley, Rashid from the Alliance, and Oliver and three brothers he'd brought along from the house.

I was *so* happy Oliver showed up, I was plenty happy to give him a five-minute back scratch.

"How'd you know I love back scratches?" he said. "You guys came up with a great idea."

I was thankful I was sitting behind him and wearing baggy pants. Scratching his wide, muscle-hardened shoulders was doing things to me.

"Thanks for coming," I told him, my voice cracking.

"No problem. We'll try to send more people your way."

Afterward, he gave me a ten dollar bill for the five minute massage, with a five dollar tip, and a goodbye hug that confused me. It was a strong hug, but kind of a brah thing with a hard slap on the back. He left, and I texted Jayson to get his butt over to the library. We had a line of a dozen people waiting to get back scratches.

Things went really well from there. Lots of Jayson and Tyler's friends showed up around eleven, and the two of them brought in steady business all afternoon by canvassing the library. Business trickled off around five o'clock, but when Ashok counted our take from the day, we'd raised two hundred and thirty-two dollars. I was really proud of the four of us. We stuck around for another hour, and then Jayson called Vinnie to see how the other groups were doing. He was super happy to tell us that the combined total for all the groups was twelve hundred dollars and money was still coming in online.

We all went to the house at eight o'clock, and Oliver and the other brothers congratulated us. They ordered pizza and told us to enjoy the night hanging out in the basement with their gaming equipment. It was stressful pledging, but I wasn't minding it one bit.

I'd never had so many friends, and like Oliver had said, I'd found a place where I belonged.

Chapter Six

I FACETIMED WITH my parents later that week, and I think I shocked them as much as I'd shocked myself with how well I was doing at college. I couldn't tell them *everything*, of course. I told them I'd passed all my midterms and gotten a B+ on my freshman seminar paper. I couldn't stop smiling while we video chatted. I said I'd made a lot of friends and I was pledging a fraternity for gay and straight students.

My mom's eyes were welling up. Meanwhile, my dad asked questions about the fraternity. He wanted to make sure they weren't hazing me.

"They don't do hazing. There's just activities we have to do. They're challenging but kind of fun." I told him about the scholarship fundraiser.

"We're real proud of you, son," my dad said. "You just be careful with that fraternity. We hear stories. I know it's probably just a few bad apples, but we're your parents and we worry."

I didn't know how to explain to them that Tau wasn't the kind of fraternity that made pledges drink alcohol until they dropped dead. Or I guess I didn't want to bother. I was having an amazing time in ways they couldn't understand. It was complicated. Neither of them had gone to college, and my older brother dropped out of community college and got his license as a construction worker. I knew they were sacrificing to pay my out of state tuition. I'd overheard them talking about taking out a second mortgage on their house. But I couldn't really have a conversation with them about what college meant to me. It was more than setting myself up for a good career, and I just felt like they'd think I was being selfish.

Later that week, there was a big party at the house for Halloween. Jayson had a great idea to go as Harley Quinn from DC Comics. He talked me into going as a slutty unicorn with some costume he'd found online. It involved a unitard with a hood for the silver horn, and it showed a lot of my chest and legs.

"You can totally pull it off," he assured me. "You've got like the perfect twunk body."

He was the creative one, so I wasn't going to argue. I'm also not bragging, but since I started working out with Oliver, I was popping in places I hadn't thought I was capable of popping. I filled out that slutty unicorn costume, and Jayson got my face, arms, and legs sparkling with glitter gel. We both looked hawt for that party.

The night started out great. There was a wild vibe in the air with everyone dressed up in crazy costumes, and the house was tricked out with red lanterns, creepy decorations, and fog machines, and they had a deejay. We met up with Vinnie, Scott, and Tyler and stormed the dance floor like party animals. Ashok and some of the other pledges joined us. I'd somehow lost my fear of dancing and let loose, jumping and grinding to the beat. I worked up a sweat, and I was happy when the guys decided to take a break outside to cool down and chug some water.

While we were chilling, my glance strayed to the annex behind the house. It was a two-floor colonial style unit, almost a mansion of its own, right on the property. I remembered Oliver saying that twelve of the brothers lived there. Lights were on, but every window was shut with blinds.

Tyler noticed me staring. "That's where all the fun happens."

"What do you mean?"

"Sex parties. The guys who live back there are hardcore."

"That's just a rumor," Jayson said.

Tyler drew on his vape pen and croaked, "Whatever."

I'd never heard that rumor. I thought about the two twinks Oliver had introduced us to at the Retro Rave party. Jacob and Daryl. Oliver said they lived at the annex, and they had seemed kinda shady. But we were all fraternity brothers and shouldn't be talking bad about each other. Sex parties sounded like a ridiculous exaggeration to me.

While the other guys went on talking about the rumor, I spotted Oliver coming out of the back door in a skimpy Thor costume. Some girl dressed up as Wonder Woman was hanging off his side. Oliver smiled at her, and I felt like I'd been slugged in the gut. They weren't just being cuddly in a friendly way. I could tell by the way they looked at each other and were so comfortable with all their body contact.

I should have looked away, but I couldn't stop staring. I was shell shocked. Then Oliver glanced my way, we made eye contact, and he took the girl's hand in his and strolled over to our group. He gave each of us a fist bump.

"This is Lilah," he said.

She was a pretty, dark-haired girl. I hated her. Oliver wrapped his hand around her waist, and after a little small talk, I couldn't handle it. I took off back into the house, and then I went out the front door and staggered down the block until I had some privacy. Then I crouched down crying.

I hadn't even noticed Jayson had followed me out. He tried to get me to talk.

"I'm sorry, Ethan. It was a shitty thing for him not to tell you."

I wiped my eyes with one of my stupid arm hoofs. "I'm such an idiot."

"You're not an idiot."

"Yes, I am."

"No, you're not. You can't choose your feelings."

He was right about that. My heart was throbbing painfully for Oliver. But at the same time, I hated him. I stood up. "I can't go back in there. Just tell people I got sick or something."

"What are you gonna do? C'mon, Ethan. You should be with your friends."

"I can't." I looked down at my feet. I was so embarrassed, I was trembling. "You think everyone knows now?"

"They know something's going on with you. But I don't think they know it's about Oliver."

Just him saying the name again had my stomach aching. I appreciated Jayson for seeing if I was all right, but I just wanted to disappear from the world. "Thanks for checking on me. But I'm gonna go home. I don't want to be around people."

"You sure?"

I nodded.

He pulled me into a hug. "Text me when you're back in your room."

OLIVER DIDN'T LIKE me. My heart had been gouged and run over by a steamroller. Then, at times I felt like a fool. I mean, what did I expect? He'd never want someone like me, and now I knew he wasn't even gay.

My cell blew up with texts from people, asking if I was okay. I answered Vinnie and Ashok, just to say I wasn't feeling well, but I'd be fine. Then Oliver texted me. I turned my phone to silent and put it in my nightstand drawer.

I never wanted to see him again. I was too hurt and too embarrassed. The next morning, when Jayson Facetimed me, I told him I was quitting as a pledge.

He stared at me in horror. "Why?"

"It's not for me."

"Ethan, you love being a pledge."

I shrugged. "It was all right."

"I'm so not letting you do this. Because of Oliver? No way." His camera went out, and I heard vague noises.

"What're you doing?"

"Texting Vinnie. I was calling to let you know we're going out for breakfast at the diner. I'm telling him to meet at your room first. We're having an intervention."

I really wished he hadn't done that. I didn't want to have to tell Vinnie and Scott how pathetic I was. But the deed was done. I quickly grabbed a shower and dressed. As my emotions settled, I pulled myself together to face the guys. I went down to meet them in front of the dorm so I wouldn't look like such a drama queen.

Vinnie and Scott pulled up in Vinnie's old Ford sedan. They looked alarmed and wanted to know why I was quitting as a pledge.

I realized it wasn't right for me to lie to them. I let them know the truth.

"Honey, you got your heart broken," Vinnie said. He pulled me into a hug, and then he looked squarely at me. "But we're not letting you quit Tau over it. Brothers before lovers, remember?"

That had been the name of one of our pledge challenges. We had to dress a blow-up sex doll like it was our boyfriend or girlfriend, run it over to a post where our pledge partner was tied up, untie him and tie our 'boyfriend' to the post, then race to the finish with our partner, all in two minutes or less.

Jayson came along, and we hopped into Vinnie's car. They all said I'd be crazy to give up pledging. Jayson even told me that if I quit, he was quitting too. I definitely didn't want to be the reason he quit pledging. The guys really lifted my spirits. I started feeling better, and then, at the diner, I got coffee and a big plate of pancakes and bacon. After a few forkfuls of pancakes with maple syrup, I'd chilled out completely.

"All right. I won't quit."

Everybody around the table slapped five.

"It's not going to be easy." I sighed. "Oliver's at every pledge event."

Vinnie glanced at me. "Maybe you should talk to him. To clear the air. It'll make you feel more comfortable around him in the long run."

I was nowhere near being able to do that. Vinnie backed off from the suggestion, and we had a great time wolfing down our food and looking at photos from the party. I missed a lot of fun, and when I saw a pic of me, I was really sad I'd run out. I'd put so much time into getting dressed up. I looked damn good. I needed to manage my emotions better. I'd been kind of childish.

When Vinnie and Scott mentioned they were meeting up at the athletic center on Monday after classes, I asked if I could join. They said that would be great. Later, I texted Oliver to say I wouldn't be going to the gym with him in the mornings anymore. I said it was a schedule change and left things at that. He wrote back right away, asking if I wanted to talk, but I said no.

Chapter Seven

I MANAGED TO avoid Oliver for the next few days. We had another pledge meeting and a challenge that week, which was one of those blindfold "trust" activities where we had to get our partner through an obstacle course and then eat a plate of disgusting foods like pig ears and dead grasshoppers. That was gross, but it was almost entirely just interacting with the other pledges. Whenever Oliver glanced in my direction, I pretended I didn't notice. I know it was immature, but I thought it was the best way to get over him. I was purging him from my life so I could heal from the heartbreak. Vinnie and Scott still thought I should talk to Oliver and try to be friends, but Jayson understood what I needed to do. I figured by the time initiation was over, my feelings for him would wear off. Then, I could just act normal around him.

It was working. Well, little by little. I still thought about him sometimes and got sad and angry and jealous, and once or twice I couldn't stop myself from checking his Insta. He'd started posting photos of him and that girl, Lilah. Every time I looked, I regretted it. Love makes you do really stupid things.

Our pledge class had the job of planning Tau's winter formal party, and we were all over at the house one night, figuring out the layout for furniture and decorations. I remember there was a lot of commotion that night because some assholes stole the rainbow flag in front of the house, replaced it with a "TWAT" sign, and left a blow-up sex doll, violated in disgusting ways, on the lawn.

Everybody was pissed, and unfortunately the perpetrators had driven off before anyone saw them. Peter gathered everyone in the house to say he shared our anger. He told us it was probably a hazing prank another frat had put their pledges up to, and he didn't want anything cleaned up until public safety and a reporter from the local TV news came by to see it themselves. That happened pretty quickly, and while the guys from the exec council spoke with the authorities and a news team outside, our pledge group speculated about who was responsible.

Jayson remembered the stupid joke Shawn had made about TAT missing a 'w.' I hadn't crossed paths with Shawn much that semester, but I had seen him wearing a 'Zeke' jersey on campus, which meant he was rushing Zeta Kappa Epsilon. Some people thought for sure Zeke was behind the prank. Others said there were a half dozen jock frats that probably would've done it. Anyway, when the exec council finished with the news team, Oliver came around to ask for volunteers to help clean up outside. Everybody raised their hands, and Oliver said we could knock off for the night once we were done.

The news coverage was all over social media the next day, and even though I'd been at the house and seen things with my own eyes, I couldn't believe it had happened. I mean, I'd always known that hateful people existed, but the attack on Tau was personal to me now. It took place on campus, which was supposed to be safe for everyone, and I was proud of being a Tau pledge. Oliver texted us that day to say we had a special meeting that night, and someone from the student counseling center was going to be there to help us talk about it.

At the meeting, I didn't do much talking, but it helped to listen to other people. Vinnie said he wished we could retaliate against the people who'd attacked our house. Tyler spoke about having been bullied in high school for being gay, and some other guys had similar experiences, including Jayson who'd never told me that. Ashok brought up that a lot of Asian and Middle Eastern students felt unsafe on campus, and a pledge named Ray, who was Black, said it was the same for him. I remembered Jayson's experience with his suitemate. I felt for him in a deeper way, like my eyes had been opened to what that must've been like for him. I should've realized that before.

It was a really good discussion, and we all stuck around after the counselor left the meeting. I think the incident brought our pledge group even closer, and people wanted to say how they appreciated each other. I told Jayson and Ashok I was sorry what they went through, and we talked about looking out for each other more. I was proud of all of us and feeling empowered. Then Oliver popped in on us.

"Hey, you got a minute, Ethan?"

My gut wound up. All the self-confidence I'd been feeling flew out the door. Maybe he just had something to say related to pledging, but I still dreaded being face-to-face with him.

He stood there while I hesitated. Then I nodded and followed him to a spot in the back of the house, away from people.

"You doing okay?" he asked.

"Oh yeah."

"That's good. It was a shitty thing that happened, but it looked like the meeting went really well."

"Uh-huh."

An awkward silence passed. Oliver grinned nervously. "That's not what I wanted to talk to you about actually. Did I do something to piss you off."

I stared off to the side.

"You seem uncomfortable around me, and it's like out of the blue." He tried to pry out eye contact. "We used to be chill, but for the past few weeks, you haven't answered my texts. Something's going on. I feel bad but I don't know why I should feel bad." He blustered a breath. "I don't know. Did I overstep a boundary in some way? Or say something that hurt your feelings? I've been racking my brain, and I swear I have no idea. It's cool, whatever it is. I just thought we oughta make peace even if you're over being friends."

The tension kept mounting. I took a deep breath. He'd always been super nice to me. I couldn't keep acting like a jerk, especially after the pledge group had reaffirmed how important it was to respect each other. "You didn't do anything. It's me. I didn't want to tell you because I thought it was going to make things awkward between us. But I guess they couldn't get any more awkward than they already are." I breathed again. Being alone with him brought up so many feelings, including a pathetic hope that maybe he could like me the way I liked him. But that was me being stupid. I steeled myself. "I like you, Oliver. Like more than a friend. So, when I found out you were dating Lilah, I decided it was best if we stopped hanging out."

I'd never seen him shocked before. He seemed to be unable to speak. Unfortunately, like every one of his expressions, it was painfully cute.

"I should've said something earlier," I went on. "Maybe then I could've gotten over it and not have made such a drama out of it."

"Ethan, I'm really sorry." He pushed back his hair. "I had no idea."

We were quiet for a while.

"Is there anything I can do?" he asked.

I shrunk into myself. "No."

"If I'd known...well, maybe I shouldn't have invited you to come with me to the gym. I thought we were just pals."

That kinda hurt. "Why didn't you tell me you were straight?"

"Because I'm not. Entirely. It's complicated." His face colored. "You thought I was gay?"

"Well, yeah. You told me about that guy who got you into working out and building up your confidence to be yourself."

Oliver's eyes bugged. Then he shook his head. "Brad and I weren't together like *that*."

"And you're kind of touchy-feely with guys," I said. "Someone told me earlier in the semester you were fooling around with a guy who came by the house." I wasn't trying to give him the third degree, but he was acting like I was. Or maybe he just felt guilty. "I didn't..." he started to say. "Are you talking about Brooks?"

"I don't know. One of my friends saw it."

He shifted his weight and didn't look at me. "It was probably Brooks. But nothing happened. We hooked up once a long time ago." He glanced around. "How 'bout taking a walk with me?"

I followed him out back and around the house. I guessed he had something to tell me he hadn't told many people. It was kind of freaking me out. When we were a few houses down the block and nobody was around, he turned to me.

"Ethan, I feel like a real jerk. I didn't mean to, but I can see I led you on. And it hurts me too because I really enjoy spending time with you. You're like the little brother I never had, and I don't want to lose that. But I also don't want you to feel uncomfortable being around me."

I peeked at him and looked away. A scary thought occurred to me. Was he warming up to tell me I should leave the pledge class?

"I didn't tell you about my sexuality because I haven't figured it out myself. And I know you're figuring out your own stuff, so I also didn't want to confuse you." I watched him carefully. "But now I feel like I owe you an explanation. It's not a secret. Most of the other brothers know, so you should too."

He gave me a tight grin. "I told you when I joined Tau, I found my community. But not in the sense of having the same attraction as the other guys. It was being around people who accept me for who I am. Guys who don't care if you're not masc or a jock. Or if you're into something different, y'know, in the bedroom. I guess it's more about gender expression for me." He pushed back his hair again. I could see he was having a hard time explaining things.

"I've had, I mean I do have sex with men," he said. "As a casual thing. I don't think I could do it with a guy I had feelings for. I mean, non-sexual feelings. And I'm attracted to women, both physically and emotionally. So, in terms of relationships, it makes more sense to me to date women."

"So, like, you're bi?"

"More like pansexual. And my thing is being submissive. I've fooled around with bi guys and bi women and gay guys and transgender women, and a transgender man. I think, when I squint into the future in terms of who I'd settle down with, it would probably be a transgender woman, or a cis gender woman. If she was okay with being more dominant in the bedroom. Or maybe a polyamorous relationship is what's right for me. I'm still figuring it out, like I said."

I was thinking all of this would have been helpful for him to say a long time ago, but I could tell it meant a lot to him to share. Anyway, it took away some of the hurt I was feeling. I didn't understand everything he was saying about his sexuality, but it was sinking in we weren't cut out to be together that way.

"Does Lilah know?"

He hesitated. "She doesn't. And we're getting to the point where I should tell her." He razzed a breath. "I'm pretty nervous about it, actually. She knows Tau has a lot of gay brothers, and I told her I've been with guys. She's cool with that. But I don't know how she'll react to the other stuff."

He was quiet for a while.

"Thanks for telling me, I guess. I hope it works out for you with Lilah."

"Thanks." He lifted his hand, probably to squeeze my shoulder like he used to, but he cut the motion short. "You're an awesome guy, Ethan. You think we can still hang out?"

I nodded. Then I explained I'd started going to the gym with Vinnie and Scott later in the day.

"Pledge brothers should do things together. I'll miss the company, but I'm happy for you." He looked at me and smiled. "And

Ethan, you're going to find a guy who's *so* into you. You're a really genuine person." He smirked. "And your body is getting tight, boy."

We headed back to the house. I felt a big weight lifted off of me.

I NEVER WOULD'VE believed I'd become a gym rat in college, but after almost three months of going to the athletic center four times a week, I can't deny that's what I was. It really wasn't bad once I knew how to use the equipment, and I enjoyed the social time with Vinnie and Scott. The two of them had been working out since junior year of high school, and they were built, but they weren't snobby about it. Vinnie joked that he only went to the gym in order to get laid. He took a lot of racy photos of himself for his Grindr and Insta. We didn't talk about it directly, but I think it was on all of our minds that building muscle was a way to deter the haters, after the hazing prank. Anyway, the three of us motivated each other.

After Oliver made that comment, I did start noticing people giving me looks, and it wasn't in the mean way I was used to. Girls looked at me and smiled when I walked through campus. A couple guys at the gym peeked at me from time to time. Then, on a Friday night, Vinnie drove a bunch of us to a nightclub in Asbury Park where they had an eighteen and over night for college students. I dressed in a pair of stretch jeans and a tank top to show off my arms. When we all went onto the dance floor, an older guy started hitting on me.

I wasn't looking to hook up with anyone. I was still pretty scared of doing that, especially with someone older. But I didn't mind the attention. A little while after the older guy gave up trying with me, a kid closer to my age danced up on me and put his hand on my butt. That felt a little too nervy to me at first, but he was cute, and I'd seen lots of people messing around on the dance floor. It didn't mean anything. Vinnie and Scott got kind of raunchy with each other dancing sometimes, and they were just friends.

So, that night, I danced real close with the kid with a crew cut and a stubbly beard and let his hands wander wherever he wanted. He asked me to come out to his car with him, but he split quick when I told him I was with friends and not looking to fool around.

Then later, we met a pair of guys from Fairleigh Dickinson University, and they were super cute and flirty. When we headed back to the dance floor, one of them danced in front of me really close, and later he turned me around and pressed up so close, I could feel the heat from his groin against my behind. His friend got in front of me, and they sandwiched me. That was really crazy, and extremely hot, and then they started kissing me and kissing each other while we danced. They were both hot and thin and toned. I was having a great time. I mean, I guess I would've preferred my first kiss to be with someone I'd gotten to know better, but fooling around on the dance floor was a lot of fun.

When we drove back to campus that night, the other guys gave it to me good.

"Ethan, you're like an entirely different person now," Tyler said.

Everybody laughed.

"You went from prude to slut in ten seconds, dude," Scott joked.

"Well, I wasn't going to say anything," Jayson piped in. "But this bitch shamed me for hooking up for blow jobs at the beginning of the semester."

Vinnie howled, and the rest of them cracked up.

Tyler elbowed me in the ribs. "So, what's the tea, Ethan?" I was between him and Jayson in the back seat. "Are you like pregnant now? And if so, do you know who the baby daddy is?"

I was burning up in the face. "Was it really that bad?"

"Yeah." They answered in unison.

Jayson placed his hand on mine. "But we're happy for you."

"It's good to see you cutting loose," Vinnie told me.

"Just be safe, okay?" Jayson said.

"Did you exchange numbers with those guys from Farleigh?" Tyler asked.

"I did. But we're really far from each other. I'll probably never see them again."

I wouldn't have minded seeing them, but I was fine if it never happened. I was just trying new things, and I was glad my friends supported me. Pledging Tau was the best decision I'd ever made. I had an amazing friend group, and I was actually meeting guys who thought I was attractive.

TUESDAY NIGHT, BEFORE Thanksgiving break, I was at the house with Ashok, finalizing the digital invite for the winter formal. The big party was only two weeks away. I couldn't believe it. Time had speed warped that semester, and the final initiation challenge was a week after the Winter Formal. After that, the brothers would decide which pledges were invited to join the house.

Ashok was great at digital publishing. I just helped with the copy and gave my opinion on fonts, colors, and the overall look of the invitation. We had a great looking invite, incorporating winter colors and a graphic of two snowmen in tuxedos for the background. Ashok emailed it off to the executive council for final approval. Then we sat back in our chairs at a table in the den. I was tired. I'd had a quiz in bio that day, and I was going home to Pennsylvania first thing in the morning. It wasn't going to be much of a break. I had lots of school work to do.

"Are you bringing anyone to the formal?" Ashok asked.

"Me? No. I don't think anyone is." I thought it was strange that he asked me that question. None of the pledges mentioned bringing a date. "We spend all our time together, so it's not like we're ever meeting people outside of Tau. Are you bringing someone?"

"No."

I glanced at him. He looked like he had something on his mind.

"Do you ever think about hypotheticals?" He didn't wait for me to answer. "Like, if you could bring one of the pledges or the brothers to the formal, is there someone you'd like to go with?"

I shrugged nervously. "Jayson's my best friend. I guess I'd go with him."

Ashok looked away. "I mean, if you could go with someone you really liked. More than a friend."

I hadn't thought about that. Between getting over Oliver and just having fun with Jayson, Vinnie, Scott, and Tyler, it really hadn't crossed my mind. I told Ashok that, leaving out the part about my crush on Oliver.

"That makes sense." Something was still eating at him, and then it finally came out. "This is awkward. But I told myself I was going to do it." He sat forward a little and looked at me. "If we weren't in the same pledge class, I'd want to go to the formal with you. Do you think when initiation is over, you'd ever want to go on a date?"

A pit formed in my stomach, but I don't know why. Ashok was a really great guy, and Lord knew, no one had ever asked me on a date. He didn't get my heart racing like Oliver did, but he was cute, and we always had a lot of fun together. But out of nowhere, the situation had me feeling guarded.

He filled the silence. "I'm sorry. I shouldn't have said anything. I just thought I'd give it a try."

"There's nothing to apologize for."

He powered down his laptop and started packing up his stuff. "You don't have to be nice about it. I guess I misinterpreted things."

"You didn't." That kind of blurted out of my mouth. I didn't want to hurt his feelings. But now I had to explain what I meant without making the situation worse. I mean, I could've said I'd had this massive crush on Oliver that I was still getting over even though he'd made it clear he was mainly into women, but Ashok wouldn't want to hear that. He had such a pained look on his face.

"Please don't feel bad about asking me to date," I said. "I'm just not focusing on that right now. It's not you. It's me."

"I shouldn't have said anything." He finished packing up his things and stood up from the table. "How about we forget this ever happened?"

I felt like a total A-hole. "Sure. If that's what you want."

He glanced at me and nodded. Then he said he was going home because his mom was picking him up early in the morning for Thanksgiving break, and he walked out.

Chapter Eight

I DIDN'T EVEN tell Jayson what had happened with Ashok. Ashok had asked me to forget it, and I wanted to respect his privacy. I felt bad for a little while, but to be honest, my head was all over the place. Over Thanksgiving break, I took a look at my assignments, and I realized I'd gotten really far behind with my classes. I had a ton of make up work to do, and soon enough, I'd have final exams and final papers. Meanwhile, it was a busy time for pledging. At the end of my first week back at New Jersey State, we had the Winter Formal.

Everything turned out great, from the food to the decorations. Our pledge class hauled in a ten foot Christmas tree and got it looking spectacular with lights and ornaments. We put together a red carpet area for photos, strung lights all through the house, catered in a kick-ass spread of passed hors d'oeuvres and a buffet, and had white rose boutonnieres with pine sprigs for everyone. We all looked amazing in suits and ties. The brothers brought dates, but most of us pledges went stag. My heart dropped a little when I saw Oliver with Lilah, and I felt awkward around Ashok. We said hello, and then he veered away from me for the rest of the night. Anyway, I had a lot of fun dancing and hanging out with Jayson, Vinnie, Scott, and the other pledges.

Late one night the following week, in the middle of finals, we got Swedish flagged. Oliver had told us we'd have one final challenge before they decided who was getting initiated. Twenty out of twenty-two of us made it to the parking lot of the Environmental Sciences building. The rumor was two kids got kicked out for drinking at the formal. The rest of us huddled together in winter coats. We were all loopy from nerves.

The minivan careened into the lot, and two masked brothers ordered us inside, hostage-style. They took us on a long drive, and when they finally let us out, we were in some forested park.

They moved us down a trail with flashlights. It was the first time I truly felt scared during one of the challenges. We had to be in the middle of nowhere, which was the perfect place to haze us in some humiliating way, and they'd taken our cell phones.

The air was cold and damp. We headed deep in the woods. It smelled piny with an undercurrent of decaying maple leaves, and then I heard the sound of moving water. It got louder, roaring, as we traveled farther and the trail got muddier. Finally, the guys called us to a halt and shouted orders.

"Strip down. Put all your clothes in the bags. Then get in alphabetical order and follow us to the death dive."

I did what I was told. It was so dark, I could barely see people a foot or two away from me, and it was probably just a few degrees above freezing. Nobody complained. Everyone must've been as terrified as I was, which made things even scarier. I dreaded being naked around other people, and far worse, I didn't like the sound of "death dive."

The brothers gave us garbage bags for our clothes, and we got into a line along a muddy, wooded trail covered with fallen leaves. We'd gotten good at sorting ourselves out alphabetically. I fell in the middle, which was both good and bad. I didn't have to go first, but the anticipation was excruciating. I covered myself with my hands for privacy while every part of me was shivering.

Through the glow of flashlights, I put some things together. We were at the bank of a rocky river near a waterfall, based on the echoing roar and fizz. The water at the top had to be shallow. The brothers who had brought us there were standing in the middle of it with their flashlights. They called out for Sam Augustine, and along the line behind him, we all perched around and squinted to see what was going on.

I heard a scream of terror, and it got eaten up by the roaring water. My heart started beating outside of my chest. Then I felt like all my insides were going to be expelled in a really gross, embarrassing way. The line inched forward. One by one, they called up a pledge, and I heard another horrified scream that disappeared into the night. When just two guys were ahead of me, things came into sharper focus. They were bringing people to the edge of a waterfall and making them jump into a sightless depth.

Steve Jokavic went ahead of me, and then it was my turn. I trudged into the ankle-deep water numbly and tried not to look over the edge.

One of the brothers barked at me, "Leavitt, do you pledge your loyalty to Tau Alpha Theta?"

I didn't want to die, but a greater part of me was committed to doing anything they asked to earn my place at the frat. In just a span of months, the pledges and brothers had become my new family. "Yes, sir."

They pointed me to the very edge of the watery cliff. I couldn't tell how far it was to the bottom or where I was going to land. Everything was pitch black below. All I could discern was raging water and disembodied screeches and howls. Did I mention I was scared of heights?

I prayed to God and jumped off. I felt the rush of accelerating gravity, saw my life flash before my eyes, and then I plunged feet-first into icy water. I fought back to the top, gasping for precious air. If I hadn't been so pumped up with adrenalin, I might have died from hypothermia. But as it was, I hollered for joy. I was alive, kind of hyper-alive from the rush.

Voices called out to me from the river bank, and a group of shadowy figures helped me climb up and patted my back and shouted in my face triumphantly. Someone handed me a big fluffy towel, a robe, and slippers. They had a portable heater a little farther up the bank. I headed over there to warm up with the other pledges and cheer on our friends as they made the dive. I guess they'd taken us to a state park with a big river gorge. Believe me, none of us were mad about it. Jumping blindly from that forty foot waterfall was the most bad-ass thing I'd ever done.

After the last pledge did his jump, the woods behind us lit up with flashlights. A rowdy commotion gained up on us, and then the other Tau brothers emerged from the trees. Peter, Jamal, Tomas, and Oliver. Then more of the guys came along. I think it was the entire frat.

"Congratulations Pledge Class 2022," Peter shouted. "You all made it. Welcome to Tau Alpha Theta."

We attacked each other with hugs and howled. The brothers came around and shook our hands. Then we all got in one big rugby circle, jumping up and down and chanting: "T-A-T."

Chapter Nine

I'M NOT GOING to play it chill. I was insanely happy with myself. I'd come to college a total nobody, and I hadn't even dreamed how awesome college could be. I was part of the coolest fraternity in the world. I had fifty-something amazing friends. I didn't just have a social life. I had a hectic, crazy social life. Between meeting up with Jayson and Tyler, going to the athletic center with Vinnie and Scott, and getting together with everybody at the house at night, I always had something to do.

The initiation ceremony was a big deal. All the pledges dressed up in suits and ties, and every single brother was there along with a good number of alumni, some of whom had traveled from out of town. We had to recite the Tau oath, which involved our promise to uphold the fraternity mission and always be there for our brothers. Then Oliver called us up to the podium one by one, people cheered like at a commencement ceremony, and Peter gave us our fraternity pins. They took a group photo of the pledge class and put it on the frat's Insta, and I couldn't stop sharing it with my friends and family. All the pledges were doing that. Peter told us they'd get the photo framed, and it would go up on the front hall where they had class photos going back thirty years.

Afterward, they had a buffet dinner in the dining room, and people congratulated us and we ate and joked around. I felt really special. We'd made it, and Peter and all the brothers were really welcoming. Jacob and Derek had been eyeing me, but after what Tyler had said, I steered away from them. Maybe that was shady on my part. The gossip had gotten into my head, I guess. If it was true, I didn't want to get a bad reputation from associating with guys who had sex parties.

Then a heated argument broke out from the hallway.

"Fuck you. I won't sit by and watch your liberal agenda ruining Tau's reputation. This used to be a place people could feel proud of."

"Luke, I think you should leave."

"You realize what you're doing? You're grooming young men into your amoral lifestyle."

"He said you should leave. We'll be informing national about your behavior."

"Another pervert? Well, fuck you, too."

I glimpsed a man in the hallway storming out the front door with a loud slam. Luke Renfield? I recognized Peter's voice in the argument, along with an older man, maybe one of the alumni.

The party was silent for a moment, and then it sounded like some of the senior brothers had gathered in the other room to talk about what happened. I was mad curious, but just as I was about to walk over there, Oliver came into the room to address everyone.

"Guys, Luke does this every year. But this is going to be the last time. We're filing a complaint with national's Board of Trustees so he'll be banned from coming here."

People cheered. I was happy too, but I also had a lot of questions. What kind of person shows up at a gay/straight fraternity every year just to harass people about being gay?

Oliver must've noticed I was upset. He came over to me while the rest of the guys went back to chatting.

"You okay?"

"Who is that guy?"

Oliver frowned. "He's a world class pain in the ass." He drew me over to the side. "Don't let his bullshit ruin your night. It's a celebration for all you've achieved."

"What's his deal?"

"Supposedly he was an okay guy back when he was a brother in the 90s. He was ROTC, and after he graduated, he did a long tour in Afghanistan. He was Special Forces, and I guess he saw a lot of bad shit." Oliver rubbed his face. "I don't know if that explains anything, but people say that changed him. When he returned to civilian life, he got involved in conservative politics. Like really alt-right conservative politics. Most of the alumni like that just resign, but Luke wants to make it his cause to bring Tau back to the old days when it was 'straight and Christian.' He's harmless. Just has a big mouth."

It made me mad that the guy tried to ruin the initiation ceremony every year because of hatred. Then Oliver put his hand on my shoulder and gazed at me in his protective way. That triggered my bitter feelings toward him again. I thought I'd gotten over them, but I was wound up. Like, he didn't have to act like I needed to be handled with kid gloves as though I was so hopelessly heartbroken over him.

I told him I was going to head back to my friends and walked away.

THAT SEMESTER, I admit, I let my school work slide a little. We all did. Pledging took up a lot of time, and it felt like it was more important than keeping up with classes. So my finals didn't go so great. Overall, I got a C- in Bio, a C in American History and B minuses in my other classes. That put me on academic probation and with a lot of hard work ahead of me to raise my GPA to the 3.2 required for the physician assistant program. But all things considered, I was glad I hadn't done worse. At the end of term, the only thing I cared about was the celebration party the brothers were throwing for our pledge class. It was the night before I'd be going home for winter break.

The party was crazy. They had the place set up like a dance club with a deejay, lights, and a foam machine, and everybody was throwing off their shirts and dancing. I was feeling confident enough to do the same. I'd earned it after working out all semester, and maybe it sounds conceited, but I was proud of the way I looked. I danced up to Vinnie and Scott, and we twerked on each other and the two sandwiched me between them and things got sexual. We only liked each other as friends, but they were both really attractive. I guess we were caught up in celebrating making it into the frat and just being able to be ourselves. We were grinding and feeling each other's bodies, and the three of us made out on the dance floor.

The whole night was this amazing blur. Like I said, the energy was wild, like it was New Year's Eve. Everybody wanted to party since we weren't going to see each other over winter break, and I think there was a bit of an edge to the celebration for those of us who were gay. Nobody was talking about it, but being sexual with each other felt like a big fuck you to that homophobic Luke Renfield guy who'd been such an asshole at initiation. I mingled with just about everybody, and when I spotted Ashok, I darted over to him with a big smile on my face.

I was like ninety-nine percent sure he saw me, and then he stared down at his phone and sped off in the other direction. I guess he was still pissed at me, which kind of hurt, but so much was going on, I didn't let it bother me.

Later, I was dancing with some other guys, and someone pressed up behind me with his crotch against my butt, kissed my neck, and ran his hands around my chest. That felt really great, and while we were dancing, a cute twinky kid danced up in front of me with a friendly smile. He put his hands on my waist and pressed his hips into mine. I did a double take. I hadn't recognized him at first. It was Jacob. He was wearing a lot of eye makeup, and I'd never seen him with his shirt off. He had a lot of tattoos.

I looked over my shoulder and saw his friend Daryl grinding on me from behind. My guard was up for a few seconds, remembering the rumor that they participated in sex orgies in the annex. Pretty soon though, I was feeling like I didn't want to be rude and slip away from them. Everyone was grooving with everyone. We were all brothers now, and Jacob and Daryl were both really cute.

When the DJ mixed in a track with a slower beat, Jacob leaned into my ear. "You want to get something to drink?"

I nodded. My shirt was soaked with sweat, and I could use some water to cool down.

He took my hand to lead me over to the bar, and Daryl followed along. I was surprised they were being so friendly. They'd never talked to me at any of the other parties, but I guessed maybe it made a difference now that I was officially a frat brother.

Over at the bar where it was quieter, they re-introduced themselves.

"Ethan," I said. "We met at the rave party."

Jacob, the twinky kid, ran his hand along my bare shoulder. "You really filled out since then."

Daryl, the shorter, punky-looking Black guy, joined him in admiring my body.

"Thanks." I was blushing really hard and feeling things from being so close to them.

We got bottled waters and tossed back some slugs. The two guys were looking at me flirtatiously. I didn't know what to say.

"You're a freshman, right?" Jacob said.

I nodded.

"Congrats on making it through rush." Jacob glanced at Daryl. "We went through it as freshmen, too. We're seniors now. It's an awesome organization, right?"

I blushed and nodded again.

"You ever think about living here at the house?"

I twitched my nose. They were eyeing me encouragingly. "Maybe next year," I said. "I've got a housing contract for the dorms."

Jacob scowled. Daryl eased up closer and roamed his hand down my back.

"I bet you'd like living here better," Daryl said. "You're really hot. All the best guys live at the house. Two rooms in the annex are going to be free in the spring. You can bring some of your friends."

I was stunned and flattered, though I didn't know how that was possible. "My parents are paying for my housing plan, so I'd have to see if they can afford it."

"The cost is about the same. Maybe less with a roommate."

"Really?"

"It could save your parents some money," Jacob said. "And it's no big deal breaking your housing contract with the dorms. The university says it is, but they always back down. You just tell them you found a more affordable option."

I liked the idea of living in the house, though it sounded complicated. I mean, I really had no idea how such things worked, and out of state tuition and room and board was a lot for my parents. Plus, those rumors about the annex had me worried.

Jacob gave me a killer smile. "You're a real hottie. Talk to your parents about it over winter break." He gave one of my nipples a tweak, which got me squirming and smiling. He asked for my phone so we could exchange numbers. Then the two eased away from me and gave me parting grins. I realized Oliver had stepped over.

Oliver had a concerned expression on his face. I was officially a brother, so I wasn't sure what the big deal was. I turned away from him, and I took a draw of my water.

"How's it going?" he asked.

I shrugged.

He came up close, trying to make eye contact. "You made it as a pledge. I'm really proud of you, but be careful with Jacob and Daryl."

"Why?"

He drew a breath and skirted my gaze. "It's just...well, some of the guys who live in the annex...it can get a little sketchy back there."

That hit me the wrong way. Oliver had basically been leading me on, and now he was saying I shouldn't trust two other guys who were showing an interest in me?

"I just saw they were getting kind of aggressive with you and wanted to make sure you were okay," he said.

"They weren't getting aggressive."

Oliver said nothing.

"How's Lilah?" I asked him.

He hesitated. "She broke up with me." He smiled wistfully. "Turns out she wasn't so okay with everything."

"I'm sorry." Then I considered something else. "Is that why you're so interested in talking to me lately?"

"Ethan, you're my little brother. I'm just looking out for you."

The sincerity on his face was cute, though something inside me was changing. I was a brother now, not some lost kid who needed his special attention.

"You don't have to."

"Maybe not, but I want to."

I looked at him squarely. "Don't." I finished my last gulp of water, gave him a nod, and went to find Jayson, Vinnie, and Scott.

AT THE END of the night, Vinnie and Scott drove Jayson, Tyler, and me home. That party had stirred up a lot of drama to talk about. Jayson was crushing on this kid Alex from our pledge class. Tyler had hooked up with Frankie, who was one of the upperclassmen brothers, and Scott had spent most of the night with Luis. They were all giving each other shit, and no one mentioned what had happened with me and Jacob and Daryl until they dropped off Jayson and Tyler, and I was alone with Vinnie and Scott in the car.

I could see Vinnie's eyes on me in the rearview mirror. "So, what's up with you, Jacob, and Daryl?"

I blushed. "Nothing." I told them what they'd said about moving into the annex, and I peeked at the two of them to see what they were thinking.

"That sounds hot," Vinnie said.

Scott didn't say anything.

"They said I should see if any of my friends were interested." I chewed my lip. "I mean, I wouldn't do it by myself."

Vinnie cocked a look at Scott. "How fucking awesome would that be to live at the house?"

Scott still didn't say anything.

"They said it's about the same cost as living at the dorms. Maybe less. But I need to talk to my parents." I pushed back my hair. "I wouldn't do it unless you guys were into it. And Jayson. They said it's cheaper if we double up."

Vinnie smiled enthusiastically and gave Scott a playful nudge. "I'm in. What d'you say? It'll be a hell of a lot better than living at home. I bet we can both swing the rent from waitering."

Vinnie and Scott had part-time jobs at a restaurant on the Jersey Shore where they made pretty good money. There was something else to consider, however.

"You remember what Tyler said about the annex?" I said.

Vinnie scoffed. "You know what that is? Haters."

Scott turned back to me. "You seen the guys who live there? Danny? Shannon? They're the best looking brothers in the house."

"Queens get jealous," Vinnie said. "I'm sure the stories get blown out of proportion."

"You think?"

"Hell, yeah." Vinnie smirked at me in the rearview mirror. "And if it's true, that's not the worst thing in the world, is it?"

I laughed a little though it made me uncomfortable. Anyway, it was a long shot. I'd need a roommate, and the only person I could think of who might be interested was Jayson. Not to mention, I'd have to convince my parents it was a good idea.

Chapter Ten

WINTER BREAK WAS kind of endless and boring. I mean, I didn't mind spending time with my family, and I got to hang out with Kathleen and Gary, who I hadn't seen since the summer. But honestly, I missed Tau like mad. I felt like I'd become a different person since leaving home. That maybe sounds a little weird. I'd only been gone for four months, but it felt more like a lifetime had passed. I'd grown up, made totally different friends, made out with guys, jumped blindly off a forty foot high waterfall, not to mention I could bench press one hundred and fifty pounds for ten reps, and I didn't mind my shirts being a little snug around my chest and shoulders. I went through the motions with family get-togethers. When I met up with Kathleen and Gary at Denny's, they teased me about turning into a frat brah. It was funny at first, but as they talked about the same old things like snobby classmates and the latest RPGs, it was like we had nothing in common anymore.

Meanwhile, I texted with Jayson and Vinnie a lot. They were feeling the same way being back in their hometowns. We all just wanted to get back to school and hang out with everybody again.

One morning after the holidays, I had breakfast alone with my mom and dad. It was prime time to talk to them about my housing plans. I told them about the opportunity at Tau. My mom said nothing. I could tell she wasn't thrilled about it. My dad seemed open to the idea.

"They said it's the same cost as the dorms?"

"Less if I double up. I've been talking to a friend about sharing a room."

I ate some eggs and bacon. Jayson had said he'd have a conversation with his parents about leaving the dorms and rooming together in the annex. Vinnie and Scott were all-in to take the other room Jacob had mentioned. But something I said wasn't sitting well with my mom, and finally she said something.

"They've cut back your father's hours at the lumber company." She stood up from her chair and started clearing dishes from the table. "Your parents aren't made of money. It would've been a lot more affordable if you'd gone to one of the colleges in-state."

I hadn't expected her to be so harsh. She was the one who pushed for me to go to a small, private college where the tuition was even higher than New Jersey State.

Dad looked at her. "It's not so bad." He glanced at me. "If this is what you want, we'll make it work."

"How, Terry?" My mom turned to me. "And they don't give out college degrees for joining a fraternity and partying every night. You need to pull up your grades to get into your major. How're you going to do that living at a frat house?"

I stared down at my plate. I knew they'd gotten my grade report, and I felt real shitty about letting them down. "It was my first semester," I said. "I promise I'll do better in the spring."

She rolled her eyes. "Well, you're going to have to put an effort into it. And that means more studying and less socializing. I don't think living at the fraternity is a good idea."

Raw emotions poured out of me. "Joining Tau is the best thing that ever happened to me. You'd rather I be a loser for the rest of my life?"

My mom turned stricken. "Who said you're a loser? Honey, I'm just saying you've got to meet us halfway. You wanted to go to that university, and we took out a second mortgage on the house so we could pay for it. I'm glad you made friends and you're enjoying yourself, but there's got to be a balance between your social life and your classes."

I didn't need to be lectured about that. I knew what I needed to do. I just wished she could appreciate how much I'd accomplished by being initiated at Tau. I'd never worked harder on anything in my life.

My dad broke the tension. "If this is what Ethan wants, we'll figure it out." He looked at me firmly. "Ethan's going to work on those grades."

I stood up from the table because I was ready to explode. "I'll get a second job and pay for it myself. This means a lot to me, okay?" I walked out of the kitchen.

"Hey. Ethan," Dad called after me. "We're just trying to have a conversation."

I kept going. But I stopped in the living room and overheard them talking.

"We can't go through the same thing we did with Tim. And back then, we both had full-time salaries."

"I told you, I can pick up shifts at Home Depot," Dad said.

"Why can't you take my side for once? It's not just about the money. He's off having the time of his life at school. He's not going to get anywhere unless he applies himself."

"He'll come around. Y'know, it's not a bad thing he's made some friends. He had a tough time in high school. Look at where he's at now. He's really shaped up. Joining a fraternity has built his confidence."

"For crying out loud, Terry, he could do that at an in-state college without sending us into massive debt. We're paying for him to get an education, not to turn into a fraternity jock."

I didn't want to hear any more. I shot off to my bedroom upstairs.

WHEN I GOT back to school, I was even more determined to move into the frat and prove my mom wrong. I wasn't going to college just to party and waste their money. I could live the frat life *and* get good grades. I was registered for a lighter course load in the spring, and I talked to Vinnie about getting a job at the restaurant where he and Scott worked. I'd wait tables on weekends to contribute more to my tuition and housing, if things came to that. I couldn't believe my mom had turned on me completely. It was like she had no idea who I was anymore.

I texted Jacob about the rooms he mentioned. He told me the four of us should come over the first Friday after the semester started.

That morning came, and we were all mad excited. I told the other guys we should probably dress up, just a bit, to make a good impression. No sweats or shorts or beat up sneakers, you know? Vinnie drove us all over, and we were looking good. He found a spot to park down the street, and we walked up the driveway behind the house to the two-story, white shingled backhouse.

I knocked on the door. The place was dead, and I worried for a minute Jacob had forgotten he'd told me to come at ten o'clock. It was right in our text thread. I was panicking.

Then we heard some heavy-footed steps. An alarm code beeped, and locks clicked and jangled. The door flew open, and we all got a pleasant surprise.

A tall, built dude, wearing nothing but thigh-length, fitted boxer shorts stood at the door. His shaggy blond hair was sleep tossed. He squinted at us.

I could feel my voice threatening to crack, but I pushed out words. "We're here to see Jacob."

He blinked a couple times. "Oh man. I forgot. You're the fresh meat that just got initiated."

Now *I* was blinking. I think I'd seen him before, wearing a lot more clothes. I still hadn't formally met all the brothers. Some of them like Jacob and Daryl didn't come to all the house events.

"Fresh meat. *Fresh*men. It's what we call freshmen," he explained. He stood aside and waved us in. "Jacob's probably still asleep. I'll wake him up. We all sleep in on Fridays."

He had an amazing body. Like zero body fat, and he waxed his chest and stomach so he was completely smooth. I pulled my eyes away so I could walk past him, and the other guys followed me. The guy shut the door, clicked and bolted like three locks and entered an alarm code. Then he led us into the house.

"I'm Grant. I've got the front bedroom on the first floor. It's one of the biggest bedrooms in the house, but lemme tell you, it comes with a major trade-off." He looked me dead in the eyes. "Anybody comes to that door, at any hour, day or night, I gotta hear it." He scratched his head and yawned. "Not to mention, I've gotta hear every damn thing that's going on in the kitchen and the living room."

I gave him a friendly smile and glanced around. It was a sunny day, but the place was really dark. The windows were covered with total blackout blinds. I guess they kept the blinds drawn until everyone was up and about. I saw what looked like a living room in the front, and we passed by stairs to the second floor and some closed doors off the hall. The place smelled like men. Not in a gross, stinking locker room way. But it was a bit stale, and I could smell a hint of body spray and the scent of guys who just rolled out of bed. I wasn't minding it. It actually had me feeling excited.

Grant led us to a big kitchen with white and black tiles and a granite counter in the middle. It was cleaner than I expected for a houseful of college guys. No dishes in the sink, and all the surfaces looked clean.

That's where we each introduced ourselves and shook Grant's hand. His vibe was disinterested. Maybe he thought he was too cool to hang out with freshmen. He pointed his hand at me like a gun and said he'd drag Jacob out of bed. We watched him disappear down the hall to the back of the house.

Alone, grins crept up our faces.

"Kinda wild, huh?" Vinnie said.

Jayson mouthed. "*He's hawt.*"

"Right?" Vinnie said. "I'm like, why haven't we been introduced before?"

Jayson was getting that silly, antsy look like he was about to burst. I prayed the two could hold it together so we wouldn't make fools out of ourselves. Oliver had told me only upperclassmen got to room at the house. I was suddenly crazy nervous they were all going to think we were too juvenile and stupid.

"Hey. Look. What's all that for?" Scott drew our attention to something high up on one of the walls. Like a camera? I saw two others in corners of the room.

"For security, probs," Vinnie said. "You saw they've got a really serious alarm system."

Jayson pivoted around. "What have they got in here that they need so many security cams?"

I was wondering the same thing, though it seemed like it would be rude to ask, at least right away. The big main house had an alarm system, but the guys always forgot to use it. With over a dozen people living there, someone was always going in and out of the house at all hours. They had one security camera in the front of the house and one in the back. It was a little weird the annex was geared up like a bank.

While we were peering around the kitchen, we heard a lazy shuffle from the way we'd come, and a guy stumbled in completely naked. I thought he had to be drunk at first. But the sleepy look washed off his face real quick when he realized he didn't have the kitchen to himself.

"Jesus Christ." He backed up against the wall, covering himself with his hands. The four of us jumped away from him on reflex. The guy spotted an apron hanging on the wall and grabbed it. Though not before I'd seen cock, balls, and pubes. I was drenched. The guy was just as beautiful as Grant.

Just then, Grant came back with Jacob, who was thankfully dressed in a T-shirt and board shorts. Jacob's gaze landed on the naked guy fumbling to tie on an apron, and his face hardened.

"Dude, I told you people were coming to look at the rooms today."

The guy scowled. "I just came downstairs to make a cup of coffee."

Jacob gave him a look, and then the guy skulked out of the kitchen in his apron, giving us a scorching view of his backside.

Jacob came over to me with his hand stretched out. "Ethan. What up, boss?" I shook his hand, still kind of reeling. "Guess you may as well have gotten that introduction to the house. Some of the guys are comfortable *au naturel*." He looked at me, earnestly. "You're cool with that, right?"

I was just about 101 percent sure I was. I nudged Jayson, Vinnie, and Scott to introduce themselves. Grant drifted down the hall back to his room and shut the door. Jacob took up a space leaning against the counter.

"You guys are all friends?" he said.

"Mm-hmm."

He was slyly studying us. "You understand Tau's policy about confidentiality?"

We all nodded vigorously. For rush, we'd taken oaths to not talk about anything related to initiation and what the brothers did at the house. For a moment, I wondered if we'd been lured into another pledge challenge. Though Oliver had said, after the initiation ceremony, we were full-fledged brothers.

"Cool," Jacob said. "I'll show you the rooms and give you a tour." He hesitated for a moment. "Just remember, everything you see is strictly confidential."

My eyes widened. I'm not sure why. It just seemed like a weird thing to say, but he probably meant the housemates liked their privacy. I tried not to look at the other guys in case they were making us look dumb. Jacob waved us along to follow him upstairs.

I noticed more of those little mounted cameras up in corners along the way. That was odd, but otherwise, everything looked normal and surprisingly tidy. It was an old house with a lot of character like the main house. High ceilings, moldings and brass ceiling lamps. Jacob brought us to the upstairs hall, which had hardwood floors and a patterned runner carpet. He pointed out closed doors to bedrooms, took us into the shared bathroom, which had a really nice walk-in shower along with a bathtub, and then he showed us the two double bedrooms. He had to click on the lights because the windows were covered by blackout blinds. They were pretty much the same size as my dorm room. One had bunk beds. The other had two single beds on either side of the room. I exchanged glances with the guys. I was pretty sure we were all thinking we could work with the rooms.

Jacob walked us back downstairs. "You've got access to all the facilities in the main house, like the gaming room in the basement and the terrace and the barbecue. For a couple thou extra per semester, you can get the frat's meal plan with three chef-cooked meals a day." He shrugged. "Most of us just buy our own groceries and use the kitchen. It's cheaper that way. We all pitch in for Sunday dinner and special occasions." He smirked. "Danny, who you met, makes a great baked ziti and arroz con pollo."

I blushed, remembering. I wondered if he also cooked in the buff. Everything was sounding great to me. Jayson and I could rent our room for $1,500 apiece per semester, and we could ditch our meal plans at the dining hall and save money by buying groceries for a couple hundred per month.

Vinnie asked about parking, and Jacob told him he could get on a waiting list for the house's four car garage and park off-street in the meantime for free. The rent included utilities and Wi-Fi, and Jacob said they had cable and all the streaming services for the TV in the downstairs living room. Everything was sounding better than living in the dorms. I was ready to break my contract and put down the deposit my dad had given me. Then, when we were back in the kitchen, Jayson asked a question.

"What are all the security cameras for?"

"The protection of our residents is really important." He glanced at me. "I made the offer to Ethan first, so I'll be sure to fill him in on all the policies."

Jayson shot a look my way. I gazed at him steadily to let him know I'd give him all the details.

"You seem like great guys," Jacob said. "There's just some things I'd like to go over with Ethan on a one-to-one basis."

Vinnie and Scott shrugged and said that sounded cool. Jayson looked at first like he was going to make a bigger deal about it, but he relaxed a little. "My parents are paying for my housing, so I just need to give them all the information," he said.

"Gotcha. It'll all be spelled out in the rental agreement," Jacob said.

"When are the rooms available?" Vinnie asked.

"They're vacant right now," Jacob said. "Why don't you guys grab breakfast while Ethan and I discuss things. There's a great bagel place just down the street."

One by one, the guys looked okay with that. I told them we'd catch up later on campus. We gave each other handshakes, and Jacob saw Jayson, Vinnie, and Scott to the door.

I REALLY HAD no idea what was going on, but I felt special. Jacob wanted to talk to me personally. I'd never been the leader of anything, and it was cool to step up for my friends.

After they left, Daryl came into the kitchen. He asked if I wanted a cup of coffee, and I said sure. Daryl got their brewer going and poured me a mug. He even put milk and sugar in it for me. Then Jacob told me to come along to the first floor living room, and I sat down on a well-used sofa while the two of them took oversized chairs across from me. Daryl brought out his vape pen and offered me a drag. I politely declined.

Jacob hadn't mentioned Daryl being part of the conversation. It was a little awkward being with the two of them after we'd all gotten hot and heavy at the initiation party last month. I didn't know what to say, and they were both just looking comfy and casual.

"So, what do you think of the place?" Jacob asked.

"It's great. Vinnie and Scott are looking to move closer to campus. And me and Jayson have been wanting to get out of the dorms. We've both got not so great roommate situations."

I watched the two of them exchange a look. Daryl was wearing a loose tank top that gave a peek of his pierced nipple. My brain was getting scrambled. Their vibe was hard to read, and they were taking their time getting to the subject of housing policies and the rental agreement. Were they looking to fool around again? Had Jacob asked to talk to me privately to say the rooming situation wasn't going to work out? My old insecurities were coming back to me. They were upperclassmen. They probably thought I was a dweeb.

"I think you guys could really fit in here," Jacob said. "But it's not for everyone. You seem cool, and you've got an amazing body. Where'd you grow up?"

"Lancaster, Pennsylvania."

"A small town boy." He and Daryl exchanged a look of amusement. "Do you consider yourself open-minded, Ethan?"

I nodded, though I wasn't sure what he was getting at.

"What about your friends?"

I cleared my throat. "Yeah. They're open-minded." I smiled. "You kind of have to be to get through rush."

Jacob nodded, though he looked like I'd said something stupid.

"Jacob's asking 'cause we've got an entrepreneurial situation going on here," Daryl said. "It's not required for guys to participate in it, but residents have to be chill with what's going on."

That sounded serious in a super vague way. Was I supposed to be following what they were saying? They kept peeking at each other, which was making me nervous. *Oh God.* I hoped they weren't running some weird pyramid scheme.

"Have you heard of the site *Frat House Secrets*?" Daryl asked.

I shook my head.

"But you're familiar with *Only Fans*, right?" Jacob said.

That I did know. Jayson had told me about it, and a couple times, when I was alone in my dorm room at night, I'd watched videos of guys to do, you know, like my business.

Jacob looked at me, deadly serious. "I'm going to tell you something, Ethan, and it's really important that it stays confidential. Do we have your trust?"

I shifted in my seat, sprouting sweat. "Oh. Totally." I looked at Daryl and nodded to him too.

"This house *is Frat House Secrets*," Jacob said. He sat back in his chair. "The two of us started it a little over a year ago to make some extra money. That's what the cameras are for."

Call me slow, but I still had no idea what he was talking about.

Daryl leaned toward me. "It's a subscription service. Like *Only Fans*, except we run it ourselves so there's no middle man."

All at once, I put it together. I nearly giggled out loud. My inner spaz was coming out. It felt like the room was closing in around me, and I was simultaneously itchy all over.

"So, like...you run a...*porn* site?"

"It's adult entertainment," Jacob corrected me.

"We create live, reality-based content for subscribers," Daryl said.

"Nothing hard-core," Jacob cut in. "Mostly, subscribers just pay to see Ivy League frat boys strutting around the house naked."

"New Jersey State's not Ivy League."

Jacob and Daryl exchanged a weary glance.

"We tell them we're from Princeton," Daryl said.

Well, that made sense. Sort of. Actually, none of it made sense, and I wanted to bolt out of there.

"You look kind of shook, Ethan," Jacob said.

"No. No. It's just...a surprise. We...Jayson and me. And Vinnie and Scott. We were just looking to room here is all."

"We're not saying you have to get naked on camera," Jacob said.

"Unless you want to," Daryl added. "Some of the guys pay their rent just doing a few scenes a week."

"Really? Wh-what do you mean by a scene?"

"A few guys get together in the kitchen. Just horsing around or doing regular stuff like making dinner or playing beer pong."

"It's a peek into fraternity life after dark," Jacob said. "That's what the clientele are into."

"They pay just to see guys like hanging out?"

Daryl knit his hands together and leaned toward me. "They sure do. To get a look at hot frat brahs in the buff. We've got over ten thousand subscribers at thirty bucks a month."

My brain exploded. Even I could do that math. Three hundred thou a month. They only had twelve guys living there. No matter what the split was, that wouldn't just pay for rent. It would cover tuition, living expenses, and money to put in the bank.

Daryl smiled some more, looking at my gobsmacked face. "And that's just subscribers on our basic plan. Guys who pull in premium subscribers make an extra two to three thou a month, plus tips."

I had questions about that, but I was too scared and embarrassed to ask. What they were talking about was way beyond my knowledge base, life experience and possibly my comfort-level. But I'm not going to lie, I was mighty intrigued by the kind of money they were talking about. I didn't want to be judgy. I mean, I'd gotten a lot more comfortable with my body. Showing it to strangers wasn't such a bad way to make some cash, was it? If what they were saying was true, it was ridiculously easy money.

"All you have to do is regular things, naked?"

"That's up to you," Jacob said. "But yeah. Some of the guys just do a few everyday scenes per week, like I said."

I gulped. "And it's legal?"

"You're over eighteen?"

"Yeah."

Daryl exhaled from his vape pen and turned to me. "What you should do is check out the site. We've got some free teaser scenes on Pornhub. See if it's something you're comfortable with."

"No pressure," Jacob said. "If you don't want to participate, you and your friends can sign the housing agreement and put down your five hundred dollar deposit for the semester. No problem and no hard feelings."

He and Daryl stood up and studied me. "Just remember, we've taken you into our circle of trust. You and your friends can't say a word about it."

I took another gulp, shook their hands, said I'd get back to them, and walked out of the house like I'd been spun around a centrifuge.

Chapter Eleven

I TEXTED THE guys to say we needed to talk. Two seconds later, they wrote back and wanted to know what happened right away. It wasn't something I could explain through texting, and even though I was bursting to tell them, it felt too complicated and serious to try to talk about on FaceTime. I told them to meet me at the bleachers at the track outside the athletic center. Nobody would be there on a Friday afternoon in January. We needed privacy for the conversation we were about to have. Like a square mile's worth, though I couldn't think of anyplace more remote than the track.

Vinnie, Scott, and Jayson beat me there, and right away, they were all over me.

"You better spill, gurl. You got us all on pins and needles," Vinnie said.

"Did you have sex?" Jayson asked.

"What? No." I drew them over to sit down in the stands. I didn't know where to start so I kind of gave them the blow-by-blow since they'd left the house. Then I got to the crazy part and just blurted it out.

"They're running a reality porn site called *Frat House Secrets.*"

Vinnie snickered, and he and Scott gave me goofy looks like I must be putting them on. Jayson pulled out his phone and googled the site. He knew I wasn't capable of putting anyone on.

He turned his phone screen to me. "This it?"

I wasn't sure since I hadn't tried looking for it myself. I should have. My head had been in the clouds. I took a closer look. Jayson had found the site on Pornhub. They had a small collection of short, teaser videos like Daryl had mentioned, but the weird thing was the actors' faces were blurred. You could see plenty of skin and I recognized the interior of the house, but I guess they protected the identities of the guys for privacy. The videos had a caption with

110

the website and a message: Subscribe to see ALL of the frat boys unaltered.

"Holy fucking fuck," Vinnie said.

"This is what the cams are for?" Scott asked.

I nodded soberly.

"Did they ask you to take your clothes off?" Jayson asked.

I scowled at him. "No."

Vinnie grinned big. "I would've done it."

"Is it just me or is this kinda sketchy?" Scott said. "They could get in serious trouble with the university."

I'd thought about that. Jayson looked it up on Reddit. "It says they can't kick you out for doing porn unless you're using the school logo or affiliating with them in any way."

"Do the other brothers know about this? Like Peter?" Scott said.

I hadn't asked, and I told him so.

Jayson looked at me. "Did they take you aside because they want *you* on the site?"

"No. Well. Sorta." I raised a shaky hand to push back my hair. "I guess they wanted us to know what we're getting into. But guys, whatever we decide to do, we can't tell anybody."

"Did they make you sign a non-disclosure agreement?" Jayson asked.

"No. But it's in our oath of confidentiality."

The guys nodded. Then we all got on our phones like lunatics to check out the videos. We were dead silent for a while. The housemates were hot. All cut up and smooth. I think I recognized Danny in one of them based on the free show he'd given us earlier. There was nothing hardcore at all. They just did a lot of huddling together in their underwear, and wrestling, and in one of them, they were getting ready to drop their shorts, but then the video cut out.

"It's teaser stuff," Scott said. "Guess you have to pay to see the guys in action."

"I think I've seen these before," Jayson said.

Vinnie laughed out loud. "These boys are *pros*." He looked at me. "Seriously, they want you in on it?"

"They said it was an option. Not just for me. For all of us."

"Anyone able to open the website? It keeps telling me 'site not found.'"

We all tried and got the same message.

"Maybe it's temporarily down for maintenance," Vinnie said.

"This video was uploaded to Pornhub just yesterday," Scott pointed out. "I'd say they're active. Maybe they're just having trouble with the site."

"Well, what did you tell them?" Jayson asked me.

"I didn't say anything. I wanted to talk to you guys first. Jacob said that was a good idea. He said we should take a look at some of their vids and like, decide for ourselves."

Vinnie snort-laughed.

"They've got a lot of subscribers," Scott pointed out. "Did they say how much money they're making?"

I took a dry swallow. "About three hundred thousand a month. Or a little more, I think. They mentioned something about premium content and tips."

The guys' eyes bugged.

"What's the split?" Scott said.

"They didn't say."

"Jesus, that's a lot of money," Vinnie said.

Jayson set down his phone. "Wait. You guys are actually thinking about doing it?"

Nobody answered at first. Part of me was still in shock. I'd been wanting to live at the frat house so bad, I couldn't really think through things clearly. Meanwhile, Vinnie and Scott kept looking at each other.

"All right. I'll just say it," Vinnie said. "Scott and I have experimented a little on *Only Fans*."

I stared at them in disbelief. For a second I wondered if everyone was doing porn except me.

"Don't judge," Vinnie said.

"It was just something we did over the summer," Scott added.

"Oh. My. God," Jayson squealed. "I could've jerked off to you. Please tell me your porn names aren't CadeNViktor, Joey Squared, or ThirstyStepBros."

I looked at him pleadingly to calm down. I hadn't seen anyone around the track, but he could get loud enough to be heard all the way back at the dorms.

Scott shook his head. "We took it down before fall semester."

Vinnie grinned at Jayson. "You like stepbrother porn?"

"It never went anywhere," Scott went on. "We got like four followers and eighteen bucks."

"I can't believe this." I glanced at Jayson.

He raised a palm. "I've never done porn. I sent one dick pic in all my life. Last semester. To Andrew."

I'd never even sent a dick pic to a guy. I'd never received a dick pic. When it came to sex, I was always the last one to do anything.

"It's not that serious," Vinnie said.

"I'm not judging you, but I don't think I can do it," Jayson said. "My parents don't even know I'm gay. If they found out I was on a porn site, they'd murder me."

Scott gave him a glare. "You think any of us want our parents finding out?"

"No. But mines are paying my room and board."

"None of us will have to worry about room and board if we move into the annex," Vinnie said. "Shit. I won't be waiting tables anymore. I'll tell you that."

Things were getting a little heated, and it was making me antsy. I turned to Jayson. "None of us have to be on camera if we don't want to. Jacob told me."

"*You* want to do it too?" Jayson said.

I dodged his gaze. "I don't know. I mean, it's *a lot* of money. You know my situation with my parents. It would help a lot to contribute to my tuition. And Jacob said some of the housemates just do a few scenes a week. And it's not like full-on sex. They just do regular stuff around the house and like wrestle a bit."

"Without any clothes on," Jayson pointed out.

"I've seen these kind of sites," Vinnie said. "It's like voyeurism. Some guys are into watching college kids in the nude."

"I'm sorry, but I can't do it," Jayson said. "If anybody recognized me, my life would be over. A neighbor from back home. A classmate from high school." He shook his head. "I can't risk anything getting back to my family."

"So, we won't do the site," I told him. "We'll just rent the rooms."

Now Jayson was avoiding my gaze.

"It's all for one, and one for all. Right?" I glanced at Vinnie and Scott. They looked uncertain. I was starting to feel like the whole thing was becoming a major problem.

"I'm not going to be the party pooper," Jayson said. "Listen. I'm totally cool with you guys moving into the house. It's just not for me. I'll put up with my suitemates for another semester. I spend most of my time with Tyler and Ashok anyway."

"Totes respect," Vinnie said. He squeezed Jayson's shoulder. "You shouldn't be pressured into doing anything you're not comfortable with."

Scott agreed with him. I kept watching Jayson, hoping he didn't hate me now. He flashed me a smile. I guess he was cool with things. But then it hit me. What was I going to do for a roommate?

A WEEK LATER, I was packing up my stuff to move out of my dorm room. I know. It was sketchy and arguably stupid and definitely insane, but I'd spent eighteen years being a social misfit. In one semester, I'd experienced acceptance, brotherhood, and guys finding me attractive. I felt like I couldn't go back now, sitting on the sidelines like I used to do. Guys had invited me to share their house. Seriously *hot* guys who thought I was good-looking enough to make money doing exhibitionist porn. I guess it fed my self-esteem, and I had a lot of lost time to make up for. That really gnawed at me sometimes. Like, what if I'd had the balls to go after what I wanted when I was thirteen or fourteen? I'd been suppressing who I was for way too long.

That's not to say I wasn't nervous to move into the house. I'd been a basket case since Vinnie, Scott, and I had met with Jacob to sign the rental agreement. There was no turning back now, kind of like jumping off that waterfall in the middle of the night. And I was lying to my parents. I mean, maybe not blatantly. I told them I was moving into the annex behind the frat house. They just didn't know what went on there and that the reason I didn't have a bill to pay was I'd signed off on doing three scenes a week in exchange for rent and a stipend of seventeen hundred dollars a month.

Jacob suggested I tell them the semester's housing was covered by my fraternity dues as a special deal for freshmen with financial need, so that's what I did. I didn't like deceiving them, but in the end, I justified I was saving them a lot of money. It was two hundred dollars per scene! I embellished Jacob's suggestion by saying the frat was also paying for my meal plan, and in exchange for working around the house, I had plenty of money for books and everyday expenses and would even set aside some monthly payments for my out-of-pocket tuition. My dad had a few questions when I told them, but nothing too hard to explain. He was really happy I'd figured out how to cover my living costs. My mom didn't say much of anything, which was somewhat of a relief, though I could tell she still thought I wasn't taking college seriously enough.

I worried about Jayson. We were besties. We had a long talk one night, and I asked him a hundred times if he was mad. He assured me he wasn't, but it still felt like we were splitting up as friends. We'd see each other at Tau functions, but guests were strictly prohibited at the annex. We wouldn't be able to hang out on the spur of the moment, any day of the week. Meanwhile, Jacob said it was okay for me to take my room as a single. He worked the additional expense into my "contract," and said he'd double my monthly salary if I found a roommate down the road. I'd asked Tyler without getting into details, but he and his dorm roommate got along great and they wanted to finish out the year together.

All these things were spinning in my head while I got my clothes into suitcases and boxed up my school supplies. Then Shawn bounced into the room. It was nine o'clock on a Saturday morning. I'd hoped to make it out of there without seeing him.

He glanced at me in his usual snotty way, and then he took account of my suitcases and boxes.

"You're finally moving out? My lucky day."

I ignored him and zipped up my garment bag.

"Where you going? Tau?"

"Mm-hmm."

He studied me. "I bet they like you there. You've been working out. Those fag boys must be drooling over who gets to fuck you."

I snapped. I hated him so much. My body just reacted, and I charged at him and shoved him against the wall.

"Say that to me again."

Shawn beat back my hands. He still had a wider wingspan than me and probably a good thirty pound advantage.

"Don't fucking touch me," he shouted.

I got in his face and shouted back. "Don't fucking talk to *me* like that."

I caught his arm before he could take a swing at me, and I hurled my fist into his chin. His head smacked into the wall, and he was stunned. Just then, Vinnie and Scott showed up. They had said they would help get my stuff over to the house. I guess someone let them into the dorm downstairs.

They stopped in their tracks, taking in the scene. Shawn was bowing over himself and stumbling to stay on his feet. I was just as frozen as Vinnie and Scott. I didn't mean to hurt Shawn, I mean, not *that* bad. He was tending his bloodied mouth, and then he looked up at me hatefully.

"You're gonna regret this. I'm gonna destroy you."

He stumbled out the door past Vinnie and Scott. I explained things briefly, and then we hauled my stuff down to Vinnie's car.

Chapter Twelve

WE MOVED INTO the house, and everything was pretty normal for a while. Besides Grant, who we'd already met, Jacob introduced us to Shannon and Michael who roomed on the first floor. Then we met the guys who shared the second floor with us: Kyle, Luca, Rahim, and Danny, who we'd also already met, naked in the kitchen. We had dinner together on Sunday, and they all seemed like great guys.

After spending more time with Danny, my crush on him expanded. He was such a sweet, kind of clueless dude, who was always forgetting things, like his wallet and his phone. The way he ducked around the house, I could tell he had no idea how cute he was. It hurt me Jacob, Daryl and the other guys were always taking little digs at him. I think they thought he was an airhead, but I thought he was beautiful. He was just a little awkward and nervous, which I could totally relate to.

We had weekly jobs to do on a chore wheel. That first week, I was on garbage duty, and Vinnie and Scott had to clean the bathrooms. After dinner, I tied up two bags from the kitchen to take out to the bins by the driveway, and I saw Danny still had a long way to go with dishwasher duty. I summoned some courage and stepped over to him.

"You want some help?"

He looked at me like I was joking.

"I don't mind. It was my job back home all through middle and high school."

He smirked. "Okay. But you should watch out for yourself. The other guys see you volunteering to help with someone's chores, you'll be doing everybody's."

I opened the dishwasher to start fitting in plates and bowls Danny had rinsed off. I didn't want to become everyone's slave. I only wanted to help Danny. I liked being close to him. He looked great in his sleeveless T-shirt and track pants.

"How long have you lived here?" I asked.

"Since the fall." He churned on the faucet to fill a big pasta cooker with water and lots of suds. "Jacob and Daryl told me about the house last year, and it sounded like a great way to save some money."

I could've been wrong, but he seemed a little regretful. He must've caught the concern on my face.

"I'm not mad about it. I like living here. I had a hard time in the dorms." He glanced at me. "Kids making fun of me, y'know. It was kind of like high school all over again."

That blew my mind. "Why would people make fun of you?"

He snorted. "If you hadn't noticed, idiots can come up with plenty of reasons." He stopped scrubbing for a minute. "Where I grew up, if you didn't dress like a gang banger, listen to Latin hip hop, and talk about screwing girls twenty-four-seven, you didn't fit in."

"Where did you grow up?"

"The Bronx. South side."

I didn't know anything about the Bronx. But I knew about not fitting in. I told him a little about myself.

"Well, you'll be safe here. Just stay on Jacob and Daryl's good side." He lowered his voice. "Those two are the only bullies you have to look out for."

Before I could ask him what he meant, he quickly said, "So, how long have you, Vinnie, and Scott been friends?" I caught him glancing at one of the cameras in the corner. Was he trying to tell me something? Were we being watched?

"Oh. Vinnie and Scott have known each other forever. I met them at the first pledge event. They're super cool. We just hit it off right away."

"Cool."

He was quiet all of the sudden. I reached for something to say. "So, do you have a lot of friends? Here at the house?"

"Oh, they're good guys. I get along with everyone." He rinsed the pasta pot a last time and handed it to me to dry.

I leaned in to ask him quietly. "Does it ever get weird? I mean, being naked around each other so much and...y'know...the other stuff?"

He blushed a little. "How do you mean weird?"

I thought about how to put it. "Well, like, does it change your relationship with the other guys?"

"Not for me," Danny said. "As soon as that camera light goes on, I'm in business mode. It's reality-based entertainment, not reality." He gave me a playful grin. "You'll do fine."

I hesitated. My face was heating up because I wanted to ask him something more specific. "What if you like have feelings for one of the other guys? I mean, do any of the housemates date each other?"

"Yeah. Luca and Kyle are boyfriends. Me and Rahim's room is right next to theirs so believe me, I know a lot more than I need to about their relationship. And other guys have dated, and there's lots of casual sex going on when the cameras are off. It's kind of inevitable, y'know? All these good-looking dudes living with each other." He grabbed a frying pan to scrub. I think something had made him uncomfortable again, and then he turned to me. "I don't do that, personally. This gig is paying for school and giving me money to send home to my moms. I've got four younger brothers and an older sister. I've gotta keep my head in the game, if you know what I mean."

That broke my heart in more ways than one.

Danny looked me in the face and spoke low again. "Hey. If you're attracted to one of the guys, you can have all the sex you want. Most everyone is easygoing about that. But if you want my advice, don't take it too seriously. We all moved in here to make money, not to find a boyfriend, right?"

I nodded, though inside my heart was collapsing. It's not that he didn't make perfect sense, but I guess deep down I'd hoped I *would* find a boyfriend at the house. Well, I'd been naive, like always. I forced a grin. "Thanks. For the advice."

"Any time."

While washing dishes, he'd gotten soap suds on his nose. It was really cute and made me smile. Danny gave me a look, wondering what was so funny.

"It's just..." I used my wash towel to gently dab his nose. "Soap suds."

We exchanged a smile that got us both burning up in the face. Just then, Jacob walked into the kitchen.

"There you are," Jacob said, looking at me. "I told you, after dinner, we'd go over some things about the site. Grab Vinnie and Scott and meet me back down here."

I nodded and acted casual about slowly making my way upstairs. It didn't make sense, but I had this feeling I might've gotten Danny into trouble by talking to him. I don't know. Jacob was always hard to read, and he looked amused for some reason.

But he didn't say or do anything mean to Danny while I was making my way out. I even stopped outside the door to see if I'd overhear anything.

LATER, JACOB BROUGHT Vinnie, Scott, and me downstairs to the basement. He unlocked a door with a sign that read Authorized Personnel Only, and ushered us into a dimly lit room that glimmered with computer lights and monitors. I felt dizzy from all the mounted screens. It looked like a security control room, monitoring everything in the house. Daryl sat at a desk with two computers. He gave us a wave while he tapped at his keyboard.

"This is where the magic happens," Jacob said proudly. "But listen up. This room is strictly off-limits. You fuck around in here, and you could crash the whole site."

I watched Vinnie and Scott staring at the screens, and then I stared myself. I saw Danny finishing up in the kitchen. Grant was doing crunches on his bedroom floor. Luca and Kyle were chatting with Rahim in their bedroom. I felt kind of guilty spying on them.

"The cameras are on twenty-four-seven?" Scott asked.

"Of course not," Jacob said. "We wanted to give you guys a demo so you can see how the site works."

Daryl joined in. "The reason *Frat House Secrets* is so successful is that it gives users a realistic experience." He hit some keys, and his monitor switched from whatever coding window he was working on to video of Grant's room. He tapped his mouse and dragged it to one side to zoom in the camera on Grant exercising shirtless. "From here, I control which camera feed goes live." He hit another key, and his monitor showed Michael brushing his teeth in the first floor bathroom. "A few months back, we tested out letting members choose which feed they want to see."

"*Premium* members," Jacob said.

Daryl switched up feeds on his monitor. It was Shannon's room, the big guy who went by Ashton for the site. He was stripping down and checking himself out in his mirror. Jacob went on talking, and I had to pull my eyes away.

"We go live every night from ten to midnight. You all have a three night contract, so that means you wash up, groom up and strip down by ten p.m. every Monday, Wednesday, and Thursday." He looked at each of us until we nodded soberly. I hid my terror. I'd gained a lot of confidence with my body, but guys like Shannon and Grant were built and perfect. I couldn't imagine people tuning in to see me. Not to mention, it was a show-all site. Letting other guys see me shirtless was one thing, but showing everyone what I looked like out of my underwear?

"Can I ask a question?" Scott said.

Jacob shrugged.

"What do you do if someone recognizes you from the site?"

Jacob smiled cleverly and stepped over to wring Daryl's shoulders in a brotherly way. "Thanks to this genius, the site's protected. Daryl can explain it better, but basically we use filtering software that blocks devices in a thirty mile radius from accessing the site."

"It's an adaptation of CyberGhost, sort of in reverse," Daryl said. "Instead of blocking our own IP address for tracking, the software detects and redirects users geographically. Plus we use an alternative VPN so users can't find our actual location. It's not a one hundred percent perfect system, but you can be sure it's blocking anyone logged in from campus. If you've got family or friends you want to block, just give me their IP address, and I'll add them to the list."

I somewhat followed what he was saying and made a mental note to get my parents' IP addresses the next time I was home. Whatever they were doing seemed to be working. We'd all tried accessing the website on different devices, and none of us had been able to pull it up.

Vinnie got a goofy smile on his face. "So, like what do we do? Just hang out naked?"

Jacob glanced at a digital clock on the wall. 9:59 p.m.

"You're about to see," he said.

Daryl performed some function at his keyboard. I could see a countdown on his screen. At ten precisely, a light lit up at the top of his monitor to indicate the site was live, and the screen view divided to show the camera feeds and a sidebar window that was scrolling with screen names. Daryl pointed out that was members logged in to the site. It scrolled and scrolled. I drifted closer, following Vinnie and

Scott. Daryl showed us a little counter at the bottom of the screen. Five hundred members and counting. I was excited, but my chest tightened up at the same time.

"Show time," Jacob said in a singsong voice.

Daryl pulled up the living room feed on his monitor. Three guys were sitting on the couch, only wearing their underwear. I squinted. Shannon, Grant, Danny. My gut was in my throat.

"We always start with a group scene," Daryl said. He clicked on his mouse, and the audio came on.

"Hey guys and girls," Shannon said. "Thanks for coming over on a Sunday night. For the newbies, I'm Ashton. This is Holden, and this is Felix." They both waved. "We're taking a break from school work to play Xbox."

They did some trash talk and got to playing some game. Shannon, or Ashton rather, said whoever won would get to spank the other two. But we watched for a couple of minutes, and it was just the three of them playing video games, albeit naked on the couch.

"People pay money for this?" Scott asked.

"They sure do." Jacob glanced at Daryl's monitor. "Right now, we've got over a thousand people logged in to the site. With the new interface, we can see which room they're watching the most."

Daryl navigated over to the second floor bathroom. Kyle was in the shower scrubbing up with a bar of soap. "This one wins so far."

I could see why. Kyle was gorgeous and had a tight body. He was playing things up, soaping his arm pits and chest and turning around to show his butt. Then Rahim entered the bathroom and got into the shower with him.

"Tomorrow night, you guys have your big début," Jacob said.

I pulled my eyes away from the bathroom feed and glanced at Vinnie and Scott. They'd both gone pale, and I was sure I looked the same.

"So, do we, like, get a script or something?" Vinnie asked.

Jacob came up behind him and rubbed his shoulders. "Just be natural. We'll have something to introduce you to the members." He scowled impatiently at our frightened faces. "Nothing hardcore. But you'll want to make a good impression to get some fans. And the big money is with the premium members. The more we upsell from thirty to fifty bucks a month, the better it is for all of us. Not to mention tips."

"How does that work?" Scott asked.

Daryl answered. "Premium members can view any of the rooms, and they can also enter private shows." He clicked over to a room where Luca was in front of a laptop screen. "Luca's doing a private show tonight. He can interact with members at his work station."

We could hear him talking to people while he stroked himself between the legs in his briefs. Daryl pointed out a dialogue screen where members were sending him messages, asking him to do things and giving tips of ten and twenty dollars.

Daryl shifted the view to a patchwork of twenty-some feeds. "That's something for you boys to work your way up to."

"Just focus on being hot tomorrow night," Jacob said. "And I don't mean dirty. We never mention sexual orientation on camera. For our members, it's a fantasy. The things that go on at a frat house after dark, y'know? Don't play things too eager and whatever you do, don't queen out."

I gulped. It sounded high pressure. Now, in addition to being scared of letting everyone see my private parts, I was worried I was going to act too gay. Or, the three of us wouldn't be able to stop cracking up on camera.

"Last thing," Jacob said. "Don't forget, every person who logs in to the site is a subscriber to *Frat House Secrets*, not your private fan club. That's written into the contract you signed. That means no contact outside of the site interface and no private arrangements."

I had no problem with that. My brain was fried from what I'd seen that night, and I couldn't stop from glancing at what was going on in the living room screen. The window was small, but it looked like Danny was just playing Xbox with the other guys.

"How do we know if someone wants a private show?" Vinnie asked.

"Don't worry. We'll tell you," Jacob said.

"And before tomorrow night, we need your screen names and profiles," Daryl said.

Vinnie smiled. "I'm Antonio."

"I'm going with Paddy," Scott said.

Everyone looked at me.

"I guess I'm Jeb," I said. "It's short for Jebediah. Everybody's been making fun of me for being from Amish country."

Chapter Thirteen

ALL THROUGH CLASSES the next day, I was a nervous wreck. It was almost worse than those first few minutes before I had to jump off the waterfall. I felt like I was going to die, and I was seriously asking myself why I signed up to do something so crazy.

The only time I'd ever been naked around other people was for that death dive during initiation, and the park was pitch black and I'd been covering my stuff with my hands the entire time. I had managed to skip the showers after gym class since ninth grade because it scared me so much. At the dorm, I'd always snuck into a shower stall while wearing a shirt and shorts, and I got back into my clothes as soon as I washed and dried off. Now I was about to get naked in front of all the housemates, in good lighting, with a thousand people watching me on a live feed.

For a while, I was thinking I should just tell Jacob I'd decided the whole thing wasn't for me. Per the housing agreement, I'd lose my dad's five hundred dollar deposit, but I was already thinking about solutions. I'd beg my dad to pay for me to move back into the dorms. I'd talk to the bookstore manager to get rehired for my work-study job, and I'd get full-time work over the summer to reimburse my parents for the money they spent on my housing. I just had to come up with a believable story for why rooming at the frat didn't work out.

What stopped me was talking to Vinnie and Scott that day. After classes, we met up at the athletic center as usual, and they told me they'd been stressing all day too. But Vinnie brought up we were all in this together. Just like we'd supported each other through rush, we were going to get through this next challenge. That's what brotherhood was about, and then he got me thinking that nudity was natural, and none of the housemates were going to judge me for the way I looked. He reminded me there was a big payoff in the end.

I was spiraling so bad with anxiety, it was hard for me to get excited about the money, but I didn't want to let my friends down.

We worked out hard that day, and after we showered, Vinnie and Scott threw off their towels in the locker room and harassed me to take mine off too. They joked that it was a rehearsal for later. I think I was bright red everywhere, and then they coaxed me to come over with them to a floor-length mirror. I squinted at my reflection while the two did tough guy poses and sexy poses, and eventually, I was comfortable enough to face the mirror fully and join in with the stupid stuff they were doing. I came around to thinking I didn't look *so* bad. I wished my dick was bigger when it wasn't hard, like Vinnie's. He pointed out I was a grower, not a show-er. Scott was on the small side too. Anyway, our corny rehearsal had me feeling slightly better about what we were going to do.

That night, after a dinner I barely ate, the three of us gathered in Vinnie and Scott's room to try out different pairs of briefs and help each other out with styling our hair. Vinnie had a set of clippers for grooming ourselves in other places, and without getting into specifics, I got myself trimmed up the way the actors looked on Pornhub. Jacob had told us to come down to the kitchen at nine thirty. Strangely, he said we could wear as much clothes as we wanted, which made things a little less terrifying though we were all guessing our clothes would be coming off at some point. Time sped by, and a little before nine thirty, the three of us headed down to the kitchen.

Six guys from the house were waiting there for us. Shannon, Grant, Danny, Kyle, Luca and Rahim. They were pumped up, hanging out in just their briefs, and they all cheered and slapped us five. Shannon brought out cans of beer from the fridge, and the guys cracked them open and started guzzling. I'd never drank any kind of alcohol before and worried about the frat's rules against underage drinking. But with everyone tipping back beers, including Vinnie and Scott, I didn't want to look like a dork. I took a few sips while everyone was palling around.

"You guys nervous?" Rahim asked.

I blushed. "Yeah."

"You don't have to be. We've all been through our first time before."

The other guys nodded along and gave us tips.

"It's not really that serious," Kyle said.

Luca gave me a pat on the back. "Just have a good time."

"It's just money in the bank, fellas," Shannon said.

Danny smiled at me, encouragingly. That got me warm in the face, and I was starting to feel just slightly relaxed. Then Jacob showed up.

He looked us over. "All right. Everybody's accounted for. You all ready to make people's dreams come true?"

Guys hollered "Hell yeah," and some of them slapped Vinnie, Scott and me on the butt. I was skeptical about making anyone's dreams come true, though being surrounded by so many half-naked guys was making things less terrible. Vinnie threw his arm around my neck and howled, which got me laughing.

Jacob pointed us out. "Guys, remember. Their names are Antonio, Paddy, and Jeb. You three remember everyone's names?"

With all the adrenalin pumping through me, my brain wasn't working so well. I remembered Shannon was Ashton, Grant was Holden and Danny was Felix, but my head was frozen up about the others. Rahim reminded me he was Leroy, and then Kyle said he was DJ. Luca went by Ace. All that was out of my head in seconds.

"Keep things simple," Jacob said. "Ashton and Holden will introduce the guys, and you all just follow their lead. Newbies, leave names out of it if you go blank. We'll do a full thirty minutes here in the kitchen, and then you can all go off to your regular Monday night scenes. I'll come up to check on the newbies then."

He headed to the control room downstairs. Shannon and Grant got us into a huddle and explained how things were going to roll. Vinnie, Scott, and me were going to enter the scene a few minutes in, so we stood off at the door to the kitchen while the other guys gathered by the counter. Daryl's voice came over the intercom, giving us the one minute warning. The guys wrestled down their shorts, and all at once, we were standing across from six hot dudes who were completely naked.

Little red lights blinked on from the mounted cameras. I think I stopped breathing for a moment. Then Shannon and Grant started talking to the site visitors. They welcomed them, got introductions going, and thanked viewers for their tips and messages.

"We've got something really special for you tonight," Shannon said.

"Not one, not two, but *three* new guys moved into the house," Grant said. "And we're going to introduce them to you and play a game to get to know them."

Shannon put two fingers in his mouth and whistled. "Ladies and gentlemen, meet our three new hotties: Antonio, Paddy, and Jeb."

He waved us over, and I followed Vinnie and Scott into the middle of the pack of guys.

Shannon and Grant asked us each some questions. Just basic stuff like what year we were, what we liked to do for fun, and how we felt about being naked on camera. Vinnie hammed it up. He had no inhibitions about talking to people, and he said it had always been his dream to be a stripper. Strangely enough, my nerves washed away. The whole thing felt like a group project for class, as though we were filming an amateur late night TV show. Of course, with one big difference. Everyone had their stuff hanging out except for Vinnie, Scott, and me.

Grant placed a hand on my shoulder and got a big grin on his face. "Well we've got a game to initiate you guys to *Frat House Secrets*. You guys like games?"

Vinnie answered enthusiastically for us.

"That's good. All you need is to like games and beer," Shannon said. "And taking your clothes off." He went to the fridge and brought out another twelve pack of beer. The others howled and hollered.

"You guys know how to play *Never Have I Ever*?" Grant said. He patted Scott and me on our backs. "Everyone does. Of course you do."

"But the rules at *Frat House Secrets* are a little different," Shannon said. "You've gotta take a drink when someone says something you've done. *And* you've got to take off an article of clothing."

The guys broke out in more hoots and hollers. Shannon opened beers for the three of us. "The three of you have been friends for a long time. This should get interesting."

"We might as well go in alphabetical order," Grant said. "Which means Antonio goes first."

Vinnie raised his hands in the air and did a little dance, really soaking in everybody's cheering. Then he got a scheming grin on his face, studying Scott and me, playing things up.

"Paddy and I have been friends since tenth grade, so this could get vicious. But I'll start out easy." He looked at Scott. "Never have I ever failed a driver's test for sideswiping a parked car."

Scott scowled at him. He took a slug of his beer and wedged off one of his sneakers.

"Never have I ever passed out on someone's couch and pissed myself."

I burst out laughing along with everyone else. It really was going to be brutal. But while everyone was laughing, Vinnie showed off, pulling his T-shirt over his head. I thought of something that could get both the guys.

"Never have I ever lived at home while going to college."

Vinnie and Scott eyed me coolly. They drank, and Scott took off his other sneaker. Vinnie took off his belt. I could tell he was coming up with something to get me back.

"Never have I ever dressed up as a slutty unicorn for Halloween."

He got me good. I took a swig of beer and kicked off a sneaker.

"Never have I ever listened to K-Pop while working out," Scott said.

Shit. They were ganging up on me. I drank and kicked off my other sneaker.

"Never have I ever made out with my best friend."

The room got really loud after I said that. I worried for a second I'd gone too far, but Vinnie and Scott took it in stride. Scott removed one of his socks, and Vinnie kicked off one of his flip-flops.

"Never have I ever jerked off in the dorms," he said.

That was a good one. I had to cop to it. I mean, I'd been jerking off in bed since seventh grade.

Scott got Vinnie with a crack about him freeballing it to class. I got Vinnie too, remembering a story he'd told about turning his hair puke green when he'd tried to give himself highlights. The poor guy was down to his jeans. He hadn't worn socks like Scott and me. We were all laughing a lot, and I was already feeling the half beer I drank.

A few nevers later, Vinnie put on a show shimmying out of his jeans. He hadn't worn underwear either, so he was doing the full monty and out of the game. Vinnie loved it, though. He turned around and shook his butt, and the other guys gave him some spanks. It was pretty hilarious.

Meanwhile, Scott had lost his shirt. I was out of my socks and belt. Scott and I squared off while the kitchen roared with commotion. I lost my turn because I'd run out of ways to catch him without saying something that might give away his identity.

Scott got me twice, and I had to take off my shirt and jeans. I was down to my boxer briefs. I finally thought of something.

"Never have I ever worn leopard print underwear."

Scott shook his head, took a drink, and soon after, we were both standing in briefs. Then Shannon announced time was up and the game was over. We both had to strip.

The guys stomped and chanted for us to take it off. I glanced at Scott, and we exchanged a crooked grin. We both yanked down our briefs and kicked them off our feet.

Everybody cheered rowdily. I felt like I was standing on a stage for a scene from *Magic Mike*. I know that was stupid, but with everyone hollering and slapping my back, that's what it was like. Vinnie charged at Scott and me and crushed us together. I'd never have expected it, but my face was hurting from smiling so much.

"We'll be back in ten," Shannon said. "Be sure to follow these new guys and send them tips."

Someone mentioned the cameras had gone off. Our housemates came around to congratulate Vinnie, Scott, and me and slap us five. When I had the chance, I quickly grabbed my briefs and stepped back into them.

"You guys did great," Shannon told us.

Kyle got a wrestling hold around Vinnie's shoulder. "This one's a natural. Our new exhibitionist."

They wandered off with the other housemates, leaving Vinnie, Scott, and me alone in the kitchen.

"How fucking hot was that?" Vinnie screeched.

I was amped up too and slapped his hand again.

"What do we do now?" Scott said.

The sound of a door creaking open traveled from the back hallway. We all turned, and Jacob stepped into the kitchen.

"Okay. You made it through your premiere." He looked down at my underwear. "Clothes stay off, rookie. Let's move you guys along to your next venue. You've got an hour and fifteen on the clock until we wrap for the night."

"What're we supposed to do?" Vinnie asked.

"It's your first night, so you just go back to your rooms. Most of our members will be switching over to private shows with the housemates. And Danny and Rahim have booked the upstairs bathroom."

I was confused. Vinnie and Scott looked the same.

"What are we supposed to do in our room?" Scott asked.

Jacob nudged us along to the front hallway. "Frankly, you can do whatever you want. As long as you keep your clothes off. Study. Work out. Give each other massages. We'll have some visitors who'll want to see what you're up to, but you're second string until you build up a following. Keep things relatively clean for now, you got that?"

I nodded along. That sounded completely okay to me. I wasn't feeling like I was up to getting any studying in after what we went through, but I was fine with just chilling out in my room and waiting until midnight when I could put my clothes on again. Vinnie, however, looked disappointed.

"How do we build up a following if we can't interact with members?"

"Chill, bro," Jacob said. "It's your first night. We're going to look at the analytics to decide what's the best plan for getting you camera time."

"Okay. But how do we get private shows?" Vinnie said.

Jacob faced him blankly. "You don't. For now. I've got five guys with premium followers. You earn that privilege."

"Well, how do we earn that privilege just sitting around in our rooms?"

I was wishing Vinnie hadn't said that. Jacob was making it clear he was particular about running the site, and he and Daryl were in charge. He halted at the stairs, and he didn't look too happy.

"Let me explain something to you, Fontanelli. This isn't some fourteen-year-old's Instagram we're running. We've got a business plan. We pulled in a mil last quarter, and that wasn't from letting our actors do whatever they wanted. Do you even know the concept of an audience and branding?"

Vinnie's face went blank.

"Didn't think so. So, listen clearly, our brand is bi-curious frat boys. Our standard content is young guys showing off their bodies, and when visitors like what they see, they pony up to premium. Right now, you're basic. You do your group scenes and show off a little in your room. It's not rocket science."

"I'm sorry," Vinnie said. "I meant no disrespect."

Jacob studied him. "Good." He moved us along to the second floor and took a peek here and there to see that guys were at their locations. Then he turned to us again. "Wednesday, we'll have you interacting with the housemates again. Everybody okay with spanking and some wrestling? Just the usual hazing stuff. Nothing that's going to make it hard sitting down."

Vinnie nodded vigorously. My chest was freezing over, but I managed to nod as well and so did Scott.

"Another popular scene is group showers. Just soaping each other up and getting hard together." He looked at Vinnie. "You down with that, big shot?"

Vinnie hid his face. Then he came back with a goofy smile. "I'm down with that."

Chapter Fourteen

I'D BASICALLY GONE from jumping off waterfalls to skydiving without a parachute. That week, I got my bare ass spanked by a half dozen guys, did the ice bucket challenge naked, and got greased up with vegetable oil to wrestle Scott naked in a kids' inflatable pool. It was scary at first but ridiculously fun. I mean, I'd never been so sexual with guys, and it wasn't really sexual, but it was, for me, and I'm probably not making any sense. At the time, I guess I wasn't comprehending what it was. I knew it was a show, and I knew it felt good being around so many naked men. When someone touched my body, I felt shy and meek and ticklish in an incredibly great way. I loved that attention. I hardly ever thought about the thousands of people watching, and when it did cross my mind, I felt bad-ass and sexy.

I don't know. All the teasing and touching wasn't real, but it *was* real, for me. Vinnie and Scott talked about "Antonio" and "Paddy" being characters they played when the site was live, and I could see the other guys doing that, becoming louder and more boisterous and sexual when we got together for group scenes. But it was different for me. I was still myself when I was "Jeb," and when the guys checked out my body or gave me a smile or brushed up against me or gave my butt a squeeze, I glowed inside and yearned for them to touch me more and be able to touch them more. Especially if it was Danny or Shannon or Grant.

Looking back, those experiences definitely desensitized me to being naked around other guys. After a week, it was nothing to take off my clothes and walk downstairs with Vinnie and Scott when it was time to do a scene. Doing the site together was like another level of brotherhood. Our housemates were really encouraging and made us feel like we were part of their family. Outside of classes, I ended up spending all of my time with the guys and not much at all with

Jayson and Tyler and the other people from our pledge class. I feel bad about it now, but that semester, things just changed really fast.

Vinnie, Scott, and I got more serious about our workouts and keeping to a muscle-building diet. We wanted sick bodies with popping pecs, six-pack abs, tight butts, and thick thighs. We got our first payout from the site at the end of February, and though my conscience was telling me to bank most of the money, the guys said we deserved to treat ourselves, just for the first month. I rationalized that I'd been dealing with a lot of stress, and I'd be more conservative about the money I was making moving forward. So, we ordered protein and vitamin supplements, high-end skin and hair products, clothes for Tau formals and dance parties, and designer underwear and workout outfits. Vinnie and Scott said they were doing it all to look good on camera and earn the privilege of doing private shows so they could make more cash. I just wanted to look good to the other guys. I'd never made so much money, but that month, I blew through it really fast. I can't say I was following through on all the vows I'd made to prove my mom wrong about being able to handle college. For sure financially, but I was spending a lot more time looking good for the site and hanging out with friends when I should've been keeping up with my classes.

Then in early March, we all got a harsh dose of reality. It was a Sunday morning. I woke up really early from a heated conversation going on downstairs. I went to check it out, and Shannon and Michael told me some asshole had spray-painted the fraternity's front lawn with the words: "Fagots go home." They must've done it overnight.

I went out with the two of them to help clean it up, and we met up with a group of brothers who were already out on the lawn with sponges and buckets of soapy water. That's when I overheard some of the brothers talking about anonymous calls and emails they'd been getting. One of the guys mentioned the voice mailbox for the house phone had a message, threatening to bring an automatic rifle to the house and kill us one by one.

Oliver was out in the yard. We hadn't talked in like forever. We'd barely seen each other really. I felt bad about that. He'd tried to maintain our friendship, but I hadn't been able to forgive him for not liking me back and all that drama seemed like ages ago. I missed our friendship, and I also really wanted to know his take on the incident. I stepped over to him.

"You think this is the same guys who pulled that prank last semester?"

Oliver frowned. "We don't know. There's been some chatter about Zeke being involved, but no one knows for sure."

My former roommate Shawn's frat.

"You think it's Zeke?" I asked.

"Could be. It's kind of deeper than the usual rush stuff, though. We've been getting some really serious threats." He glanced at me, and I could see him shifting into older brother mode. "We've got things covered. The Executive Council is working with public safety and the town police. We're going to make sure the perpetrators get what's coming to them."

I remembered the frat's security system. "They've got to have leads from the security cam."

Oliver's face hardened. "Here's the shitty thing. The feed from the cam is all fucked up. It's a cheap system. The Council said they were getting an upgrade after the last incident, but apparently someone dropped the ball. The cam goes idle sometimes or the recording comes out distorted. We can't make out much from either incident." He sighed. "Peter says he's got the security company bringing in new equipment first thing tomorrow."

That was really tragic and got me feeling guilty. The annex had a super high quality video recording system, and meanwhile the frat's main house couldn't even rely on their security cams to identify people who'd defaced the property on the front lawn.

Oliver must've caught that I was stressing. "It's going to be okay. We're going to get to the bottom of this. Peter's also holding an emergency house meeting tonight to talk about the incidents. There's going to be a rep from Public Safety to answer questions and talk about some safety precautions."

That sounded like a good idea. We were quiet for a while.

He caught my glance. "How's living in the annex?"

"It's great."

He hesitated. "Cool. You must have your pick of guys these days. Your workout has got your body smoking."

I didn't know what to say at first. Oliver had kind of shared his opinions about the guys in the annex, and I wasn't sure if he was trying to get into that conversation. Part of me wished I could tell him all the crazy stuff I'd done, but Shannon and Michael were close by, and I'd promised to keep the website confidential.

"Thanks," I told him. "I've been taking things slow. 'Til, y'know, the right guy comes around."

Oliver raised his fist, and we fist bumped. "You deserve that. You're a quality guy, Ethan, and dudes should earn the respect of spending time with you."

I'd never been good at taking compliments. I think my whole body turned bright red. To make things worse, I spotted Danny carrying out a big custodial broom to scrub the lawn. Every time I saw him, I got light-headed and my stomach knotted up.

"You okay, Ethan?"

I pulled myself together. I really did have something important to say to him. "I'm sorry about being such a spaz last semester. You really helped me out a lot. I don't know if I would have made it through initiation without your encouragement, but I never told you that." I scuffed my sneaker. "I'm sorry I was a jerk. I guess I couldn't control my feelings, but that's like totally in the past."

Oliver brightened. "Thanks Ethan. You don't have to apologize." He smirked. "And look how things turned out. You've got your own tribe now. I'm really happy you found a place to fit in."

It was weird. Him saying that brought up mixed feelings. Like I did have cool people to hang out with, the kind of guys I'd never dreamed of being friends with, but the website thing was mad confusing. Again, I wrestled inside over telling Oliver what was really going on. Then I lied and told him everything was going great.

Chapter Fifteen

A FEW DAYS later, when I was headed out to my Wednesday morning classes, I ran into Danny. He had his backpack on and was going to campus as well. We ended up walking together, which felt like the best thing that had happened to me in months. I really wanted to get to know him, and I hadn't found a time to catch him alone. Now, I just had to figure out how to make conversation.

"You never told me what you're majoring in." I said.

"Communications. I want to get into TV production."

"That sounds really cool."

Danny said nothing.

"I'm in the health sciences program, so I don't know anything about communications," I said. "What kind of TV production are you interested in?"

"Probably news. Or Latinx media. I'm hoping to get an internship at Telemundo this summer."

"That's awesome."

He smirked. "*You've* heard of Telemundo?"

I blushed. "No."

"Then how d'you know it's awesome?"

"Well...um...it sounds awesome." I glanced at him. "I'm sorry. Did I say the wrong thing?"

That made him smile. "I was just playing with you. You wouldn't have heard of it. It's a Spanish language network."

I nodded and glanced off to the side. I felt like I'd let him down, and I couldn't come up with anything to say.

Danny lightly poked my arm. "Relax. You're even more wound up than me. People don't generally ask me what I'm interested in. That's why I was giving you a little shade. What do you want to do when you graduate?"

"I want to get into the physician's assistant program," I said. "But can I tell you something?"

He nodded.

"I've got to get my grades up. I need a 3.2 by junior year. Last semester I got a 2.3."

"Yeah. Well, my grades aren't so great either. I'm supposed to be meeting with a writing tutor, but between my classes and working for the site, I never have time."

I could relate to that. Thinking about school was making me anxious, and I didn't want to bring Danny down.

"How's your family doing?" I asked him.

His face ticked. "I told you about my family?"

"Yeah. You told me about your mom and your younger brothers and sisters."

"Oh yeah. They're okay. We talk on Sundays. My mom's always after me to tell my brothers to keep up in school and stay out of trouble. But I don't know how much they listen. The oldest, Hector, just wants to get into working in security like his uncle. My mom wants to send him to stay with me for a weekend to get him interested in college. I've been running interference. Neither of them have any idea about the house."

I liked how much he cared about his family. I liked *him*. It wasn't just that he was hot. Danny had a good heart, and going to college meant a lot to him, the same way it meant a lot to me.

"My family doesn't know, either. I mean, they know I'm living at the frat, and my mom wasn't too happy just knowing that. She thinks I'm not going to keep up with my classes, and so far, she's kind of right."

Danny clopped my shoulder. "Hey. We'll look out for each other. No goofing off when we're supposed to be studying."

I liked that idea a lot. We'd reached the main path through campus. Soon, we'd be splitting off in different directions to our classes, and I was feeling an opportunity slipping away. I dug down deep.

"Did you hear about the new brew pub in town? I heard they've got really good food."

Danny didn't answer.

"I was thinking of checking it out. Would you like to go sometime?"

"I'm kinda keeping to a tight budget."

I tried in my dorky way to flirt it up a bit. "I asked you so it's my treat."

The expression on his face killed me. I could tell already I was way off base.

"I'd like to. I'm just mad busy." He turned to me and carefully chose his words. "You're a real nice kid. If things were different, I'd be glad you asked. I just don't do that kind of thing. You know, not while I'm working at the site." He cracked a guilty smile. "God, the way you're looking at me! Am I being an asshole?"

"No, it's cool," I lied. I remembered something he told me before, and I don't know why, but it came blurting out of my mouth. "What about hooking up sometime? I've got my own room."

Danny stopped walking and took a glance around. He waited until a group of people passed by us.

"Ethan, you're a really good-looking guy. And I get it. When I first moved into the house, I wanted to get down with everyone." He glanced away grimly. "Truth is, I pretty much did. Last semester was a free-for-all, and for a while, I thought I was having the time of my life. I don't know if all this sounds patronizing. Maybe you can handle it like I couldn't. For me, it was too confusing, and the more I did it, the shittier I felt. I was just getting my heart broken, over and over again. So I decided I wasn't going to do it unless I was getting paid. Like I said, it could be different for you if you can be with one guy one night and see him getting down with someone else the next without getting jealous." He looked me firmly in the face. "Just be careful, okay?"

I gave him a nod, and we said see you later.

I WAS FEELING really low after that conversation. First it was Oliver, and now Danny. Was I ever going to find a guy who liked me back? I didn't know what I was doing wrong. I'd built some confidence and gotten into shape, and guys were noticing me at the gym, at the frat, and around campus. They just weren't the guys my heart was set on. I was dying to be with someone, and as usual, everybody else was making connections while I was striking out.

Luca and Kyle had each other, and Vinnie and Scott kind of had each other, too. Don't ask me to explain their relationship. They insisted they were just best friends, but they acted like a couple. Meanwhile, there was a lot of bed-hopping on the second floor with them, Luca, Kyle, and Rahim. Outside of the house, Jayson had moved on from Andrew and was seeing some nursing student, Brad. Tyler was dating this kid, Sebastian. It felt like I was the only person in the whole frat who wasn't having sex and/or dating someone.

At the annex, the single guys I was attracted to barely acknowledged me outside of our live scenes. The only person who'd shown interest in me was Rahim. He made a lot of eye contact when we were filming, and he lingered around after we wrapped up scenes.

One night, a little after twelve, when the cameras shut down, Rahim came by my room in just his workout shorts. He hung around the door, looking like he was bored and wanting some company. I'd just stepped into a pair of pajama bottoms after doing a 'hazing' scene with Vinnie that involved being blindfolded while Michael and Shannon teased us with feathers and ice cubes and nipple twists to see who'd pop a boner first. I was still really wound up. I told Rahim to come in and shut the door behind him.

Rahim had a pretty face and a tight body. He didn't get butterflies swarming in my stomach, but being alone with him in my bedroom had me hot and eager. I sat down on my bed, and Rahim joined me. We didn't even talk. He started kissing me and touching my back and shoulders.

He smelled real nice, like cocoa butter and a musky body spray. I felt his shoulders and his biceps while we kissed really deep. Then he held me between the legs, and I held him. I fell back on my bed, and he pulled off my pajama bottoms to suck me. No one had ever done that before. I was tense all over, and my brain was throbbing out of my skull. Then he lifted my thighs and found my opening with his finger.

That felt strange and dirty, though I'd been wanting to be touched there for years. He pressed his mouth and tongue against me, and I curled my neck into my shoulder, burning up in the face. He asked if I had some lube, and I told him I had a safe sex packet in the top drawer of my night stand. Rahim found it, broke open a pillow pack of lube and a condom, wet my opening and slicked up his erection.

When he pressed up against me, I didn't think it could possibly work. Then I ceded little by little at first, and he tore inside me, stupefying me with the shredding pain and making me break into a cold sweat.

He topped me and made me come while he was inside me. It blew my mind anything could feel so good, but afterward, my head was scrambled. Rahim was a nice, attractive guy, but I didn't feel like he was someone I wanted to be with in a relationship. I tried to tell myself it was just sex for fun, which was totally normal. Everyone was doing it. But my anxiety was going crazy.

I got up from the bed. "I should take a shower." I glanced at Rahim on the way out, but I was feeling so crappy about myself, like

I didn't even want him to look at me, I headed to the bathroom without saying anything else.

I'D ALWAYS THOUGHT losing my virginity would be this special, momentous thing, and the guy I did it with would be "the one." To be honest, up until a few months ago, I thought it would probably never happen. Now that it had, I kind of wished it never did. Rahim was a nice guy, and it had felt good, but it was obvious to both of us it was just a rando hook-up. I felt lonelier than I ever had in my life, and it didn't matter I was living in a house with eleven people who were supposedly my "family." I was grossed out by myself and didn't want to see people.

The next day, I texted Vinnie that I wasn't feeling well and asked him if he'd let Jacob know that I wasn't up for being on the live feed that night. I skipped classes and stayed in bed, watching videos and napping off and on. Vinnie and Scott texted me all day. I didn't answer them. But when they got home from classes, they barged into my room.

"How you feeling, hon?" Vinnie sat down on my bed, and Scott hovered nearby.

I closed up my laptop and sat up a little.

"Just tired." I wasn't crazy about them seeing me in the same clothes I wore to bed. I hadn't showered that day.

Vinnie studied me. "You look like shit. You got a fever?" He put one palm on my forehead and another to his own. "You don't feel warm."

Scott scowled at him. "Like you're some kind of Dr. Fauci." He turned to me. "We texted you like fifty times. You been sleeping all day?"

I faked a yawn. I was terrible at lying. I didn't even know why I was lying. I was so embarrassed, I guess. But it was really sweet they were concerned about me. Before last night, I could talk to them about anything, no matter how personal. But something inside was holding me back from telling them what was really going on, and then I felt guilty about not being honest, which made me draw into myself even more.

"It sucks," Vinnie said. "You're gonna miss the dance off party." That was the scene scheduled that night. We were all supposed to dance like strippers. Vinnie got up and gave me a preview, doing some locking and popping, and dropping down, shaking his ass. I couldn't help smiling.

"You just rest up," Scott said. "We've got the Return to Wonderland party tomorrow."

Return to Wonderland was a big event at Tau. I'd forgotten about it. I didn't feel like going, but if I didn't, I was letting the guys down.

"You want us to get you anything? Soup? Cough medicine?"

"Alcohol?" Vinnie said. "It'll kill the germs."

I chuckled. "No. Thanks, but I'll be fine."

"We'll check on you later, 'kay?" Scott said.

I nodded, and the guys left the room.

Chapter Sixteen

I WAS FEELING a little better the next day, and in the afternoon, when Vinnie and Scott asked for help with their outfits for the party, I decided I couldn't be a lame-ass and sit out the big event. All the brothers would be there, and invites had gone out to five hundred people. Besides, I hadn't seen Jayson or Tyler in, like, forever.

If I had to describe the Return to Wonderland theme, it was Alice in Wonderland with a slutty edge. Vinnie had picked up bunny ears and a bunch of crazy stuff from some costume shop in East Brunswick. He and Scott went all out, getting their hair all sculpted and glittery. Vinnie put on a corset and fishnet stockings. Scott got into a tight pair of high-waisted striped cotton underwear with an ascot and a bunny tail. They were both fine with showing a lot of skin, and they ended up looking like very sexy, androgynous anime characters. I couldn't shore up that much confidence, but they got me into a vintage waistcoat and dress pants and, of course, I had to wear mouse ears. We headed out to the party around nine.

Things started out chill. We met up with a bunch of guys from our pledge class, and then Jayson showed up in full drag as Alice, followed by Tyler who was wearing some kind of steampunk take on the Queen of Hearts. We all got on the dance floor, and it started feeling like old times. The place was filling up and getting raucous.

We took a break to cool down, and I was hoping to catch up with Jayson. But he was a big attraction in his blonde wig and high-hemmed schoolgirl dress. I didn't want to tear him away from all the people coming up to him to say how cool his costume was. I wandered over to the bar and disastrously came face-to-face with Rahim.

It's not that I had bad feelings toward him. I'd just been trying to put out of mind what happened, and I don't know if I should've been feeling like a jerk for avoiding him, but I did.

"Oh. Hey. How you doin'?" he said. He looked a little awkward about the situation, which made me want to run off even more, but I kept it together.

"Cool. Um. How're you?"

"I'm good." He glanced around. "You got a minute?"

I shrugged. Rahim pointed us over to a quieter part of the room.

"I just wanted to say...you cool about the other night?"

"Oh yeah." I leaned closer and lowered my voice. "I didn't tell anybody. You don't have to worry about that."

He screwed up his face. "I didn't mean it like that. You just seemed kind of freaked out." He glanced at me. "I thought you were into it. But if I crossed a line, I'm sorry I misread things."

I was feeling like a bigger and bigger dweeb. "No. It was cool." I looked at him earnestly. "Really. No worries. It was no big deal."

He smiled to himself in a not so humorous way. "Why you gotta say it like that?" He leaned closer. "We messed around. And now you're gonna act like it was so below you?"

I didn't know how to handle him being confrontational. I could see I'd hurt his feelings, but I had no idea why. Did he want me to tell other people? Did it mean more to him, like he wanted to be boyfriends?

"I can't figure you out," he said. "You're looking at me like a lost puppy, but ever since that night, you've been avoiding me like the plague."

"I didn't mean to." I fumbled for words. "It's just...new to me."

He looked me over and softened a bit. "You never hooked up with one of the guys from the house?"

I nodded and skirted his gaze.

"Listen, you're right. It's not so serious. But show some respect, okay? It doesn't mean we're getting married, but it also doesn't mean you gotta treat me like a pariah. We were bros before, weren't we? We just had some private fun. It happens in the house."

"Oh, yeah. I get it."

Neither one of us said anything for a while, just staring off in opposite directions. Then he lifted his hand to bump fists. "We cool?"

I bumped his fist and looked him in the eye.

"I'm gonna find Kyle and Luca. I'm glad we had this talk."

I nodded, and he walked away. That conversation didn't have me feeling less confused about what we did, but I guess I was learning how things worked. I shouldn't have been embarrassed after we had sex, or I shouldn't have left the room so abruptly. I chugged some water, and then I thought about taking a look in the mirror since I'd been jumping around and dancing. The first floor bathroom had a line down the hall to get in. I took the back stairs up to the second floor to find one of the bathrooms up there.

I WENT TO the first bathroom I could find. A light was on, and the door was open a crack. In retrospect, I should've knocked or asked if anyone was in there. But I was in a fog of anxiety after talking to Rahim. I pushed the door open, grabbed the knob to close it behind me, and as soon as I shut it, the knob came off in my hand.

"Hey. I'm finishing up. The door's broke, y'know."

The toilet flushed. Then I heard a plunk, a frantic splashing sound, and panicked cursing. Some kid zipped up his jeans and quickly came around the side of the recessed toilet. It was Ashok. He was holding a wet cell phone in a wet hand, and he looked miserable. Then he glanced past me, and his expression changed to terror. He set his phone down on the sink.

"You didn't...?" He pushed past me, grabbed the knob hole, and rattled the door. It was locked tight.

Weakly, I showed him the knob in my hand. Boy, did he look pissed.

"Didn't you see it wasn't working?" He tried prying open the door from the side and from the bottom. Nothing worked. He stood and faced me.

"What're we going to do? We're locked in here." He looked back to his phone and rushed to get it. He shook his head. "It's dead. You startled me, and I dropped it in the toilet. I can't call anyone for help."

I felt like a massive idiot. I tried the door myself. The outside knob had fallen off when I pulled the door shut so there was nothing to attach to the useless part I was holding in my hand. I felt around the hole to see if I could unjam the door catch.

"We need a screwdriver. Or something like it," Ashok said.

I looked at him helplessly. He was still really pissed. The last time we talked, he'd walked away real fast after I basically said I wasn't interested in going with him to the winter formal. Then, he blew me off when I tried to say hi at the end of the semester party. I'm sure I was the last person he wanted to be locked in that bathroom with.

"Do you have your phone?"

I dug my phone out of my pocket and showed it to him. He looked at me impatiently.

"Well, call someone. Unless you want to be stuck in here all night."

I tried Vinnie. It went to voicemail. I tried Scott, then Jayson, then Tyler. No one answered. It was really loud downstairs, and they were probably dancing and not paying attention to their phones. I rifled off a group text and told Ashok one of them was bound to respond really soon.

It sucked dropping your phone in a toilet. I'd dropped mine in a urinal in eighth grade because I was such a spaz. But Ashok was being particularly cold. He wouldn't even look at me.

He opened the cabinet under the sink, looking for some tools, I guess, and then he searched the medicine cabinet. I sat down on a corner of the bathtub. I wasn't going to be of much help, and it seemed like a good idea to give him some space.

Ashok gave up looking and turned around. "I guess we're fucked until somebody comes up here and finds us."

"I'm sorry. I saw the door open and didn't realize it was broken."

Ashok sighed through his nose. He looked like he was cooling down some. Like me, he'd barely dressed up for the party. He was wearing a sweater and jeans and just had a temporary tattoo of the Jack of Hearts on one of his cheeks.

"Why'd you come up here anyway?" he said.

"Probably the same reason as you. There's a mad line for the downstairs bathroom."

He sat down on the opposite side of the bathtub. "Just my luck. I was already having a shitty night, but I guess things can always get worse."

That was taking things too far. "You think I broke the door deliberately? Anyone could've made that mistake. This house is, like, a hundred years old. All the doors are falling apart."

He didn't have anything to say to that. We sat in silence for a while. I checked my phone. Nobody had written back. I rested it face down on my knee.

"Why were you having a shitty night?" I asked him.

He frowned. "You wouldn't care."

I was about to rebut that, but he cut me off. "How's living at the house? I heard you're having a great time."

"Who told you that? Jayson?"

He shrugged. "People."

He was being such a snot again, I decided it was pointless to try to find out who'd been talking about me.

"We haven't seen each other since last semester, and obvs, I did something to piss you off. You gonna tell me what it was?"

"Nothing. It's my problem, not yours."

I tried to catch his gaze. He wouldn't look at me. I decided to attempt making normal conversation.

"How was your break?"

"Fine."

"How's Zi?"

"Good."

"You have a lot of midterm exams?"

"Yeah. And I should've stayed home studying instead of going to this stupid party."

A silence stretched between us again. Ashok got up and tried the door to no avail. Then he went over to the bathroom window. It was barely wider than he was. He raised the storm window and pried open the screen. I watched him plant his hands on the window sill and perch to look around. I put my phone in my pocket and got up to check it out myself. It had to be at least a twenty foot fall, straight down.

"Someone will come by and open the door," I told him.

"Maybe I'll take my chances. What's the worst thing that could happen? Breaking my leg?"

Gently, I placed my hand on his shoulder. "Hey. Is it *that* bad being stuck in here with me?"

He pulled away and stood back by the tub. "It's not like you're any happier being stuck with me."

My phone vibrated against my leg. I ignored it. "I don't have any problem with you. You're the one who raced off every time I stepped into the room last semester. I thought we were friends."

He swiped his face. "Just forget everything I said. It's my problem, not yours. I shouldn't be taking it out on you."

It was annoying that he was being so dismissive, but I could tell he was going through something, and I was feeling for him. The two of us had a really great connection during rush. It was different than with Jayson, Vinnie. and Scott. In some ways, it had felt deeper. We'd had a lot of one-on-one time and talked about how we both felt like social misfits. That's why I didn't look at my phone to see if someone had answered me. I was concerned about Ashok.

"What's going on?"

He pivoted away from me. "It's nothing you'd understand."

"Maybe not. But maybe I would." I drew a deep breath. "Ashok, I'm sorry if you're pissed at me. About the winter formal. I mean, if that's why you're pissed. It was the last time we really talked. I was trying to explain why I wasn't taking anyone to the party. And you just bailed. You never gave me a chance to explain."

He sucked his teeth. "What was there to explain?" He shook his head. "You know, I thought Tau was the answer to my problems. I'd finally found a place where I fit in, and I'd finally find a boyfriend. But I don't fit in, and no one wants to be more than friends, or friends with benefits, at least with me. It's all kind of bullshit. 'We're gay and straight and everything in between.' As long as you're beautiful and have a sick body." He buried his gaze in the floor. "Tonight I was supposed to meet up with this kid I've been talking to. And when I found him at the party, he was making out with one of the brothers. A tall, built guy like you and all of your friends." He looked up at me. "So, I get it, Ethan. You're not into me that way. Join the club."

My heart melted. He was being much too hard on himself, and while I had some friends and got myself in shape, I felt the same way a lot of the time. Really, I hadn't connected with anyone in an emotional way, like I had with Ashok. He was awkward and excitable just like me, and if it hadn't been for my stupid crush on Oliver, I wouldn't have minded pursuing things with him.

"Ashok, I always thought you were awesome," I said. "I was going through a lot of things last semester. But if I could go back in time, I wouldn't have been so spazzy about you asking to go with you to the winter dance."

He kind of winced like I was putting him on.

"I'm serious."

"Aren't you with that crazy hot dude Danny now?"

I blinked. Of course, it wasn't true, and I was thinking that some gossip must've gotten out of hand. I'd told Vinnie and Scott about my crush on Danny. And Jayson. Maybe they'd mentioned it to other people and it had gotten twisted around like the two of us were seeing each other.

"I'm not with Danny. I never was. And I'll tell you something else. Yes, living at the house can be great. But I don't feel like I fit in either a lot of time."

He narrowed his eyes at me. "You look like you fit in." His face darkened. Something amusing was on his mind, and then he said it. "I was kind of surprised to hear that you're living in the annex. Is it as wild as people say?"

"What do you mean?"

"People say you have to get spit roasted by all the brothers to move in."

My jaw dropped. I knew about the rumors that a lot of sex was going on, but that was a really mean story for people to be making up. "That's what people say?"

I must've looked really freaked out. Ashok was kind of cowering from me.

"You think *I* let all the guys spit roast me to get a room?"

"I didn't say that. I was just repeating what other people said."

I glanced upward and shook my head. "So, everybody thinks the annex is a non-stop gang bang."

"I don't know. Is it?"

I glared at him. "No. It's not."

"Well, is it true they keep the windows covered so they can film guys having sex with each other? And that you have to, you know, give it up to all the housemates?"

I stood up. I was getting heated. And while part of what he said was kind of true, I was flipping out that people were spreading such crazy stories.

"Who told you that?"

"Look. Ethan, chill."

My voice raised thunderously. "I'm serious. Who the fuck told you that?"

Ashok slipped in his seat and fell back into the tub, taking the shower curtain along with him. My heart did skips. I hadn't meant to scare him so bad. I hurried to help him disentangle himself from the shower curtain. He was red-faced and massaging the back of his head.

"You okay?"

Lying crossways in the tub, still half covered in the vintage He-Man shower curtain, with his feet sticking out, Ashok laughed hysterically. That got me laughing too.

"You scared me," he said.

I glanced at the shower faucet and got an evil idea. I grabbed the handle. "You want to be scared?"

"No. Ethan. No."

I chuckled. "Just kidding. You need a hand?"

He clasped my hand, and I tried to help him out of the tub. It was pretty ridiculous. He was still tangled in the curtain and wedged on his upper back. I had to step one foot in the tub to get some leverage. Ashok swung one leg in too, and we managed to get him upright. Then the bastard struck out for the faucet, and I got doused with cold water from the shower head.

I cursed and grabbed him to get him under the shower spray. He shrieked and wrangled with me, and we both ended up getting soaking wet.

"What was that for?" I demanded.

Ashok giggled. "For getting us locked up in here and making me bang my head."

"I told you, it was an accident."

"It's cold," he complained.

I wrestled a lock around his arms. "That's your fault."

It was a crazy, annoying thing for him to do, but neither one of us could stop smiling at each other. Then a big commotion burst out by the door.

"Is this the one?"

"Ethan? You in there?"

I looked at Ashok, and we both erupted in laughter. It sounded like Vinnie and Scott. "Yeah," I called back.

The door rattled.

"We're going to get you out."

I turned off the water. Not that the damage hadn't been done already. Vinnie and Scott fumbled with the door, and then with a big thud, it flew open. The two guys stepped in and set their eyes on Ashok and me.

"Jesus. What were you trying to do? Flood the bathroom to get somebody's attention?"

VINNIE AND SCOTT rounded up some clothes for us to change into, and separately, Ashok and I got dried off and changed in the bathroom. I let Ashok go first, which was generous of me considering it was all his fault. When I finished toweling off and stepping into someone's sweatpants and T-shirt, I was happily surprised the troublemaker had waited for me.

"They said we can use the dryer in the basement."

We carried our wet clothes and sneakers down two flights of stairs, through the crowded basement rec room, and into an unfinished laundry area with one overhead light. We decided to just dry our sneakers since that was what we needed the most. My feet were freezing on the concrete basement floor. Ashok stepped over to an old, discarded woodshop table and hopped up. I figured we had at least a half hour to wait, so I sat down next to him while our sneakers banged around in the dryer.

Neither one of us said anything for a while, just sitting there with our legs dangling off the table. Then Ashok cleared his throat.

"I'm sorry."

"You should be," I told him.

We exchanged scowls. Then Ashok started giggling, and I started giggling.

"All right. It was pretty funny," I said.

"You threatened me first."

"I was *bluffing*."

"You made me fall back and hit my head."

"That was your fault. I didn't push you."

We were quiet again.

"Okay." Ashok raised his hand and gently scratched my shoulder. "I guess you deserve this. To make up for getting you all wet. And generally behaving like an asshole."

That shoulder scratch felt so good. It reminded me of our fundraiser while we were pledging.

"Okay. I guess this makes up for it. I forgive you. But you're going to have to scratch my back until our shoes are dry."

He swatted my back lightly. But then he maneuvered around to scratch my back with both hands.

"So, how's the semester going for you, really?" I asked him.

"It's all right. I did pretty good on my prelim exams. Except for Chemistry. But everyone bombed that exam, and the professor said he'd take that into consideration if we do well on the midterm. I've got a lot of studying to do for that."

I smiled wistfully. "Sounds like you're doing a lot better than me. I'm on academic probation. I'm supposed to get a B+ average this semester, but I'm barely pulling a C-."

"Why? From skipping classes and partying too much?"

I looked down at my feet. "Kind of. I mean, it's not so much the partying. It's like I know what I have to do. Go to class. Pay attention. Take notes. Keep up with the readings. But I just can't do it." I pushed my damp hair back. "I don't know. Sometimes I think maybe I'm not cut out for college."

Ashok stopped scratching. "You're thinking of dropping out? What're you going to do?" Before I could answer, he laid into me. "That's crazy, Ethan. What you need to do is apply yourself. You got into this college. Of course you're cut out to be here."

"I'm not smart like you. And my classes don't really interest me. Like I thought I wanted to be in health sciences, but I don't know if that's what I really want to do." I snorted. "It's really sad. Science and math are, like, my worst subjects, and I'll have three more years of those classes. My mom's probably right. My parents are just wasting their money."

"You're giving up too easily. They have a tutoring center on campus."

I knew about that. My advisor had told me. I had made an appointment once, but I didn't go.

"You could change majors. What do you want to do?"

I'd thought about that question a lot. I couldn't come up with an answer, and when I told Ashok that, I started getting emotional. "Everybody else knows what they want to do with their life, and I have no idea. It makes me feel like a loser. Like, what if I'm not good at anything?"

"Maybe you just need some time to figure it out. Talk to your advisor. Or take one of those tests where they match up your personality and skills with possible careers."

I know he was trying to be helpful, but it was just making me feel lame. "Until I get off academic probation, I *can't* change majors."

"All right. So you work your ass off and get off probation."

I sighed.

"Ethan, you're not a loser. If you want, we could study together sometimes," he said. "I mean, like, if you wanted to. Y'know, to help you stay focused."

I turned to him. I was feeling pretty miserable, but it made me smile how he looked super cute when he got shy. "You really want to study with someone who's probably gonna bomb out on probation?"

"If it'll make you stop thinking about dropping out of school, sure."

"Then, that'd be great. And I promise I won't turn it into a pity party about how sad my life is. Thanks for listening."

He grinned and rested his hands. "I won't complain about how unpopular I am, either. No one wants to hear that. It's such a downer, right?"

"I don't mind. Everybody needs to vent, don't they?"

"Then we'll set a timer. You get to complain about school for seven minutes. I get to complain about guys for seven minutes. The rest of the time we study."

"Okay. But only if we really need to vent."

We smiled at each other. I reached out my hand, and we shook on it.

"And Ethan, I'm sorry I said those things about the annex. It was just rumors. You know how things get exaggerated."

"It's okay." I glanced at the dryer. Our wet sneakers were still making a racket. I smirked at Ashok. "But you're still supposed to be scratching."

He gawped at me. But then he went back to scratching my back. It was really nice. Not just the back scratch, I mean. It was nice spending time with him.

Chapter Seventeen

ASHOK AND I started meeting up at the library after classes on Tuesdays and every Sunday. It worked out well since those were off-nights from being on the live feed for *Frat House Secrets*. Honestly, I wanted to quit doing scenes. It had been exciting for a couple of weeks, but the fun of horsing around with the housemates in the nude wore off. It took up my time three nights a week, and it started to feel like work.

I guess that's the point. Acting for the site *was* work. It was paying for my room and meals. That's why I didn't quit. I couldn't ask my parents to start paying for my housing out of the blue, especially since I'd lied to them about getting a housing scholarship. I felt lousy about that, but what could I do?

Meanwhile, Ashok and I got closer. I really looked forward to our study time. We caught each other up on our lives, got a little flirty sometimes, and we really did get down to studying, which helped with my classes. Ashok was a much better student, but I felt like I could be myself around him. He was really socially conscious too. In response to the attacks on Tau, he'd volunteered to start a workgroup to raise awareness of anti-LGBTQ harassment on campus. He organized an information table at the student union and spoke on a panel. We talked about those things too when we got together. I admired him.

To tell the truth, I enjoyed spending time with him more than with Vinnie and Scott. I mean, they were great friends, but they were into looking a certain way more than I was. Plus, they were really into partying with the housemates. I had to stay disciplined to pull up my grades that semester. I couldn't be staying up late and drinking every night.

I wanted to tell Ashok what happened at the annex. I felt kind of shitty about keeping it from him, but it was *a lot* to explain.

As well as we got along and didn't judge each other, I was afraid he'd think I was gross, not to mention I'd be outing the website and everyone associated with it. I told myself I'd just get through the semester. A group of us had started talking about getting an off-campus apartment together next fall. That was Jayson, Tyler, Tyler's roommate, Ben, and Ashok and his roommate, Zi. I figured then I could put spring semester in the past and start over, living more honestly. I told Jayson how I was feeling one night when we finally found a time to talk over FaceTime.

"You turned into a totally different person," he said.

"What do you mean?"

He cocked a glance at me like I was stupid. "Ethan, when we met at the start of the year, you were scared to do anything with a guy. And you basically morphed from twink to muscle twunk in like thirty seconds."

I knew what he meant, but it still made me feel defensive. "I like working out now. That doesn't make me a totally different person."

"You're doing porn. You never would've done that last semester."

"It's not porn. It's make-believe for guys who are into frat boy fantasies. It's just horsing around. I'm not having sex on camera."

Jayson rolled his eyes. "Ethan, you know I'm not judging you. You look amazing, and if your destiny is to be a muscle queen, maybe you should just own it. It's not the worst thing in the world."

"You changed too," I said. He was currently wearing pixie dust pink lipstick, blue eyeshadow, and had a hair cap on after taking off a wig.

He took a makeup cloth to his face. "I'm experimenting with gender. I think I'm more they than he."

I grinned. I'd had a feeling about that when we first met. "That's really awesome."

"It is, right? Tyler's telling people he's gender fluid, too. It's not such a big deal these days, is it?"

"I think it's cool."

"Thanks. And I guess it's pretty cool the two of us can still be friends even though we're completely different."

I took that in. "People can look different but still be a lot the same on the inside. You know what I mean?"

"Yeah. I suppose. I mean, if you can deal with my feminine energy, I guess it's only fair I deal with your masc energy."

"*I* have masc energy?"

"It's not like neon lights, but yeah, you give off masc energy. You and all the 'bros' at the house. Like Vinnie, Scott, and Oliver."

I didn't know what to say to that.

"It's not bad. It's just who you are. Believe me, I know you're a storm cloud of insecurities on the inside, but maybe you've found yourself. You're a stud, Ethan. And not in a dickish way, like you look down at other people. I'm happy for you too."

I didn't feel like a stud. I guess I understood what he meant otherwise. I mean, I was happy with my body most of the time, and I liked looking like a guy. The few times Jayson put makeup on me for parties, it had been fun, but for me it was putting on a costume for a party. With Jayson, it was how he wanted to look all of the time. I was super proud of him.

A curious and silly thought occurred to me. "Does Ashok give off masc energy?"

Jayson took a pause from removing his make-up. "Low wattage, but yes. You two are the perfect all-American gay, cisgender couple."

I guffawed. "We're not a couple. Are people saying we're a couple?" A shocking thought hit me. "Did he say we're a couple?"

"No. But it's obvious you two are into each other."

I wanted to ask him more about that, but I decided not to be a pain. "What about you and Brad?"

"We broke up. I don't think he's into the gender fluid thing."

"I'm sorry."

"Don't be. It's his loss."

"Totally."

"My therapist says I should put a pause on dating and focus on getting comfortable with my gender stuff."

That sounded like a good idea. "So, should I still call you a Gaysian Jayson?"

"*You* can call me that. But not around other people."

I smiled. He smiled back. We stayed up with each other until one in the morning. I'd missed him like mad. I was really happy we were still such great friends.

I NEEDED TO be around people like Jayson and Ashok. They really got me in a way that Vinnie, Scott and all the guys from the annex didn't. Not that I suddenly disliked them or didn't consider them my friends. They were cool people. But I'd been trying to fit in, and I didn't really fit in. I wasn't into partying and showing off for the video feed. I'd much rather spend a quiet night with Ashok and Jayson and Tyler. I missed a lot of things from last semester, including my talks with Oliver. We started texted again, just little conversations. He asked if I'd like to go jogging sometime, and I was really looking forward to that. Anyway, I felt like my life was starting to make sense again. Then everything went sideways when one of the housemates, Kyle, disappeared.

I heard about it on a Friday when I got home from my Philosophy class. Most of the guys were gathered together in the living room, which was weird. As soon as I stepped in, everyone wanted to know if I'd heard from Kyle or if I'd talked to him the night before. Kyle and I were friendly, but we weren't close. He was a cute, curly blond-haired sophomore, but besides doing some stupid scenes of strip beer-pong for the camera, we hadn't spent much time together. Everyone in the room looked really stressed.

"No one's seen or heard from him since we filmed last night," Vinnie said. "He's not answering texts, and his phone just goes to voicemail."

That was worrying, though I figured there was room for a reasonable explanation. Maybe he went home for the weekend? I didn't know much about Kyle, but he could've hooked up with somebody the night before and was just having some fun. Some of the guys did that, and Kyle and Luca had an open relationship.

Luca looked really wrecked, however. "I told you guys. We have tickets to a concert tonight. Kyle wouldn't just bail on that without letting me know."

Just then, Jacob and Daryl came into the room.

"Guys, I know you're all worried about Kyle," Jacob said. "We just went through the security camera feed from last night."

We all stared at him in anticipation.

"Kyle left the house a little after one thirty. That's all we know."

"We should go to the police," Luca said.

Jacob raised his hand. "Now hold your horses there. Kyle's an adult. He's probably fine, and he'll be bouncing in here any minute."

"You think he might've had a Grindr date?" Scott asked Luca.

Luca shrugged. "I don't think so. He hasn't done that in a long time."

"But he could have," Daryl said. "You two share the same room. He didn't mention anything to you?"

Luca shook his head. He glanced at Rahim and Danny. "I would've been in their room around one thirty."

People were quiet for a moment. Based on the blushes on the three of their faces, I could read into what that meant. Luca and Kyle both did a lot of fooling around. Then Rahim got into it with Daryl.

"If he went out at one thirty in the morning for a Grindr date, that's even more reason we should go to the police. He could've met up with a sketchy guy."

"Or he could've been attacked by the people who've been harassing the house," Luca said.

Shannon and Michael spoke up in agreement about reporting Kyle's disappearance to the authorities. Jacob raised his voice over them.

"Listen up. You're talking about going to the police, having a detective come through the house looking for physical evidence, interviewing each of us, and then what happens?"

Everybody fell silent.

"That's right, brainiacs. We're running a business that could get us kicked out of the frat, kicked off campus, and expelled from school." He gazed across us sternly. "Kyle's going to turn up. There's no point wasting the police's time when he hasn't been gone for even eighteen hours. Personally, I think the graffiti and the phone messages are the usual fraternity hazing BS. The jock frats get off on that, but they've never had the balls to try to physically hurt anyone from Tau." He shrugged impartially. "You want to look into some places Kyle might've gone, that's not a bad idea. But do it discreetly. You got it?"

Most people nodded. Luca and Rahim said they'd scout out some places around campus, and Michael and Shannon volunteered to check out the bars in town. Grant offered to ask around the frat house in a low-key way. At that point, I was thinking Kyle was sure to turn up somewhere. Then another incident happened.

Saturday, I woke up to my phone blowing up with texts from Jayson, Ashok and Tyler.

WTF. Did you see the video on VidShare?

I heard what happened. Are you okay?

Is everyone alright at the house?

I had no idea what they were talking about, and then Vinnie and Scott burst into my room.

Vinnie had his phone in his hand. "Did you just wake up?"

"Yeah." I sat up in my bed. "What's going on?"

He came over to me and showed me his screen and played a video. It was dark and kind of grainy at first with indistinct sounds in the background. Then a light shone on a banner that had been hung across the frat house.

"Groomers Academy: We Recruit Your Sons."

There was laughter, and then the video cut out.

I looked at Vinnie and Scott. They were flushed and keyed up. I still didn't get what happened.

"They pranked the house again," Scott said. "This time they recorded it and posted it on VidShare. People have been posting it all over Insta and Twitter."

VidShare was a sketchy site where anyone could post anything anonymously. I asked Vinnie if I could look at the video again. It sounded like a small group of guys, though they were careful to not show themselves in the recording. My heart fell. That banner wasn't just a prank. It was a hateful distortion of what Tau was all about.

A group of us went over to the main house to see if the other brothers had more info. We ran into Oliver first, and he told us they'd photographed the banner before taking it down earlier that morning. Two guys had found it when they were headed out for an eight o'clock class on campus, and then the VidShare post had come to everyone's attention. It must've happened between four and seven-thirty in the morning. Some guys at the house had been out at bars, and others had stayed in, playing poker in the basement, but everyone had turned in for the night around four.

"Public safety is working on getting the video deleted," Oliver said. "They've been by, along with the town Sheriff. We're also putting out a statement on social media. If any of you saw or heard anything last night, it would be helpful to the investigation."

None of us had anything to say. We'd all spent most of the night looking for Kyle around campus and in town, and some of the guys had been scheduled to go 'live' from 10 to midnight. I was pretty sure everyone in the annex had called it a night by one or two in the morning.

Later, we got a text from Peter calling for another emergency meeting that night. Everyone showed up, and the director of public safety was there to tell us they were working with the town's police department. They hadn't identified the threatening callers or the people who had vandalized the frat, but they were actively investigating the incident. They had the house's security camera feed from last night, and luckily, the Executive Council had recently contracted with a new security company that had installed equipment that actually worked. She went over the same basic tips for personal safety she'd covered a few weeks ago, like traveling in groups and always letting someone know where you were if you went off on your own.

I don't think her briefing had any of us feeling better, and then Peter spoke about Tau's commitment to fighting hate and that he was going to be interviewed by a local news station to bring attention to the incidents. We all agreed that was an important thing to do. I was kind of reeling after the meeting. I went down to the rec room with Ashok, Jayson, Tyler, and Ben. I didn't even realize I was spacing out until Ashok came over to talk to me.

"You okay?"

"Oh...yeah. I'm okay."

"You don't look it," Ashok said. "And that's perfectly normal. What these people are doing, with the vandalism and the threatening phone calls, that's a direct attack on our safety. It's an attack on every LGBTQ+ student's safety."

I nodded along, but the thing is, I was worried the most about Kyle. He could've been lured out of the house by the same person, or people, who were threatening the frat. Most of the brothers didn't even know he was missing. Just the guys at the annex. Jacob warned us not to say anything, so I couldn't even tell Ashok what was on my mind.

Ashok clasped my shoulder. "But did you hear? We're all staying over at the house tonight in solidarity. Every Tau brother." He grinned. "It's going to be one big sleepover."

"Really?"

I was impressed, and gradually it hit me that was going to be a lot of fun. Brothers from the dorms and off-campus apartments brought sleeping bags and pajamas. Two sororities came to the house with homemade cupcakes and cookies, and guys from Chi Kappa Zeta stopped by later to say they were looking out for us. The night turned into one big party, and something like sixty people crammed into bedrooms and spilled down to the living room to sleep on the floor. Ashok and I laid out sleeping bags on a fluffy area rug in one of the dens. We stayed up talking until early in the morning, and we got a little physical, just brushing each other's arm, holding hands, and finding each other's foot and leg under the sleeping bag. It felt natural and really nice being close with Ashok that way.

"Would it be okay if I kissed you?" he asked.

I was nervous, but I was also really happy. I nodded. Ashok leaned toward me and our lips met, just lightly at first. Then he got some motions going, and I got some motions going, and we made out open-mouthed and felt each other's bodies a lot more. I'd been with Rahim and fooled around with some guys, but it was my first time kissing someone I had deep feelings for. That was different in a really good way. Like it tugged my heart and made me feel so warm and safe.

After a while, we just lay face-to-face and looked into each other's eyes. I was buzzing with so many feelings, I forgot all the things I'd been worried about.

"So, what do you think?" Ashok asked.

"About what?"

He smiled shyly. "Like, do you want to be more than friends?"

I brushed the side of his hair. I loved the waves in his thick, glossy locks. "Yeah, I'd like that." I peeked at him. He was smiling really hard.

"Then we should sleep like this." He turned over and brought my arms around him so we were snuggling chest to back. We fell asleep like that.

Chapter Eighteen

I WAS BACK to being super happy again. What can I say? That year was one long rollercoaster. Becoming boyfriends with Ashok was unexpected, but it was everything I'd been dying for. For twenty-four hours, my head was in the clouds.

Ashok liked me. I couldn't stop thinking about it, and we texted each other all day long the next day. I wanted to spend all my time with him. It was like my heart needed him, and it hurt on Sunday that he had some big project to finish for his physics class while I stayed back at the annex. I'd fallen for him hard. Every hour we couldn't spend together felt like an eternity. I couldn't wait to see him the next day after classes.

Then Monday night, when I rushed home from hanging out in Ashok's dorm to make it back in time to do the website thing, I found most of the housemates hanging out in the living room again. I could tell that something serious was going on.

Vinnie and Scott filled me in. "Danny's missing."

"Since last night," Scott said. "He's not answering his phone."

Vinnie rubbed his neck. "We're waiting for Jacob and Daryl to tell us if they can see anything on the security cam."

I didn't want to believe it at first. But Vinnie and Scott looked so stressed, it sank in really quick. Danny had disappeared out of the blue, four nights after Kyle. I glanced around the room. Grant, Shannon, Michael, Luca, and Rahim were slumped on the sofa and chairs like they were at a funeral. I felt fragile. Tears welled up inside me.

I waited around with everyone until Jacob and Daryl showed up to share any information they had. When they came up from the basement, I could read on their faces they didn't have good news. I'd never seen either of them looking shaken up.

"We got Danny on camera, around one thirty in the morning," Jacob said. "That's when he left the house. Out the back door."

Rahim shot up on his feet. "You gonna tell us what's going on?"

"Yeah. But we need to remind you all about the confidentiality agreements you signed first. Everything discussed here falls in the non-disclosure category."

Jacob pried out eye contact from each of us. I just wanted to hear what they knew about Danny. Rahim was riled up, however. "You gonna talk about confidentiality agreements when two of our boys gone missing in less than a week? Where's Kyle? He hasn't turned up like you said. We wanna know what the fuck is up."

Daryl headed him off. "Chill, okay? We're gonna get to that, but this is sensitive information. You gonna show us you can handle it like a man?"

I thought Rahim was going to pop off again. Luca got an arm around his shoulder, telling him to let it go, and that seemed to help. He got Rahim to sit down with him, and then Jacob and Daryl took seats across from all of us.

"So, everybody understands what happens in the annex stays in the annex, right?" Jacob said.

He waited for each of us to verbally confirm that, which we did.

"Kyle and Danny were doing out-calls off the site," Jacob said.

I blinked and looked around. Everyone in the room seemed to know what he was talking about. It was weird. Some of the guys bowed their heads. Meanwhile, I had no idea what was going on.

"Which, besides being a violation of their contracts, it's illegal in New Jersey," Daryl said. "If the police find out, we're all looking at some serious legal trouble."

I was getting the picture. Sort of. Then Luca broke in.

"What are you saying? Kyle went to meet somebody Friday morning? Who?"

The room blew up with questions from people wanting to know what user Danny was talking to and people saying they needed to take whatever information they had to the police. Jacob had to raise his voice to be heard.

"Guys. Listen up. We've got a user name and an IP address. But that's not much, and I'm gonna explain to you why. The IP address comes up as Naples, Florida. It's either a spoof address or somebody was talking to them from Florida and setting them up to meet someone locally. We tend to think it was the former. They also used a fake credit card to access the site."

Grant jumped in. "You gotta have a transcript of their chats. What did they say?"

"Their handle is Mr. Pain," Jacob said. "Same guy who's been chatting with both Kyle and Danny. He's been offering them money to hook up for several weeks. Kyle told him he'd do it Friday morning. Danny, just last night. But then he gave a cell phone number and took things offline. Without their phones, we have no idea where he told them to meet."

Everyone fell silent. Once again, I wasn't sure what was happening. I was thinking either I was dense or everyone was in on a secret nobody had told me.

"So, what now?" Rahim said. "This is some FBI shit. If you can't ID the guy who played Kyle and Danny, we gotta bring in people who can."

"That would involve turning over the website to the authorities," Daryl said. "I want you all to think about that for a minute." He looked at Rahim. "Kyle and Danny aren't the only ones who've been making extra cash off the site."

I glanced around. Rahim hung his head along with Luca, Vinnie, and Scott. I was floored.

Shannon burst out. "What the fuck, guys? Who's been hooking up with users?"

Nobody said anything. The tension in the room was suffocating. I looked at Jacob and Daryl. They ran the site. They had to know everything.

Michael joined Shannon indignantly. "Seriously. Show of hands. Who's taking cash for real-time sex?"

Rahim copped to it, and little by little, the others did as well. Luca. Grant. Vinnie glanced at Scott, and they both did.

Vinnie muttered to me, "One time. This guy in Atlantic City asked to meet at his hotel, and we did."

Shannon and Michael were really pissed. I felt betrayed by Vinnie and Scott too, but I was also in shock and having a hard time keeping track of things with everyone talking over each other. Then Shannon laid into Jacob and Daryl.

"You guys had to know this was going on. That's fucking cold. Are you getting a take?"

Before they could answer, Michael burst out. "This is bullshit. All of you fucked the rest of us. I'm one year away from graduation, and I'm probably going to jail instead. Kyle and Danny, they're not even going to have it that good."

"Nobody's going to jail if we stick together and be smart about this," Jacob said. "Now listen, the past is the past. We keep things legit moving forward, and we focus on the future. That means we seal things down tight. No authorities. No talking to the exec council or any of the other brothers." He glanced at Daryl. "And as of one hour ago, *Frat House Secrets* has gone dark permanently."

I was shook, big time. Not because the website was over, but by the fact no one said anything about Kyle and Danny. I guess I should've been braver and spoken up myself. Two of our housemates had probably been lured into meeting a psychopath. But I couldn't bring myself to say a word. I was still reeling over the fact I'd had no idea all these things had been going on.

LATER THAT NIGHT, Vinnie and Scott came to my room while I was trying to study. I wasn't sure if we were friends anymore, but they looked really remorseful and eager to say something. I told them they could come in.

Vinnie spoke first. "Listen, Ethan. Don't hate us. We made a mistake. It was stupid and selfish, and we know it put everyone at risk. But we didn't mean to get anyone in trouble."

I closed up my laptop. "How long were you making extra money off the website?" I glanced at Vinnie. "Did you talk to Jacob about it and work out a deal?"

Vinnie strained to explain. "Some of the guys told us they were using the site for 'bonuses.' It sounded harmless for once in a while. We didn't think we should mention it to you 'cause you didn't seem interested."

Scott stepped in. "It was one time. This guy who was in town for a convention in Atlantic City. We'd done a private scene for him, and he wanted to meet us."

"It was one thou just to drive down to Atlantic City, spend an hour with him in his hotel room and drive back," Vinnie said.

My anger kicked in. "With a total stranger. That's really smart." I looked at Scott. He was supposedly the more level-headed of the two. I couldn't believe he would do something so dumb. And Danny. He was helping out his family financially. Did he need the money *that* bad?

"We used the cash to get a new radiator for my car," Vinnie said. "I know it was risky, but it was easy money and a lot of the guys were doing it."

"Like Kyle and Danny," I said.

Neither of them said anything.

"I don't get it. I mean, besides the fact it's against the frat's code of conduct, you had to know Jacob and Daryl would find out. They're constantly monitoring the site."

Vinnie gave me a not so friendly look. "You've been cool with stretching the frat's code of conduct ever since we signed our housing contracts to move in here. So don't be acting all holier than thou."

It was the first time we'd had a confrontation, and I hated confrontations. Not that I wanted to smooth things over or give in to what Vinnie was saying. I was just all kinds of nervous, and I guess he had me feeling guilty myself.

"You want to know the truth? I wish I'd never moved in here. I wish I had a time machine, and I could go back to that day at the start of the semester." I hid my face. "I never wanted any of this."

"So, what're you going to do? Report us to the frat?" Vinnie said.

I heard Scott arguing with Vinnie to chill out. It had occurred to me that the right thing to do would be to tell Oliver everything. Even if it meant I'd get thrown out of Tau, it would clear my conscience, and things had gotten really serious. Kyle and Danny could be dead, and nobody cared.

"Ethan, listen," Scott said. "We all made a big mistake. And we're scared, just like you. But we're still brothers, right? We've got each other. We just need to figure this out."

"How?"

Scott sat down next to me on the bed. "We could come clean to the other brothers. If you want to."

I glanced at Vinnie. He didn't look mad anymore, just scared. From the start of pledge, I'd always looked up to him. In my heart, I couldn't believe he'd do something to harm anyone intentionally. If we went to the frat's leadership, we'd all be kicked out and expelled from school. I was just about ready to accept the consequences for myself, but could I do that to two guys who'd had my back all year?

I threw up my hand. "I guess I'll do whatever you guys want to do."

Vinnie stooped down in front of me. "Thanks. 'Cause you know, if you really wanted out of all of this, I'd go to Peter and tell him it was all my fault. That I pressured you to move into the annex, and it shouldn't jeopardize your status in the frat."

"It's not all your fault." I chewed on my finger. "We all fucked up. And now we're going to have to deal with whatever happens."

He clasped my arm and looked me in the eyes. "Like Jacob said, we'll ride things out. Maybe Kyle and Danny will turn up, and it'll be no big deal. If not, we stick together and take things as they come." He sat down on the floor. He looked really beaten down as things were sinking in. "My parents will cut me off if things come out. But I saved up a little money in the bank. Maybe we can rent an apartment together. Figure things out from there."

My parents were going to go ballistic. Then I started thinking about how horrible it was going to be when Peter, Oliver, and the entire frat found out what we'd done. And Ashok. I'd ruined so many things with one bad decision.

Scott sat down next to me on the bed. "We don't feel any better than you about lying to the frat. How 'bout this? We sleep on it. Make a decision in the morning."

That sounded like a good idea. I was mentally and emotionally exhausted. I guess there was a tiny sliver of hope that public safety would turn up something from their investigation of the hate crime against the fraternity that might be related to Kyle and Danny's disappearances. Vinnie, Scott, and I hugged, and they went off to their room.

Chapter Nineteen

I DIDN'T SLEEP so well that night. I kept worrying about Danny and Kyle and feeling like I'd let them down by doing nothing to help them. I was super confused, and "sleeping on it" wasn't doing any good. I'd made an oath to always help a brother in need, which ought to mean that we should be trying to track down the two guys who were in the most trouble, right? But on the other hand, if I came forward with what I knew, it would ruin Tau and get everyone in serious trouble. It was the biggest moral dilemma I'd ever faced. In my heart, I knew the right thing to do. At the time, I'm ashamed to say, I wished the problem would just go away. Tau was my family. It was all going to go up in flames, and I was going to be partly responsible for that.

I went to my classes the next day like a zombie, then around eleven o'clock my phone blew up with texts. First was a group text from Peter about another special meeting that night with public safety. They had news about the homophobic banner incident. Then Jayson, Ashok, and Tyler asked me if I knew what was going on, which, of course I didn't. Then I got dings from Vinnie and Scott saying they'd heard the police had made arrests, and they were holding a televised press conference. It was going to be on the twelve o'clock news.

The six of us met up at the dining hall to watch the coverage. We grabbed a table in a back corner, and we were all so nervous, we didn't even go to the food line. Jayson got his laptop propped up on the table, and we huddled together to watch the streaming news.

It was a top news story. I held my breath while the anchor led into it with the headline in the corner of the screen: "NJ State Frat Charged with Hate Crime." They cut to the sheriff at a podium in front of the police station. He said they had arrested four members of Zeta Kappa Epsilon earlier that morning. Video surveillance had caught an SUV pulling up to the Tau house at three a.m. Sunday morning, four young men stepping out of the vehicle with a ladder and hanging the banner across the house while recording what they were doing. The police traced the SUV back to a member of Zeta Kappa Epsilon, and through their investigation, the four suspects had come forward and also confessed to the lawn graffiti earlier that semester and the incident in the fall. They were withholding their identities pending an order from the district attorney. The news anchor then read a statement from Zeke asserting that they were cooperating with the investigation and they were obligated to hold accountable any of their members who committed acts of discrimination or harassment. They said that they denounce all forms of bigotry and hatred. The news cut to the weather.

"That's total bullshit," Jayson said.

"It's no big surprise," Tyler said. "Zeke's, like, the most homophobic frat on campus."

I completely agreed with him. My former roommate Shawn was a proud Zeke brother. Whenever we walked by a group of them, wearing our Tau sweatshirts, they laughed at us, and I remembered Shawn's last words to me.

"I'm going to destroy you."

"At least they caught them," Ashok said.

I glanced at Vinnie and Scott. "Maybe they're involved in what happened to the other guys."

If I had stopped and thought for a half-second, I wouldn't have said it. It was such an airhead maneuver. Jayson, Ashok, and Tyler stared at me like I'd either lost my mind or been holding back juicy gossip. Vinnie and Scott looked in the other direction.

"What other guys?" Jayson asked.

"What else happened?" Ashok said.

My temples were perspiring. I couldn't take back what I said, and I was such a spaz, I couldn't manage to say anything.

"Y'know. The threatening emails and phone calls," Vinnie said. Our eyes met for a breath. I nodded along.

"Well, probably they're involved with that," Tyler said. Mercifully, the conversation moved on to Tyler and Ashok speculating about what could and should happen to Zeke and the four vandals specifically. I kept my mouth shut, but it was awkward, and I felt really bad about keeping the Kyle and Danny situation from three of my friends. Including my boyfriend. It must have been showing on my face because Jayson kept looking at me while everyone else was talking.

When we got up to head to our afternoon classes, I drifted over to Jayson and quietly asked if we could talk. He told the guys we both had something we needed to print out at the computer lab. I hugged Ashok goodbye, feeling like a villain, and we said we'd see each other at the house meeting that night.

Jayson and I made it as far as the second floor stairwell before he stopped me and gave me his shadiest eyebrow quirk. "Gurl, you're looking guiltier than an altar boy who just gave the priest a hand job."

I gaped at him. "Ew. That's totally gross."

"Well, spill," he demanded. "What *was* that at the table?"

I took a breath to gather some courage, and then I led him down the second floor to the gender neutral bathroom. Luckily, it was unoccupied. We stepped in, and I locked the door behind us. Then I sat down on the toilet with my head in my hands and told Jayson everything.

I knew Jayson was going to freak out. He had every right to, and I deserved every bit of it. I was just a little worried his voice was traveling outside the door, down the hall, and through the offices of the Center for Student Engagement next door.

"Like, when were you guys going to tell the rest of the frat? Did you go to the police?"

I shook my head. Then I got teary and covered my face.

Jayson stooped down next to me. "Ethan. Okay. I'll give you ten seconds to pull yourself together. Then you're going to explain. I mean, you *have to* explain. I'm not bullying you, but this is serial killer shit. You can't keep it to yourself."

Gradually, I filled him in on my predicament. That's not even a strong enough word. I felt like I'd been living in a torture cage.

"So, you all swore to silence. Vinnie *and* Scott?"

"We didn't swear to silence. We were going to sleep on it. Then we were going to tell Peter. Or something."

Jayson stood back and studied me. "You didn't tell anyone? Not even Ashok?"

I was melting into a puddle of guilt. I wiped the tears from my eyes with my shirt sleeve and glanced at him. "You're my best friend. Right?"

"Yeah, you're my best friend. It's fucked up big time what you're telling me, but I'm not like going to break up as friends with you and stop following you on Insta."

I appreciated that. I relaxed a little and asked him what he thought I should do.

"One hundred percent, you guys have to tell Peter."

I nodded. "We'll get kicked out of the fraternity, but it's the right thing to do. I'm such a sleaze."

"That's a little harsh." He glanced at me. "Is there like video of you masturbating on the site?" His eyes popped. "Did you do video of penetration?"

"No," I told him firmly. "It's just stupid stuff like I told you. Like wrestling and taking our clothes off."

He curled his mouth. "Well, I'm sure it's no big deal then."

"How's it not a big deal? We've been using the annex to make frat boy porn."

He gazed at me squarely. I didn't know why. "Ethan, you think Peter *doesn't* know about it?"

"How would he know about it?"

"He's the president of the fraternity."

"So?"

"You think he's not aware people are using the back house for a porn site that's pulling in hundreds of thousands of dollars a month?"

"Wait. You think Peter's known all along?"

"Think about it, Ethan. You guys are paying rent and buying expensive clothes while none of you have jobs. And the only guys who live there are buff dudes who keep the shades down over the windows twenty-four-seven. Peter's probably getting a cut. There's rumors around the house. It's kind of an unacknowledged secret."

My mind was blown. Then I remembered the gossip Ashok had mentioned. It made sense now. Jacob and Daryl had made a big deal about confidentiality agreements, but I could see how it looked from an outside perspective. My anxiety spiked all over again.

"Jacob and Daryl are shady," he went on. "I had a feeling from the beginning."

My eyes bulged. "You never said that."

"Maybe it was just *kind of* a feeling."

"You could've told me that before."

"You, Vinnie, and Scott were all over the idea of moving in. I didn't want to be judgy." He smoothed out his tucked-in floral blouse. "But I'm saying it now. There's something creepy about them, and it's even creepier they're telling you guys you can't say anything about Kyle and Danny disappearing when they know some user from the site's involved."

I didn't disagree with that. Jacob and Daryl had always made me feel like they were holding back something, and they pretty much treated everyone like crap. Now I was getting paranoid. Like maybe they knew more about Kyle and Danny's disappearance than they had told us. They knew guys were meeting up with users. They hadn't cared that it was dangerous. They only cared now because their business was in jeopardy.

"If Peter knows about the website, you think he knows Kyle and Danny are missing?"

Jayson shrugged.

"I don't think he does," I said. "Jacob and Derek were really insistent we don't say anything to executive leadership."

"Then probably he doesn't. Which is why you need to tell him. ASAP."

I pushed back my hair. "Okay. I'll talk to Vinnie and Scott, and we'll tell him tonight."

"Are you going to tell Ashok?"

I gulped.

"He's really into you. If you care about him, you should let him know. Before everybody knows."

I bowed my head again. "He's going to hate me. Everybody's going to hate me."

"Ethan, don't have a meltdown." He came back over to me, trying to calm me down.

"I fucked up. Really bad. Tau is probably going to be disbanded because of this. Because of me."

"You made some bad decisions, and now you're going to make them better. If you want to get technical, I'm responsible too. I knew about the site and didn't tell anyone."

I scowled. "That's different. I, like, signed a contract. I broke the code of conduct. And I know whatever happened to Kyle and Danny is a lot more serious, but basically, my life is over."

"Maybe they'll be lenient with you," Jayson said. "I mean, you've only been doing the website for a couple of months, right? It's not like you created it. It would've been going on whether or not you moved into the house."

That sounded like wishful thinking to me. I looked up at him. "One hundred percent serious, if you were Ashok and I told you all this, what would you think?"

He shrank up his face and took his time answering. "One hundred percent serious? I think I wouldn't be totally shocked. About the website, I mean. There's been a lot of gossip going around. So, like, if I knew that and still wanted to be your boyfriend, I think I'd probably be okay about you doing porn. But the bigger issue is having known about Kyle and Danny and not doing anything about it. I think Ashok is going to have a problem with that."

I nodded, and then I started sniffling tears again.

"Ethan, listen, we're besties. I've got your back." He squatted down and clasped my hand. "And the other guys will come around. We made an oath to look out for each other."

That made me feel a little better. There was no way I could get through what I needed to do by myself. I stood and went to the sink to splash some water on my face and pull it together. Jayson hung around my side. He was grinning like he had something else to say.

"So, like, maybe this isn't the right time, but remember how we said we'd both find boyfriends this year?"

I glanced at him in the bathroom mirror.

"Well, you're dating Ashok, and I started dating somebody."

"No."

He scrunched up his brow. "Whatever. Glad you're happy for me."

"I *am* happy for you. I meant like no, shut up. Not no, you can't." He still looked moody. "I'm just kinda surprised because you said you were taking a pause from dating."

"I took a pause. But then things kinda just happened. He's like the first person I ever dated. *Really* dated. Not like Andrew or Brad who basically just wanted to hook up for oral sex." His face turned red. "And he's the first Asian guy I ever had a relationship with."

My jaw dropped. "Oh. My. God. That's awesome."

He smiled. "My therapist says it's awesome, too."

I was super happy for him. We hugged, and Jayson told me all about Hye, who he'd met in his bio class. They'd gone out for coffee and then they went to some student film screening together and stayed up late talking in his dormitory lounge. Hye invited him to a party the Korean Student Association was having, and after, they kissed and Hye asked him if he wanted to be boyfriends.

That was all insanely cute, and I was really grateful I had a friend like Jayson. It made what I had to do next just a little bit easier, knowing that whatever happened, we'd still be friends.

I RAN TO my statistics class, and after I got settled in, I sent two texts. First, I asked Ashok if he could meet up at four at the cafe in the arts and sciences quad. Then I texted Vinnie and Scott to say we needed to talk before the house meeting.

I was crazy nervous about my conversation with Ashok. Everything felt surreal that day. Since word had traveled about the incident between Zeke and Tau, I overheard people talking about it everywhere, and kids looked at me funny, knowing I was a Tau brother, I guess. Or I could've been imagining it. I got to the cafe before Ashok, and I found a two-seat table in the crowded room. My stomach was twisted up really bad. I spotted Ashok walking in and I waved to him. He came over, threw his book bag down, and took a seat.

Telling Jayson the truth had been hard, but it was nothing compared to confessing everything to Ashok. I nearly chickened out while we sat in awkward silence. I could tell Ashok was nervous too. It had to be obvious I had something serious to tell him. So, after we got iced coffees and sat down again, I took the plunge.

"Remember when you asked me if we all get together for group sex at the annex?"

His eyes widened.

"We don't," I rushed to say. "But there's things going on I haven't told you. I wanted to. I really did. I didn't have the courage, and I know that's not an excuse, so, like, anyway, I'm telling you now."

I couldn't look at him while I stumbled through the story of how I'd ended up doing frat porn for my room and board. Ashok was silent. I raised my eyes for a half second.

"I wanted to quit the site weeks ago. I just couldn't figure a way out. I needed the money to pay for housing this semester, and I told myself I'd just get through it and save up some money to live off-campus with everybody next year. Then things got more complicated." I tried to get a read on him. "So, if you think I'm totally gross and don't want to have anything to do with me, I understand."

He sighed. "Ethan, I don't think you're gross. I'm kind of at a loss for words. I mean, you could've told me when I asked about the annex at the Wonderland party."

"I know. I'm sorry. I just never thought I'd be in this kind of situation. Jacob and Daryl made us sign a confidentiality agreement."

The more I explained things out loud, the worse I felt. It was all so underhanded and sleazy. I didn't know what to make of the look on Ashok's face. He didn't seem disgusted, but he definitely had things on his mind.

"You're an enigma, Ethan Leavitt," he said.

I grinned nervously. "How do you mean?"

"When we first met last semester, I thought you were shy and sheltered. Then you got into going to the gym and hanging out with guys like that, and I thought you were turning into one of *those* kind of gays. I figured you'd never waste your time on someone like me. Then, when we got locked in the bathroom together, I thought

I prejudged you. You seemed genuine and innocent, and I remembered all the things I liked about you in the first place. But now, I don't know what to think. Like, which Ethan are you? The one who's into gaming and blushes when he gets a back scratch, or the one who breaks rules and shows his dick for money?"

I hadn't been prepared for him to get so deep. Don't get me wrong. I appreciated it. He was spot on, and I knew I had some soul searching to do. I just didn't have an answer for him, and I felt bad about that.

"Y'know, before I came to college, I had these high hopes for what it was going to be like. I thought I'd leave behind the lame person I was in high school, come out, make friends, be popular. And then I rushed at Tau, and all that kinda happened, really fast." I pushed back my hair. "I guess I got caught up in that. Hanging out with good looking guys. Having people actually like me. But I don't feel any different on the inside. I'm still mad insecure. And I'd never think you were someone I didn't have time for."

"I don't get how you could get involved in something that could ruin the fraternity."

"I'm not proud of it. It was stupid, but when I talked about it with Vinnie and Scott, it seemed like the best solution to my problems. My dad got his hours cut at work. My parents were having problems paying for me going to college. I know it's sketchy, but it was like an easy way to take the burden off them."

"I'm not saying I think it's wrong to make money that way." He scratched his ear. "But you had to know it's wrong to do it on Tau property. And not just you. All the brothers who are doing it."

I felt another meltdown coming on, but I pushed through it. "You're right. I screwed up. I don't deserve to be a brother. I'm telling Peter everything tonight before the house meeting, and then I guess I'm moving home."

We were silent for a while. Then Ashok leaned over the table and put his hand on mine. "Ethan, I don't think you're a bad person. That's going to take a lot of guts to come clean."

I peeked at him.

"I don't hate you," he said. "People make mistakes. I wish you hadn't made them, but I appreciate that you told me."

I was thankful he was taking things so well. Then it hit me. In a couple of hours, my college life would be over. I'd be dismissed from Tau. I'd have to either tell my parents the truth or come up with some story to explain why I couldn't live at the house anymore. I'd have to move back home immediately, withdraw from all my classes, and I'd probably never see Ashok or any of my friends again. And it could be even worse when the police started investigating Kyle and Danny's disappearances. The university and the whole world would probably find out I'd been involved in the sketchy site.

"You might not have to go home though, would you?" Ashok said. I was so weighted down by the disaster, I couldn't answer, and Ashok went on a mile a minute, in problem-solving mode. "What do you think will happen when you tell Peter? It's against the code of conduct, but it might not be an automatic expulsion. I mean, the whole website thing puts Tau in a vulnerable position, no doubt, but maybe the Executive Council will want to handle it internally. They'll want to consult with lawyers. You should get a lawyer, too. You're basically like a whistleblower, right? You were only involved with the website for a couple months. It was a breach of ethics, but the situation should be relative."

He exhaled sharply. "Look at Zeke. They've got brothers committing hate crimes, and they've sealed up everything tight and they're not suspending anyone. That's like a hundred times worse than doing porn. It's a victimless crime. Not even a crime. It's not against the law to do porn unless you're underage." He misread the misery on my face. "I know. It's going to look bad for Tau's reputation, but there shouldn't be a double standard. There's probably lots of people at other frats and sororities doing sex videos. It's worse because Jacob and Daryl monetized it, on frat property, but times have changed. There shouldn't be some big stigma attached to it. You've been working really hard at school, and you were using the money to pay for college expenses. Nobody was getting hurt or exploited."

He was being a really great friend, but all the while, I was sinking deeper and deeper with guilt. I hadn't even told him the biggest reason why I had to let Peter know about the website. I breathed in some more courage. I could see the tension building inside him as I told him about Kyle and Danny.

"So, at the party, you, Vinnie, and Scott all knew Kyle went to meet someone for sex the night before and never came home, and you didn't tell anyone?"

"No. I mean, we just knew he hadn't come home. We didn't know why he left. Even his boyfriend, Luca, had no idea." I tried to explain Jacob and Daryl had only told us about the suspicious website user yesterday.

"It doesn't matter. He's a brother. We should've all been searching for him as soon as Luca said he was missing."

I felt like such a jerk. I thought about explaining how everything was confusing to me at the time, and people were worried about overreacting and getting everyone in trouble over nothing. But I knew that would just sound like a lame excuse.

Ashok looked at me, red in the face. "Tau's been getting violent threats all year, and you guys didn't think you should report two brothers disappeared? Ethan, you know better than that, don't you? I mean, what do you think it's going to look like for all of us when the police, their families find out you all kept running the site, knowing that someone was using it to target guys from Tau?"

I had no words.

"I guess I figured out which Ethan you are," Ashok said. "You guys screwed all of us, and you sat on information about two brothers who probably got lured into an ambush by homophobes, just so you could continue making money streaming porn." He grabbed his book bag and stood up from the table. "Y'know, I actually felt bad for you for a minute. But it's not just you who's going to lose the frat and have to drop out of school. What do you think my parents are going to do when this comes out?"

I stared at him in horror. He rolled his eyes and stormed out of the café.

Chapter Twenty

I COULDN'T BLAME Ashok for reacting that way. He made me feel like a terrible human being, but I had to start taking responsibility for what I'd done. I lied to him. By not speaking up about Kyle and Danny, I'd basically conspired with Jacob and Daryl to save our asses rather than doing right by our fellow brothers. Everything was going to come out eventually, and I'd made the entire frat look bad. Ashok deserved a better boyfriend than me. I'd gone totally out of control that semester, and I didn't even recognize the person I'd become.

Anyway, I guess that conversation toughened me up. Thirty minutes later, when I met Vinnie and Scott at the athletic center to talk, I made it clear we were telling Peter everything before the house meeting. I said we should ask him if we could publicly resign from Tau and apologize to everyone. It was the only right thing to do.

Vinnie said we should get legal representation first. I told him to go ahead if he wanted, but I was going straight to Peter. Vinnie and Scott glanced at each other, and then Scott said I was one hundred percent right, and they were onboard. We didn't bother to do a workout. We walked out of the locker room to head back to the house.

While we were walking home, Vinnie turned to me. "Did you hear? I'm pretty sure one of the guys from Zeke is your former roommate. Shawn Hurley?" He swiped through his phone. "Zeke put out a statement on Facebook."

I took the phone from him and read the post. It was two long paragraphs that sounded like they'd been written by a lawyer and included the usual apology language Tyler had predicted. But the second paragraph included the full names of three brothers who had been expelled from the frat due to "egregious misjudgment," though it didn't actually say they were responsible for vandalizing Tau. The last sentence just said Zeta Kappa Epsilon was cooperating in the police's investigation, and they were committed to seeing justice served for the victims. Shawn's name was there.

"What a fuckhead," Scott said. "Remember when the big man ran out of your room like a little bitch?"

Vinnie took his phone back. "He threatened you, remember? Make sure you mention that when you talk to the police. Those scumbags are probably responsible for Kyle and Danny disappearing."

I had plenty to say about Shawn's homophobia if the police needed testimony about that. I wasn't shocked he'd been one of the vandals. But was he the kind of person who would kidnap people and possibly murder them? I didn't know what to think. It was almost unbelievable the homophobic pranks and the luring of the guys were coincidental. But then again...

"You really think those guys targeted Kyle and Danny through the website?"

"I do," Vinnie said.

Scott shrugged.

"I don't know if it makes sense," I said. "The one thing, catfishing the guys took a lot of planning and technical finesse. Jacob said the user had a spoof IP address and a fake credit card, and they'd been trying to pick up guys for weeks. But the other things, like defacing the house, that's, like, an impulsive prank. And they weren't so swift about it. The police ID'd them in like twenty-four hours. And Shawn and his friends must've copped to it right away."

"I dunno, E," Vinnie said. "They're the only suspects on campus I know."

I thought of something else. "Jacob and Daryl also said they use some kind of stealth program for the site so nobody in a thirty mile radius can access it."

Scott rolled his eyes. "Jacob and Daryl say a lot of things."

I stared at him, waiting for more. He exchanged a glance with Vinnie. That always meant they'd been keeping something from me. They halted on the campus path for a confidential huddle. "Jacob and Daryl set us up with that guy from Atlantic City," Vinnie said. "They're full of shit about the 'website agreement.'"

"What do you mean?"

"They say you can't trick off the website, but they totally want guys tricking off the website," Scott said. "It's good for their business."

An icy chill passed over me. I literally froze while they went on talking.

"They're not even college students," Vinnie said.

"You don't know that," Scott said.

"Okay. But that's the rumor. You ever seen either one of them going to classes? And Rahim said they graduated, like, two years ago. He saw them in some old yearbook."

"Guys, what the hell is going on?"

"Vinnie's speculating," Scott said. "We don't know for sure."

"You never thought about mentioning this to me?"

"It's gossip. It didn't seem important."

Vinnie added, "Besides, you've been spending all your time with Ashok."

I looked at him crossly. "Well, back up. You're saying Jacob and Daryl have basically been pimping out guys through the website?"

They each skirted my gaze.

"I can't believe this. I can't believe *you*. Is everybody tricking off the website? Am I like the only person who doesn't know about it?"

Vinnie tried to lay his arm on my shoulder. I pulled away.

"We only did it that one time," he said. "And it's not everybody. There's kind of like a 'first-string' and a 'second-string' in the house. I mean, by choice."

"Totally by choice," Scott said.

"Who's first-string?"

The guys glanced at each other, which I wasn't having. "Kyle and Danny. Obvs," Vinnie said. "Luca, Rahim, and Grant. The rest of the guys just do their thing like you."

He was talking about more than half of the guys in the house. I was pissed. Then I was terrified. When all that came out, was I going to be implicated in a prostitution ring?

"Daryl bleached the site yesterday," Vinnie said. "So, if they have to turn things over to the police, we're protected. And the clients are protected."

"What about the guy who was after Kyle and Danny?"

"They said they'd save that info for the cops."

I don't know if I'd fallen into a sinkhole of paranoia, but it hit me as super sketchy. How did they know what Daryl had or hadn't deleted off the site? Then I thought of something even sketchier. "If Jacob and Daryl are setting you guys up with users, does that mean they set Kyle and Danny up too?"

Vinnie shook his head. "They wouldn't do that."

"Why? Because they have such high ethical principles? You said they're even lying about their ages."

Vinnie got a little heated. "They wouldn't set up any of the guys with someone shady. They're mad pissed. You saw that. They lost their entire business 'cause some psychopath duped Kyle and Danny."

I wasn't so convinced, and I had a lot more questions. Peter had to know Jacob and Daryl weren't students, if they were lying like Vinnie had said. Why would he allow all this to go on? I felt so betrayed.

Then we got back to the annex, and I was sucked into a new bizarro dimension. We walked in, and everybody was in the kitchen looking pale and restless. Shannon explained. Jacob and Daryl were gone, and they'd cleared out all their equipment from the control room and all the webcams in the house.

THEY MUST'VE MOVED out in the middle of the day. Grant had been the last one to leave the house, around twelve thirty, and Luca and Rahim had come back from classes around four. They noticed the webcams were gone, and they went looking for Jacob and Daryl. Their rooms in the back of the house were cleared out, and then they trekked down to the basement and found the control room emptied. Everybody was freaking out, especially Rahim.

"I say we report their asses right now. Get the FBI to hunt them down."

Shannon argued with him. "What're we reporting? The site's gone."

"Nothing ever disappears completely from the internet," Rahim said. "A tech can probably do some shit with cookies, can't they? We all have contacts who accessed the site."

Nobody looked encouraged by what he was saying, and I could piece together why. He was counting on users who'd paid for porn to cooperate with the investigation?

"This is bad," Michael said. "They fucked us. And you can bet they held on to video of all of us so they can sell it on some other platform." He dropped his head. "They took all evidence the site existed. We can't do shit about it."

Luca piped in. "I don't know. Like Rahim said, if we report what happened to Kyle and Danny, the police can get some hacker from the FBI to track them down."

"Dude, there's no website to report," Shannon said. "What exactly are you going to say to the police?"

"We know Kyle and Danny disappeared," Luca said. "We know they met some guy who goes by Mr. Pain off the website. Regardless of Jacob and Daryl taking off with their equipment, we all know the site existed."

Shannon, Michael and Grant looked at him like he was an idiot. They were the older members of the house.

"Guys, I'm just saying..." Grant started. "We don't even know the deal here. Could be they're on some Mexican beach with Kyle and Danny right now drinking margaritas."

Rahim got in his face. "Danny wouldn't fuckin' do that. You know that's bullshit."

Vinnie and Scott got in the middle and eased Rahim back.

Shannon raised his voice. "All he's saying is there's a lot we don't know." He eyed his pals. "And maybe they did us a favor. If there's no evidence of the site, there's no reason to bring in the police or the executive council. If we can agree to lock this down, we just get through the next few weeks, and then we can all go our separate ways next year, and no one has to know what went on at the annex."

Two factions emerged. On one side, Shannon, Michael and Grant, the upperclassmen, wanted to ride things out and hope to save their skins. Then, there was Rahim and Luca who were mad worried about Kyle and Danny and wanted Jacob and Derek held accountable for what they'd done. Vinnie, Scott, and me stood back, all kind of shell-shocked. As the argument went on, I felt like Vinnie and Scott were warming to the idea of not reporting anything. I was confused. I understood the whole scenario had changed with the website disappearing, but I didn't feel great about locking things up, like Shannon had said.

After a while, everybody quieted, reaching no consensus. I blurted out what was on my mind. "I'm telling Peter. I promised my friends I'd do it." I glanced at Vinnie and Scott, hoping for some support.

"You're going to stir up some major shit," Michael said, looking at me in a not so friendly way.

"Kyle and Danny could be in serious danger—"

Grant cut me off. "Or, they could be rolling in cash along with Jacob and Daryl. Think about it, guys. The only thing we 'know' about their disappearances came from Jacob and Daryl. You gonna tell me that's not suspect? Meanwhile, who got paid this month?"

My contract with the site included a seventeen hundred dollar stipend. I hadn't really been worried Jacob hadn't sent me that month's money by Venmo. It was just a few days late, and I figured he had a lot going on. But now it was looking like I was never going to see that pay, and it hit me pretty quickly the other guys were owed a lot more money. Grant said he hadn't seen a cent he'd made from private shows that month. Rahim said the same, and then Vinnie and Scott chimed in. They hadn't been paid for any "extra work," and Jacob had promised them they'd get the money at the end of the week. In total, it sounded like Jacob and Daryl had run off with tens of thousands of dollars. The mood in the room was changing again. I felt bad for my housemates, but I'd made a promise to Jayson and Ashok.

"I'm sorry guys, but I've got to tell Peter." I looked at Grant. "Maybe Kyle and Danny are safe somewhere, but maybe they're not. I can't live with that."

"You're willing to take a gamble you're doing the right thing?" Michael said. "While fucking all us over after we already got fucked over royally?"

"I won't mention anyone else," I said. "It's something I have to do for myself. I made an oath to Tau, and I broke the rules."

Michael snorted. "You implicate yourself, you implicate all of us. You understand that, don't you?"

I felt like I was shrinking while everybody looked at me. Then finally, Vinnie and Scott came around to stand beside me in support.

"We told Ethan we're reporting things to Peter too," Vinnie said.

I really thought for a minute Michael was going to try to pound the shit out of me. Everybody looked really unhappy. Then Shannon held up his hands. "You don't leave us a choice then. We've all got to go to Peter. So we don't look like fucking punks."

The way he said it, the way he looked at me, I was feeling unsafe. I noticed Rahim staring at me aggressively as well.

"It shouldn't come from you." He glanced at Luca. "We've been friends with Kyle and Danny since freshman year."

"And listen guys," Grant broke in. "Since there's no more website to report, we can say they hooked up with Mr. Pain through Snapchat or whatever. That'll get a missing persons reports going, which is what we want. We don't have much else information anyway."

Michael pointed at him. "You're fucking brilliant." He turned to me. "You got that? There's no reason for you to go crying to Peter about how sorry you are for breaking the rules. You signed up for this like all of us did."

I started shrinking again. Then the doorbell rang. Everyone shut up.

Chapter Twenty-One

SHANNON SAID HE was answering the door. Michael and Grant followed him, and the rest of us kind of pretended to act casual while we listened intently for whatever was happening down the hall. I heard a familiar, friendly voice. *Oliver*. I crept over to the kitchen door. Guys called out to me in hushed voices, and then someone shushed them. I was so nervous, I had to listen in.

"I just came by to let you all know the house meeting's canceled," Oliver said. "The text notification system is down. The house network is down, too. It probably won't be up until our IT guy can have a look at it tomorrow morning. You should check how your network is working. Anyway, we managed to get one of the brothers in the dorms to send an email to everybody, but we figured we'd let you guys know in case you missed it."

I heard Michael say his phone was disconnected from the Wi-Fi. Shannon told Oliver we'd check things out. Then Michael said, "How come the meeting got canceled?"

There was a pause. "Officially, the exec council decided it was better to push things back until they get more information from the police. They're waiting on some news from the Sheriff's office. But, well, I don't want to freak you guys out...but there's an internal investigation going on. Did you guys notice a van parked back here this afternoon?"

"A van? No," Shannon said. "Everyone was out of the house today. We were just getting together for dinner."

"A woman from the cleaning crew mentioned it," Oliver said. "She said two guys were loading it up with computer equipment that they might've stole from the house. Are Jacob and Daryl around?"

I stepped out into the hallway. I couldn't help myself. I was worried Shannon, Michael, and Grant weren't going to tell the truth.

I locked eyes with Oliver, and then the other three noticed me. Before I could say anything, Shannon started talking again.

"As a matter of fact, we haven't seen Jacob and Daryl since this morning." He scratched his ear. "It's kind of weird. Kyle and Danny have been AWOL for a couple of days, too."

"Really?" Oliver said. "Huh. Well, thanks. I'll let the exec team know." He glanced at me and waved. "How's it going, Ethan?"

I waved back. It felt too awkward to say anything with the other guys around.

"Well, let me know if any of your housemates happen to remember anything about a moving van. Or if those other guys show up. Most of the house ran off to a bar night in town, but I'm around."

"Totally," Shannon said. "Bar night, huh? Peter and the big guns went to that too?"

"Oh yeah," Oliver said. "It's an interfraternity event, so all of them have to put in some facetime. It's down at Shooters if you want to check it out."

"Thanks. We may just do that."

Shannon, Michael, and Grant bumped fists with Oliver, and Oliver left.

I TRIED TO pass the guys to get up to my room. I was pissed they hadn't told Oliver the whole story, and I just wanted to be alone and clear my head. But the hallway was narrow, and Michael stepped in front of me.

"You know the deal now. Nobody's talking to Peter tonight."

"Whatever."

I went to get around one side of him. Shannon blocked my way with a big smirk on his face.

"You heard?" Shannon called back to the guys in the kitchen. "Bar night at Shooters. Who's in?"

"Sounds like a plan to me," Michael said.

Rahim stormed over to them. "That's grimy what you said about Kyle and Danny."

Shannon faced him. Another fight was brewing. It gave me the opportunity to slip by him and head up the stairs. I heard things heating up along the way.

"You need to relax. All I said was they went AWOL."

"You said it like they left with Jacob and Daryl."

"I said it like how it happened. And now Oliver's gonna go straight to Peter. If he's worried about the situation, he'll report it to the police. That's what you guys wanted, isn't it?"

"Y'know, Kyle didn't pack up one thing to take with him. Neither did Danny. Does that sound like they skipped off for a vacation to you?"

"I'm so over this. You guys do whatever the fuck you want tonight. We're going to Shooters."

The commotion faded away while I stepped down the second floor hall and closed myself up in my bedroom. I felt like I was in a non-stop nightmare. I hated fighting, and there was so much tension in the house. I didn't even want to talk to Vinnie and Scott about it. They were supposedly my closest friends, but it was like I didn't know them anymore. They'd been keeping so many things from me.

I sat down on my bed and pulled my phone out from my jeans. The only person I could talk to was Jayson, though I needed a minute to figure out how to explain things to him. My whole plan to talk to Peter had gone up in flames, and I didn't want Jayson to think I was making up excuses. I supposed I could go to Shooters to try to talk to Peter there. But he was hanging out with presidents of other fraternities. He'd probably have no interest in talking to me privately.

While I had my phone in my hand, agonizing over these things, my phone dinged and a text message flashed on my screen. I swiped it open.

Oliver: *You okay?*

Without really thinking, I wrote back: *Kinda sorta.*

I watched his text ellipsis.

Come up to the house. I've got half a chicken parm hero with your name on it.

K. Gimme like 15.

He liked my text. I set my phone down and went to my window, which looked out to the lot in front of the annex. I listened to sounds from downstairs. I wanted to wait until Shannon and Michael went off to Shooters so they wouldn't hassle me about going to the house. A few minutes later, I heard muffled voices and then the alarm system bleeped and the front door whooshed open. The floodlights blared on in the lot. I watched them walk down the drive and disappear into the night.

Then footsteps gained up on my room, and someone pounded on the door.

"Ethan?"

It was Vinnie. I stepped over and opened the door. He was standing there with Scott.

"Well, this sucks," Vinnie said. He brushed past me and entered my room. Scott followed him. I really wanted to head over to talk to Oliver, but what could I do?

"Everybody's gone apeshit," Vinnie said. "Rahim says he's moving out. Luca, too."

He and Scott paced around my room.

"It's fucked up what Jacob and Daryl did," Scott said, glancing at me.

I didn't say anything.

"Yep," Vinnie said. "We gotta look out for ourselves now."

"One hundred percent," Scott said.

"Like, all the shit that went down, it's like a game changer," Vinnie said. He fixed on me. "What're you thinking?"

I wasn't feeling comfortable with the two of them. Maybe I was paranoid, but I felt like they'd come by to convince me to stay silent about everything.

"I think I need some space. To figure things out." I swallowed. "Oliver texted me. I'm going to grab dinner with him."

Vinnie raised his eyebrows, but he didn't say anything.

"Oliver texted you?" Scott said.

I nodded. "I should get going." I went to grab my phone from my bed. The two of them were watching me.

"Does he want to talk to you about the internal investigation?" Vinnie said.

I shrugged.

Scott scowled. "You're not going to tell us? We're in this together."

I hadn't prostituted off the website, but I controlled myself from saying that.

"Can we come with?" Vinnie said.

I drew a breath. "I just want to talk to him for an objective opinion."

"So, you don't want us coming along?" Vinnie said.

I licked my lips. "I just need to get out of this space."

"What're you going to tell him?" Vinnie said.

A snort rushed through my nose. "I'm not looking to get you guys in trouble. We're just going to talk."

Scott studied me. "It's kind of fucked up that you'd go talking to him without letting us be part of it."

That pushed me over the edge. "What's fucked up is you two pretending to be my friends and lying to me about everything that's happening in the house."

I thought I'd shocked them silent at first. Then Vinnie got an amused expression on his face.

"God, the *drama*. Ethan, we held back telling you one little thing. I thought we were past that. Are you pissed because what I said about first-string and second-string?"

I glared at him. "I'm leaving." I went to stuff my phone in my bookbag and headed out.

"Why you gotta be like this, Ethan?" Scott called after me.

I ignored him, flew down the stairs, and stepped out of the house.

OLIVER HAD TEXTED me to meet him in the first floor living room, so that's where I went. The house had never been so quiet. It was creepy. There were always a dozen or more guys around, but I didn't see anyone. It was dead still upstairs and downstairs as far as I could tell.

When I got to the living room, I found Oliver sitting on the couch trying to get the TV working. He waved me over and pointed out the half hero he had mentioned, which was on the coffee table. I sat down and dug into it. I was starving.

"Thanks," I mumbled in between chews.

"Don't mention it." He frowned at the blank TV screen. "Everything's down, including the cable service. Pretty much everyone bailed either to catch Wi-Fi on campus or to go down to the bar."

I took another bite and wiped my mouth. "You didn't want to join them?"

Oliver eased back on the sofa. As always, he looked really cute in his Tau tank and a pair of sweat shorts. "Peter asked me to stay back. In case we hear anything from the cable company or the sheriff." He smiled at me. "I'm glad you came by. It's nice to have the company. It's been a long time since we caught up."

My face warmed. I was happy to spend some time with him as well.

"So, what's been going on?" he said. "I heard you and Ashok have been getting hot and heavy."

My stomach dropped. *Not anymore.* I was kind of dying inside because I had things to tell him that were going to make him disappointed in me. The only thing to do was come clean, so I filled him in on *Frat House Secrets* and everything I knew about Kyle and Danny disappearing. It wasn't quite as bad as telling Ashok, but it was bad.

After, he looked really shook.

"I should've told you not to move in there," he said. "I was trying to tell you. But I wanted to respect your right to make your own choices. I guess I should've gone with my instincts." He looked at me earnestly. "Ethan, I'm really sorry."

"It's okay," I said. "I'm okay, and it's not your fault." I peeked at him. "Did you know about the website?"

He shifted in his seat. "Not a hundred percent. But there were rumors. I don't know what Jacob and Daryl have on Peter and the exec council, but they've been letting them rent the back house and do what they please for a while."

Thinking about it, I was pretty sure I wouldn't have moved into the annex if Oliver had told me not to. I respected him. He was like a mentor to me, but I wasn't mad he hadn't warned me. Like he said, he sorta had, and at the time I didn't want to be lectured by him. I'd still been stinging from him rejecting me. Now I felt like an idiot for not listening to him.

"I made a really bad decision. Like the worst decision I could ever make."

Oliver sat forward and turned to me. "You also made a really good decision by telling me. Y'know, I kinda feel responsible. I recruited you, Vinnie, and Scott. If the frat imposes sanctions, I want to take the heat. I should've protected you."

"That's not fair. We're the ones who took part in the website and kept it secret." I started feeling restless as I remembered how complicated the situation was. I told him about Jacob and Daryl taking down the site and running off with the evidence it ever existed.

Now Oliver looked *really* freaked out. He stood and rounded himself. "Those assholes are the ones who came by with the moving van today."

I watched him, feeling worse and worse.

"When this gets out..." He shook his head. "They're both going to be murdered if they ever set foot on campus again."

I stood up too. He was making me nervous.

"It's so effed up," he went on. "We have to deal with all the jokes and all the hate for being an inclusive fraternity, and these guys pull this sleazy shit, confirming what people already think about us."

"The website's gone. I mean, we think they scrubbed it from the internet completely."

"That's not the point."

I buried my gaze. He looked scary angry. Then he cooled down and came over to me.

"They shouldn't have done it in the first place. And they shouldn't have gone after pledges. It just gets me so pissed off." He rubbed his face. "I'm not taking it out on you. There's just been some serious shit going on. The stuff with Zeke is like the least of it. And it hasn't stopped since they arrested those guys. We got a death threat just this morning, and we're pretty sure someone hacked into our computer systems, which is why everything's down from our Instagram account to the alarm system and security cams."

I wondered for a moment if maybe Jacob and Daryl had done it out of spite before they ditched everybody? It didn't really make sense, but the timing was suspicious.

"And Kyle and Danny took off, too?" he asked me.

"No. I mean, they disappeared. We think they got catfished by some user. Jacob and Daryl didn't want to report it. They said the guys would turn up, and it wasn't worth getting the police involved."

I didn't like the look on Oliver's face. He thought the catfish story was BS, just like Shannon did?

"The police should look into it," I told him. "They left the house in the middle of the night. They didn't take any of their belongings." I heaved a breath. "I want to tell Peter. Maybe some kind of IT expert can track down the website logs."

"Ethan, what do you think is more plausible? Kyle and Danny happened to get lured out of the house by some psycho a few days before Jacob and Daryl ran off with all the money from the website? Or they left a couple days early as part of the plan?"

For a minute, I had some doubts. Jacob and Daryl were the only ones who supposedly knew about Mr. Pain, who'd been talking to the guys at the time they left. Danny needed money to help his family. I could see the argument, but I fought against it.

"Their roommates are positive they wouldn't have done something shady. And that's *really* shady. Leaving their best friends to think they might've gotten murdered?"

Oliver gave me a dead serious look. "So, instead, they decided not to tell their best friends that some creepy guy was trolling the site, offering money for sex? If they're such honest guys, why were they tricking off the site in the first place? Ethan, when you get in bed with people like Jacob and Daryl, you start doing shady things."

I could've explained that the tricking wasn't so secret, at least among what Vinnie called the 'first-string' guys. But my brain was in knots. I didn't know what to believe. I was even wondering now if people were lying about what was going on. I had no proof of anything. Still, I knew what I felt.

"We'll report it to the police, and let them figure it out. Better safe than sorry, right? Kyle and Danny are brothers."

Oliver snorted. "If you tell the police this story, I can guarantee you they're not going to do anything about it."

"What do you mean?"

"Where's the website? Where's any record the guys were talking to this 'Mr. Pain' guy? It just flew out the door with Jacob and Daryl? And nobody saw it. Meanwhile, Ethan, we're trying to get the cops to investigate some very real incidents of harassment. It's not going to help the cause."

It felt like I was back to arguing with Shannon and the other guys. I didn't like it. It made me want to push back more.

"The two things could be connected to each other. Someone's making death threats to the house, and two brothers are missing." Oliver didn't look convinced, but I pressed on. "I'll talk to Peter. As the president of the frat, he should know, and then he can decide if he wants to take it to the police."

Oliver looked away from me. He didn't say anything for a while, and I felt like he was holding back something from me, like everyone else. Then, he glanced at me again. "You can do that. You probably should do that. But be prepared to not get the reaction you expect." He pushed back his hair. "First and foremost, Peter's going to want to protect the frat."

"Isn't looking out for two of the brothers protecting the frat?"

"Go ahead. Maybe he'll see it that way."

I studied him. "Why wouldn't he see it that way?"

"Because the whole thing stinks, Ethan. Look, maybe you're right, and Kyle and Danny are in some kind of danger. In order to do something about that, Peter's going to have to go to the police. They're going to want to interview all you guys who lived with them and get their parents involved and the media involved. When things come out about the annex, it's going to be the end of Tau."

"You think Peter knew what Jacob and Daryl were doing?"

Oliver didn't answer at first. "Maybe. Maybe not. He sure as hell isn't going to want the police or the university asking him that question."

I sat back down. Things felt so surreal, it was like I'd been spun around and clobbered in the head. I knew I'd done some unethical things, but I thought I'd joined a fraternity based on the values of brotherhood and integrity. We'd made that pledge during rush. Had I been naive?

"Regardless, I have to give Peter my resignation."

Oliver's eyes popped. "Okay...You don't have to...But if you think it's the right thing for you."

"I totally fucked up my life." I looked up at Oliver. "And for what? All the talk about brotherhood and loyalty—it's bullshit. No one gives a damn about anyone except themselves."

"That's not true. Look, Ethan, you got mixed up with Jacob and Daryl. They're the bad guys. We should've booted them out a long time ago. But the majority of the other brothers are decent people who'd lay down their life for each other."

I wanted to believe that. I really did. But there'd been so many lies on top of lies, I was questioning whether anything I'd thought I knew about the frat was real. It was supposed to be a safe space, and it felt far from safe.

Then the lights cut out, and everything was swallowed up in darkness.

Chapter Twenty-Two

OLIVER AND I called out to each other and met up in the center of the room. We pried out our phones. They'd both gone dead.

"What else could go wrong?" Oliver grumbled.

My phone battery had been at 85 percent when I left out to meet Oliver, which was like a half hour ago, tops. How'd it conk out so fast? I'd never known an electrical outage to affect cell phones. I glanced in the direction of one of the living room's windows. It was pitch black. There must've been a local power outage. I'd seen lights on at the house next door before I came over.

Oliver tapped me on the shoulder. "C'mon. There's a flashlight and candles in the kitchen."

I followed him closely as he navigated his way to the back of the house. That cavernous, empty house had been creepy before, and now it was even creepier. I knew power outages happened all the time, but I couldn't help wonder if someone cut the power lines deliberately. The same someone who was making threats and who had hacked into the network. Now, Oliver and I were blindly walking through the house, and that person could be inside, waiting for the right time to jump out from the shadows.

Luckily, Oliver knew his way around really well. He led me to the kitchen, opened a cabinet, and clicked on a big utility flashlight. While he rummaged in drawers for candles, I stepped over to a window that looked out to the back of the house. Everything was shrouded in darkness. The annex must've lost power too.

A siren blared, and my phone vibrated wildly against my leg. My heart leapt from the shock of it, and then I pulled my phone out of my pocket. Oliver's phone had gone off too, like there was a hurricane warning. We looked at our lit-up screens. A single message shone in the darkness.

Time to die.

No more than a couple of seconds later, our phones went dead again. I tried to reboot. Oliver tried too. Neither phone would go back on. It was like we'd been locked out, and someone was controlling the devices.

"Well, this is fucked up. You got any guesses what's going on?" Oliver said.

I didn't. Other than a prank, I hoped. Oliver found a phone charger at one of the kitchen outlets, but plugging his phone in didn't do any good. I drifted back to the window, wondering if the guys in the annex had also gotten the scare and maybe they'd found a flashlight too. I tried to stare through the gulf of blackness, but I couldn't make out anything.

An anguished shriek pierced through the night. I jumped back from the window. It sounded like a man's voice, from a distance, maybe from the back house.

Oliver rushed over. "What was that? Did you see anything?"

I shook my head. That was the kind of scream someone made when they'd hyperextended their knee or gotten their foot caught in a bear trap. I kept looking in the direction of the house with my ears pricked up. Still no lights or signs of anything happening there.

"C'mon," Oliver said. "Let's make sure everyone's okay."

I was thinking that was a job for the police at first, but we couldn't even call the police with our phones dead and the power out. Call me cowardly, but my next thought was we should go over to a neighbor's house to see if we could call 911 from there? However, Oliver was shifting his weight and widening his shoulders in alpha-dog mode. I took a dry swallow. Of course, the right thing to do was to see if any of the guys needed our help.

Oliver told me to stay put for a minute. He disappeared into another room with his flashlight and came back with a baseball bat tucked under his arm. He nudged me along, out the back door.

He pointed the flashlight ahead of us, which illuminated a portion of the driveway and the lower half of the annex. Everything else was in shadow. Looking around, it seemed like the power outage must've taken out the entire block. I was tense, following Oliver, and thinking about all the red flags related to the situation. Somebody had been threatening the frat. The house network had been hacked, and now we'd not only lost power but someone had hacked into our phones. *Time to die.* It could be one of the people who'd been sending death threats to the house. To tell the truth, I was petrified. But I wanted to be strong for Oliver. He was brave and didn't seem rattled in the least bit.

The door to the annex was locked, and when I went to tap in the key code, I could see the panel was dead. I guessed that was related to the power outage, though I thought the alarm system was backed up with batteries.

Oliver pounded on the door. "What's up guys? Everybody okay in there?"

No one answered. Then we heard some kind of wild shouting from deeper in the house. Both of us were shocked silent and trying to figure out what was going on. A flurry of motion gained up on the door, and somebody jostled the door knob and threw his body against the door.

"Is somebody out there? Help. We're locked in."

I recognized Grant's voice. He sounded frantic.

Oliver tried the door again. It wouldn't budge. "We can't get it open from this side either. Just hang tight. We're going to get you out of there."

He looked at me and twisted the bat in his hands. There was no way the bat was going to break through a metal door. I remembered the back door had window panels. I told Oliver about it, and then I called out to Grant.

"We're going to come 'round the back."

"Ethan? Please, you've gotta get us out of here. Someone broke in. He's got a knife."

I glanced at Oliver. I thought about the blood-curdling shriek we'd heard.

"Hey, is everyone okay?" Oliver said.

Grant didn't answer. It sounded like he'd run off deeper into the house. I started toward the back door, and Oliver followed. Along the way, I checked my phone again. It was still dead.

The back door was also sealed tight, and the key panel was down. Oliver pointed the flashlight through the window panes. The alcove on the other side was empty. We couldn't see very far down the hall. Oliver handed me the flashlight, and then he stopped short of taking a swing at the door.

"I've got no idea what's going on, but this is feeling serious. So, if you've got anything to fill me in on before I break in this door, this would be the time to do it."

"All I know is Shannon and Michael went down to the bar right before I left. Everybody else stayed back. That's Grant, Vinnie, Scott, Luca, and Rahim."

"Okay. Stand back."

I gave him a good six-foot radius. Oliver wound the bat behind his shoulder, and he struck the window pane with a bone-chilling shatter. After, he asked for the flashlight so he could take a close look at the damage. He'd made a jagged gash near the door, but it wasn't nearly as big as I'd expected.

Oliver gave me back the flashlight and used the bat to punch out a wider opening in the glass. Then he asked me for my hoodie. I took it off, and he wrapped the sleeve around his hand to grope through the window pane and turn the inside door knob. He pushed the door open. "You're gonna have to keep the flashlight pointed in front of me," he said.

I nodded nervously. My hand was shaking really bad, but I was going to hold the flashlight steady like my life depended on it.

We stepped carefully inside the house since the floor of the backroom was littered with broken glass. Things seemed really quiet. It made me wonder for a moment if the guys were playing a joke on us. A really awful joke. Making us think someone had been stabbed by an intruder while the power was out? Oliver inched farther into the house and I followed. The flashlight beam shone on the empty hallway to the kitchen. Where was everybody? Wouldn't the guys have come back to check on the sound of the door getting bashed in?

The door to the basement stairs flew open behind us, and someone came out from the shadows. I swung around, and the flashlight nearly slipped out of my hands.

"Thank god you guys got in. We thought you were him."

It was Grant. I recognized his voice before I managed to shine the flashlight on him. He'd given me my third or fourth heart attack that night. Oliver was breathing heavy from the scare.

"C'mon," Grant said. "I'll get Luca so we can get the hell out of here."

"Wait. First you're going to tell us what's going on," Oliver said.

Luca came up the stairs holding his upper arm, which was wound in a T-shirt. He looked dazed.

"We've been hiding in the control room," Grant said. "We need to get out of here and call the police."

"Luca, are you okay? What happened?" Oliver said.

The floorboards creaked above us. It was a small noise, but Grant and Luca glanced at the ceiling terrified. Then Grant looked at us impatiently. "Guys, c'mon. We can walk and talk."

I was feeling okay with that, but Oliver didn't move. "Who's up there?" he asked.

Grant started talking really fast in a hushed voice. "Someone cut the power. He must've already been in the house, or maybe he got in after. We were in the kitchen, and then our phones blew up with an emergency alarm and this threatening message. He came out of nowhere. He had some kind of knife, and we ran off in different directions. The two of us locked ourselves downstairs, but not before he took a slice of Luca. It's that Mr. Pain guy. He's a fucking psycho killer."

Luca struggled with his footing, and Grant caught him on his good side.

"Are the other guys okay?" Oliver said.

"We don't know," Grant said. "They ran upstairs." He helped Luca brace an arm around his shoulder.

My throat went dry. I had no idea what was going on, but based on how Luca looked and how Grant was acting, I was filled with dread.

Oliver faced Grant. "Who broke in?"

Grant glared at him. "Mr. Pain. Look, Luca needs medical attention. Ethan can fucking fill you in."

"Are Vinnie, Scott, and Rahim okay?" Oliver glanced at me. "We can't just leave them here."

"You're goddamn nuts if you go up there. We're out." Grant carefully helped Luca move toward the back door.

A tortured cry from upstairs froze all of us. "*Please. No. NO!*"

Then: "*Help!*"

The latter voice sounded like Rahim. I stared at Oliver. His face was glazed with sweat. "Look, guys. The power's out. The whole block. Maybe the whole town. By the time we find a phone and the police come, we're talking thirty minutes or longer."

Luca sputtered something and had a woozy spell. Grant caught him around the waist. I'd had the flashlight pointed off to the side, and I noticed for the first time Luca's shirt was darkened with blood.

"Okay. Get him some medical help and call the police as soon as you can," Oliver told Grant. He eyed me soberly. "We're going to make sure everyone's okay."

Grant and Luca staggered out the back door. I was terrified and confused. Mr. Pain, the user who catfished Kyle and Danny broke into the house with a knife? I followed Oliver to the kitchen and splayed the flashlight around. Most of the stools around the island counter were toppled, and appliances, cups, and plates were broken on the floor. I spotted a smear of blood on a cabinet and some on the floor tiles.

"M-m-maybe we should get out of here too," I said.

Indistinct sounds of movement came from upstairs. I held my breath, staring at the darkened ceiling, trying to detect if someone was headed in our direction. The house went still again.

Oliver pushed up close to me and lowered his voice. "I know you're scared. I am, too. But if someone's hurt up there, we can't leave them."

I knew he was right, morally. I was worried about Vinnie, Scott, and Rahim, too. I hyperventilated for maybe twenty seconds, and then, as if a switch had flipped inside me, I was, well, not exactly chill, but determined. Who the fuck broke into our house to try to hurt people? We had to stop him.

I exchanged a sober gaze with Oliver, and we crept toward the stairs to the second floor.

It was dead still at the top of the stairs. I scanned around with the flashlight. The only odd thing was that the hallway runner was bunched up, like a herd of people had run through. Oliver and I stopped to think for a moment. The intruder had to have heard us breaking in through the back door. He knew we were coming. Should we try to take him by surprise or draw him out somehow?

Oliver decided on the latter. He called out loudly, "We saw what you did to Luca. We called the police. You're not getting away. Why don't you come out and show yourself like a man?"

"Oliver?" we heard Scott cry. "We're in the bathroom. Vinnie's hurt. Real bad. Be careful. He's still in the house."

My heart bled for him. And Vinnie was hurt? I wanted to run over to the bathroom to help them, but I caught myself. We'd have to pass by two open, darkened doors on either side of the hallway to get to them. Oliver must've been thinking the same thing. He didn't budge.

"Scott? We're gonna get you guys out of there." Oliver glanced around the hallway. "Police and ambulances are on the way," he lied. "We just need Mr. Pain to come out."

We waited for maybe a full minute. I really didn't think the psychopath was going to show himself, and I don't think Oliver did either. Meanwhile, Vinnie could be dying. I looked at Oliver pleadingly.

He nudged me over to stand just a little bit behind him while he held his bat at the ready. Then we started toward the bathroom door. It was the only door that was closed. We had five yards to travel to get there, but at the wary pace we were going, that would take an eternity.

As we came up to Luca and Kyle's room, I pointed the flashlight inside. Nothing to see, at least out in the open. I swung the flashlight to Vinnie and Scott's room like I was on a SWAT team mission, flooding every inch of the place with light to find the bad guy. That room appeared to be empty too. It made sense. If the killer was going to hide, he'd probably opt to hole up deeper down the hall so it would take us longer to find him. But where was Rahim?

At the bathroom, Oliver grabbed the door handle. It was locked.

"Scott? You're gonna have to open up."

I listened to clumsy movements on the other side of the door. The lock unclicked. I swept the flashlight around us one last time. Then Oliver pushed the door open.

My eyes bulged. Scott hunched over himself clutching a wadded shirt against the side of his chest. Beyond him, Vinnie was propped up against the toilet with a king size towel bandaging his torso. His complexion was scary pale. I'd never understood what it meant to smell blood until that night. A sharp, iron scent. Blood was smeared across the sink, the floor tiles, and all over the guys' clothes.

I pushed past Oliver to help Scott ease down on the side of the bathtub. He was really weak and dizzy. Vinnie looked worse, and I had no idea what to do about that. How much blood had they lost?

Oliver's gaze was jumpy. He had to be as horrified as me, but he snorted in some breaths and collected himself. "We're going to get you guys taken care of." He pitted his bat against the floor and tried talking to Scott. "The fucker's still here? You know where he went?"

Oliver gasped, then struggled to take in a breath and collapsed onto his hands and knees. The bat clattered against the floor. I couldn't process it at first. It happened so quickly. Then it felt like the walls were closing in on me.

A man in full-on nighttime military gear stood in the doorway behind Oliver. A black ski mask, night vision goggles, black camouflage fatigues, and a six-inch hunting knife, wet with blood. Oliver's blood. He'd stabbed Oliver deep between his shoulder blades. Oliver was gasping for air and barely holding himself up with his hands on the floor.

Quickly, I helped Scott slip behind the shower curtain into the bathtub. I looked back at the killer, and we stared at each other for a breath. Then he stepped into the room and kicked Oliver hard in the small of his back, flattening him to the floor. I knew what I had to do. I lunged for the bat. I had to drop the flashlight to do it, but I got my hands around it and stood, creating a barrier between the killer and Scott and Vinnie.

"I'll fucking kill you," I shouted at the psycho. I didn't know I had it in me, but the situation felt strangely simple. I was going to destroy him or die trying. The flashlight had landed on the floor, pointing at the wall, but I guess a rush of adrenalin had my senses working 150 percent. I swung for the bastard's arm to beat the knife out of his hand.

The strike wasn't as powerful as I'd imagined. My balance was off with Oliver nearly under my feet and he shook it off with his knife still in his hand. Then, in a blink, he flew at me, stepping on Oliver's back like a springboard. I managed to brace the bat in front of me as a defense, but he got a hand on my arm. I shirked wildly away and backed into the bathroom cabinet. The killer cocked his head, appraising me.

"Time to die."

He threw a low jab at me with his knife. I blocked it with the outstretched bat, but the momentum of his body crushed me against the cabinet. In his black gear, he was an invisible phantom, but I could tell he was a head taller than me and powerfully built. I fought to push him back. He reached a hand around my arms, trying to clamp my shoulder to steady me and thrust his knife into my gut.

I tried using my legs to wrangle him back, but he pinned my ankles with his feet. I was losing my strength. The outstretched bat was nearly pressed up against my throat, giving him more and more room to land a stab into my body. Desperate, I pounded my shoulders into the cabinet. It was a cheap IKEA unit. If I could shake it hard enough, I could at least knock down the paper products stacked on top to throw the killer off.

A jumbo package of toilet paper tumbled down between us. That disoriented the killer just enough for me to shove him off with the bat and throw him against the sink. I gripped the bat with one hand

and swung for his knife hand again, but the bastard was too quick. He caught the bat and yanked it from my hand onto the floor.

I was completely screwed. I had nothing to protect myself, and in the narrow space, I'd either be mangling Vinnie or mangling Oliver with my feet trying to evade the guy. He took his time judging his next move. I thought about charging at him, but I'd lost some courage. I didn't want to get stabbed to death. I got into a defensive stance, just waiting for him to lunge at me. I was pretty sure this was the end.

Out of nowhere, I heard a hollow thud. The killer stumbled to the side and shrank into himself.

"Take that, motherfucker."

Rahim. He'd come up behind the guy and struck him in the shoulder with a hand-held fire extinguisher. The knot inside my chest unwound a little. While the killer wobbled drunkenly, Rahim got his arms under Oliver to drag him out of the crowded bathroom.

"Ethan, we got this," Rahim called out to me. "Just keep him occupied."

He grabbed Oliver under his arms. I couldn't tell how badly he'd been hurt, but Oliver wasn't doing much on his own. *Keep him occupied.* I knew I had to do something to further subdue the maniac. He was weakened by Rahim's hit but hardly out for the count. The problem was if I tried a punch or a shove, he'd end up falling down on top of Scott in the bathtub.

Then, horribly, the killer got his bearings and faced Rahim with his knife in hand. The way things were, he could easily plant it in Oliver's torso while he was propped up like Rahim's body shield.

I stooped down, grabbed the bat, and wrapped both hands around the handle. I aimed for the fucker's head and threw every ounce of my 170 pound weight into my swing. It connected and wrapped him around the sink with his head shattering the mirror. Then he slid down to the floor, at my feet, twisted over himself. I stared down at him. He was bleeding from his head, and he wasn't moving. The nightmare was over. I wasn't sure I could believe it.

Chapter Twenty-Three

THE REST OF the night was hazy from that point. I must've been in shock. The best I can remember is that we started hearing police and ambulance sirens headed for the house not long after I KO'd the killer. I found out later Grant called 911 from a neighbor's cell phone once he got Luca to safety. Thank god, the police were quick to respond.

Before the cops and EMTs got to the scene, I helped Rahim lay Oliver out in the hallway. Rahim got towels, and he kept pressure on Oliver's wound. I went back to check on Scott and Vinnie. Scott had already propped himself up in the bathtub, and he seemed to be all right. Vinnie, though, was practically unconscious. He'd lost a lot of blood, and all I could do was tighten the towel around his torso and try to keep him looking at me.

The killer's body was just a couple feet away. I kept an eye on him too. He'd been motionless for—I don't know—six or seven minutes, but I'd seen enough horror movies to not trust he was dead. At the same time, I was burning up with questions. While the police were beating in the front door to get inside, I crawled over to the killer. I grasped the bottom of his ski mask, and I pulled it off his head.

The past few days had been so freaky, part of me was expecting to find a familiar face. Like, I don't know, some things had thrown suspicion on the guys from Zeke, and Jacob and Daryl, Kyle and Danny, even Peter whose handling of recent events was kind of strange.

But the face was only vaguely familiar. It took me a moment to place it. That angry guy Luke Renfield who stormed out of the initiation ceremony. Oliver had said he was an army veteran. He also hated Tau allowing gay men in the frat. I was repulsed. I'd unmasked pure evil. A man so filled with hate, he'd tried to murder everyone in the annex.

The EMTs tended to Vinnie, Oliver, and Scott, and they got rushed to the hospital. All three of them turned out okay, which was pretty miraculous. Vinnie and Oliver were both touch and go for a few days in intensive care, but they were tough dudes. They got stitched up, had blood transfusions, and needed to be put on respirators for a while, but thankfully, Oliver came around after three days, and Vinnie was able to talk to visitors one day after that. Scott's wound was relatively minor. He was out of the hospital the next day. Luca, who got slashed on his upper arm, made a quick recovery too.

Sadly, later that week, we got the bad news about Kyle and Danny. The police tracked down a local apartment where Luke had been staying. They got into his computer and found that he'd created the Mr. Pain user account for the website. He'd catfished Kyle and Danny like we'd originally suspected. The police investigation found that Luke had strangled them and dumped their bodies in an abandoned warehouse off the thruway. They also traced the death threat emails and phone calls to Luke. He'd been obsessed with destroying Tau, and he'd been working for months on his murderous plan. The cops uncovered research Luke had done to hack into the house's server and the alarm systems. He'd disabled the local power grid and taken out our phones with spyware on the night of his killing spree. He had a manifesto, ready to send out to social media, in which he said he was proud of killing all the "perverts" and the "pervert apologists" at Tau. The cops also found assault rifles, grenades, and materials for making dirty bombs in his apartment. That night actually could've been worse.

The police did track down Jacob and Daryl, by the way. They'd run off to Texas where Daryl had family, and they were facing all kinds of legal issues now, from civil lawsuits by Kyle and Danny's families to charges of tax evasion since they hadn't been reporting their income from the website properly.

To say it was a dark and disorienting few weeks is an understatement. I had to try to explain things to my parents over the phone, and they dropped everything and drove to campus to be with me later that day. Neither one of them came down on me. They were just freaked out that I could've been killed, which was totally understandable. I appreciated them, though it was awkward having them around while Jayson and Tyler were hitting me up to meet up with the brothers so we could all be together. My mom wanted me to come home for the rest of the semester. I wasn't in shape to continue with my classes, and the university let me withdraw. My emotions were all over the place, and I sometimes felt like I wouldn't mind going home and disappearing from the world.

But a police detective told me it would be really helpful if I stuck around, and I wanted to help with their investigation however I could. I also wanted to be there for Oliver, Vinnie, and Scott, and all the guys from Tau who were grieving. I had a long conversation with my mom and dad about all of that. I knew they weren't thrilled, but after they spoke to the police about the situation, they let me stay on campus until the end of the term so long as we checked in every day.

I got to go to a vigil for Kyle and Danny a few days later, and Tau also held a memorial. It was a lot. I went from pouring out my feelings to crisis counselors, to meeting with the police, to crying my eyes out with the brothers and dodging reporters.

Word got out I'd been the one to finish off Luke Renfield, and then news outlets ran the part of the police investigation about the website. Reporters wanted to talk to me, but I didn't want to talk to them. I could tell some of the brothers thought I was a scumbag for being involved with the website, but most of them looked at me like I was a hero. I didn't feel like a hero. I just had to protect myself and my friends. I wasn't a courageous person. I did what anybody would've done in the situation.

Truthfully, in a lot of ways, my world was falling apart. Peter let me move into the main house while the annex was closed off for the police investigation, but I knew pretty soon I'd have to figure out my future. I had one semester of shitty grades to my name and no idea what to do. My college life had been all about being a Tau brother, and I was mad confused about a lot of things.

I mean, if I'd never rushed the frat, all the bad stuff with Luke Renfield still would've happened, but I wouldn't have been part of it. I wouldn't have lost friends and gotten associated with Tau forever on social media. I tried to ignore the latter, and I deleted my Insta account, though not before I made the mistake of clicking on a notification and reading a bunch of hateful comments about me being one of Tau's prostitutes and Kyle and Danny getting what they deserved and all of us being shitty examples of the LGBTQ+ community. I felt like a shitty example. It was a stupid decision to move into the annex and participate in the website to pay for my college expenses.

On the other hand, call me crazy, but even after all the dark stuff happened, I still had love for Tau. If I hadn't joined the frat, I never would've met awesome people like Oliver and Tyler and all the guys in our pledge class. Tau had helped me get over my hang-ups and be more confident as a young gay man. Anyway, they officially announced the New Jersey State Tau Alpha Theta chapter was ceasing operations indefinitely at the end of the academic year. The executive leadership team didn't really have a choice. The alternative was to let national and the university make the decision for them based on multiple code of conduct violations. So basically, whether I stayed or left the school, I was losing my identity as a brother.

The day after the memorial service, I got a surprise visitor. Peter knocked on my door and asked if he could take me out for breakfast. I'd been wanting to have a conversation with him, though I was a little nervous about it. He still intimidated me. Anyway, he said I should just throw on some clothes and meet him outside at his car.

He drove us out of town and onto the turnpike. I had a feeling we weren't going somewhere local since we couldn't have much of a private conversation around campus. We'd both been in the public eye. He pulled off at an exit a few towns away and brought me to a bagel shop. We got coffees and bagels with cream cheese and sat down at a table.

"How're you holding up?" he asked me.

I shrugged. "Okay. How're you doing?"

"I'm all right. Good and bad days, y'know?" He took a sip of his coffee. "At the memorial service, I know I talked about what a hero you were, but I wanted to tell you that more personally. You're a brave guy, and I've got mad respect for you."

That felt really good coming from him. I mean, like I said, I wasn't feeling special about what I'd done, but it was really nice of him to take the time to tell me that.

"I wish the year wasn't ending like this," he went on. "Y'know, typically, the end of the spring semester is a big celebration, and everyone leaves on a high note. This year, nobody is in the mood to celebrate anything. We want to honor Kyle and Danny, and the future of Tau is up in the air. We've all been through a trauma. But I hope whatever the future holds for you, you'll be leaving with your head held high."

"Thanks." I built up some courage to say what I'd been wanting to tell him for a while. "And I'm sorry. I should have reported it as soon as I heard that Kyle went missing. If I had, Danny would still be here today, and no one else would've gotten hurt."

Peter gazed at me sympathetically. "Don't beat yourself up about that."

"But it's true, isn't it?" Out of nowhere, a lump formed in my throat, and I was sucking back tears.

He placed his hand on mine. "Hey. It's okay, Ethan."

I shook my head and dried my eyes with a napkin. Peter kept looking at me squarely. "The only person responsible is Luke Renfield. Remember that. We can all play Monday morning quarterback. I could've mentioned Luke to the police when I first reported the harassment. I should've looked out for all you guys in the annex. Believe me, I've been wrestling with plenty of demons myself. At some point, you have to accept you did the best you could at that time, and Ethan, you did better than anyone. You got rid of that psychopath once and for all."

I felt a little steadier. I'd been wanting to say so much since everything went down, especially to someone like Peter, who I respected.

"You know, I participated in Jacob and Daryl's website."

Peter gave me an impartial nod.

"That makes me feel even shittier. Besides taking advantage of the fraternity and breaking the code of conduct, it's like I took part in something that got Kyle and Danny killed."

We were quiet for a while.

Peter sighed. "I'm going to tell you something, Ethan. You're going to run into plenty of people who're going to judge you. Just for who you are. Not anything to do with the website thing. I mean, you know what I'm talking about, right? If you had nothing to do with the website, you'd still have to deal with haters."

I pushed my napkin around in front of me.

"So, don't let that get to you," he said. "A lot of guys these days experiment in porn. I mean, showing off on social media or doing something like *Only Fans*, it's the same thing. And it doesn't make you a bad person. It doesn't have anything to do with what Luke Renfield did."

"I thought it was an easy way to pay for housing and other expenses. My parents were stretched really thin, and I thought I was helping them out. But it was disrespectful to the house and disrespectful to you—"

"So far as I'm concerned, none of you are getting a warning or a suspension. Getting terrorized by Luke was more than enough punishment." He snorted wryly. "It doesn't matter anyway. Tau's disbanding. There's no authority to take up conduct complaints."

"But that's our fault, isn't it? The website's the reason the frat's disbanding."

Peter blew that off at first, and then he said, "Jacob and Daryl owned the website. Nobody at the annex bears responsibility except them."

I glanced at him. My emotions were settling a bit. "Did you know about the site?"

I could read the answer from the shadow of recrimination on his face. I hadn't wanted to believe it, and now I felt completely lost.

"Like I said, I have plenty of my own demons to wrestle with. I'm going to tell you something so you see I understand about beating yourself up over past decisions. Maybe you're not going to like me after I do." He shrugged. "Maybe you shouldn't. My conscience is my business, and I've got to deal with it no matter what you think.

"Did Jacob and Daryl ask me for permission to use the annex for their site? No. Did they ever explicitly tell me what they were doing? No. Did I know anyway? Yes. I was on the executive council two years ago when the president told us two of our graduating seniors, Jacob and Daryl, wanted to start a monetized social media account. They'd gotten a group of alumni to act as investors, and it was just going to show off some of the brothers in a sexy way. A little skin and teaser stuff. Totally legit. Jacob and Daryl asked if they could rent their rooms a little longer while they were getting the funds together and starting up the business. They offered to donate ten percent of the company's profits to Tau every quarter."

He took a sip of coffee, averting my rapt gaze. "Aaron, the president back then, said he ran it by national, and they didn't see a problem with the proposal. We all voted to let them do it. Did I know at that point? No. Aaron was a good guy. I trusted him. Frankly, a lot of us thought Jacob and Daryl's venture wasn't going to go anywhere, and what was the harm in letting them rent their rooms until they figured out it was time to move on?"

I studied him. He was really shifty, like this was all embarrassing for him to say.

"A year later, I was voted president when Aaron's term ended, and I got access to the frat's financial statements. I saw we were getting donations of as much as fifty grand every quarter from Jacob and Daryl's 'media' company. I was excited, and I asked the two of them about the business. I wanted to thank them and get to know what they were doing. They showed me a site, and it was thirst trap stuff like they'd said. Nothing serious. But it didn't make sense a photo gallery could be pulling in so much money. There was nothing monetized about the site they claimed was their business. I talked about it with Jamal and the other guys on the exec council at the time, and nobody raised questions. I even looked up the list of investors to try to figure out what was going on. They were some of our biggest donors. One of the guys is chief of staff for a senior senator here in Jersey. Another is a partner at one of the biggest asset management firms in New York. I told myself everything had to be on the up and up."

He peeked at me for a breath. "But did I know then? Yes. Deep down. I inherited this informal agreement that Jacob and Daryl got to choose which brothers could room at the annex. I saw a pattern. I saw the blinds were always drawn, and I knew they had a policy of no guests, and they paid for a ridiculous high tech security system no house for a group of college guys needed. I didn't like it. I heard gossip about what was going on back there, and I didn't want Tau associated with any kind of adult entertainment. But I didn't act. So, you could say I'm a lot more responsible for what happened to Kyle and Danny than you. I chose to look the other way. I was scared of creating waves. I didn't want to give up the money. The upkeep on the old house was almost a hundred thou a year, so whatever business Jacob and Daryl were running was alleviating that expense and allowing Tau to pay for marketing and big events. It was taking our profile to a whole other level."

I understood that ethical dilemma, but honestly, I was crushed. I really thought Peter had more integrity. It must've been showing on my face.

"Would I have done it again? Absolutely not. It was terrible judgment on my part. I put the entire frat in jeopardy. Tau's still in jeopardy if Kyle and Danny's families decide to sue. They could go after me personally. They could go after the national board of directors. Bottom line, I could've pulled the plug on the website over a year ago, and Kyle and Danny would still be here, and I've got to live with that for the rest of my life. So Ethan, you made a little mistake. I made a big one. All you've gotta do is learn from yours."

That changed things in my head. Well, it gave me a lot to think about. We finished our bagels in silence, and then he drove us back to the house.

THE SATURDAY BEFORE finals week, Peter invited all the brothers to the house for a farewell party. It was just a low-key get-together to say goodbye with pizza and heroes. There were only twenty of us left on campus. Oliver, Luca, Vinnie, and Scott had gone home to recuperate, and a lot of the other brothers had resigned when news of the website came out so they wouldn't be associated with the scandal.

I spent some time making small talk with Jayson and Tyler, and then Tyler ran off with some guys from our pledge class to play RPGs in the basement. That left Jayson and me alone in the living room. He'd texted me throughout the ordeal, and we'd seen each other at Kyle and Danny's memorial, but we hadn't spent much time face-to-face.

Jayson pointed for us to sit down together on a couch. "This is really depressing, isn't it?"

I nodded. Peter had gathered everyone together to say a few words at the start of the night, but since then, people had spread out through the house in quiet conversations like it was a funeral.

"I'm sorry I haven't been around as much," I told him.

"After everything you've been through, believe me, I understand."

"I fucked up. As soon as I moved into the annex, I got caught up with Vinnie and Scott and all the housemates. I went along with covering up the situation when Kyle and Danny went missing, just so people wouldn't find out about the website. I feel like such a piece of shit."

"No one blames you, Ethan."

I wasn't so sure about that. Kyle and Danny's families probably did. And all the guys who had quit the frat.

"How're Vinnie and Scott doing?" Jayson said. "They never wrote back to my texts."

They hadn't written back to me the past two weeks. I only had one phone call with Vinnie since he got out of the hospital, and it was strange. I told Jayson about it.

"He sort of acted like nothing happened. Maybe it's how he's coping with things. He didn't want to talk about anything related to Tau."

"Probably his parents told him not to."

"Yeah." I hugged my knee against my chest. "I'm pretty sure he and Scott aren't coming back."

"My parents made me fill out a transfer application to Irvine Community College back home," Jayson said. "Tyler's thinking about going to Maryland State next year. It sucks. You decide what you're doing?"

I shrugged. We sat in silence. Then Jayson cracked a grin. "Remember the start of the year? I had to drag you to our first Tau party."

I smiled, remembering.

"You were my first friend at college," Jayson said. "My *best* friend. We had some really great times."

"We did."

"It's been a lot since then, but can I tell you something? I'm kinda mad Tau fell apart."

I heaved a sigh. "Same."

"It's just unfair. We made some great friends, and most of the year was awesome. Remember how both of us were ready to bail on school?"

"If I hadn't met you orientation week, I don't think I would've survived."

I kinda expected Jayson to squeal or say something funny. But he was being really serious. He just threw back a sip of his raspberry-flavored bottled water. "Are you okay?" he asked.

Between my parents, counselors, and the guys at the frat, I'd been asked that question a lot. It shouldn't have thrown me off, but it did. "Oh. Yeah. I mean, I'm getting by." I looked at Jayson kindly. "Thanks for asking."

"Ethan, you keep saying that, but you've been through a major trauma. It's okay to not be okay."

I squirmed a bit. "I'm not saying I'm okay, but what else should I say? I frickin' killed somebody who murdered two of my friends. I took somebody's life." I waved him off. "I talked about all that with a counselor. She said I was doing as well as could be expected."

Jayson kept looking at me.

"I'm fine, Jayson. I'm meeting with her three times a week. Some days are tough, but it gets a little better day by day. I just don't know what I'm going to do with myself now. Going back to Pennsylvania is going to totally suck."

"You think about coming back here in the fall?"

I sighed. I had. But I knew that was going to be a really hard sell with my parents, and if everyone else was leaving, what was the point?

"I heard Oliver's coming back," Jayson said.

I nodded. We'd talked a couple times since he'd gone home to South Carolina. Of course, I understood why he left, but I missed him really bad. At least I'd have one friend on campus if miraculously I made it back. Though Oliver was going to be a senior. We'd be traveling in different circles.

Jayson sat back in his seat. "I'm thinking about coming back too."

My eyes shot up at him. "Really?"

He grinned.

"You talked to your parents about it?"

"Ye-ah. They're totally not on board. But I've got the whole summer to work on them." He blushed a little. "I already told them I'm gay."

I bugged out. "When? You didn't tell me."

He laughed. "We had a video call a few weeks back. I had to tell them. They watch the news. We're like the most notorious gay fraternity in the country now."

He was right about that. I tried to avoid the media coverage, but when I got an Apple News notification on my phone about a "Night of Terror at a New Jersey State Fraternity," I knew the story had to be all over the place.

"How did they react?"

"They said they knew. They were waiting for me to say something, which is kind of annoying, y'know? Like they could've saved me years of worrying that I'd slip up and they'd find out."

"So, they were chill?"

"I think they're just glad I didn't have anything to do with the website." He sat up closer to me. "But it wasn't so bad. They told me they still loved me. We'll see how things go when I'm living back home. I didn't tell them anything about being gender fluid."

"I hope they can accept that. Anyway, I'm happy for you."

We were both quiet for a while.

"Think about talking to your parents too. About returning to school. This year's been outer limits cray-cray, but I don't know where else I belong."

I glanced at him. Jayson grinned. I grinned back. Then we hugged. *God*, I was going to miss him. I held on to him so long, he laughed and had to ease my arms away. When I opened my eyes, I saw he was looking beyond my shoulder. I turned, and my chest froze over. Ashok was standing there.

"Hey," Jayson called out to him.

"I don't want to interrupt anything," Ashok said.

"You're not." Jayson stood up. "I was just going to get another slice of pizza. You two want anything?"

We both told him no, and Jayson skipped off.

IT WAS TOTALLY obvious. Jayson wanted the two of us to talk alone. Ashok came over, and we stood around awkwardly. We'd acknowledged each other at the memorial, but we hadn't talked since he basically told me I was a traitorous piece of shit.

"How're you holding up?" he asked.

"Good days and bad days. Uh, how are you?"

"Same." He looked down, and then he added quickly. "I don't mean the same as you. I should've reached out sooner. I was worried that might make things worse for you. Y'know, after what I said the last time we talked." He drew a breath. "I'm really bad at handling these things."

I looked him in the eyes apologetically, though I couldn't bring out the words. Ashok shifted his weight. I wasn't sure why he was so nervous, but ever since the big incident, a lot of people acted nervous around me.

"Well, I bet you have a lot bigger things on your mind, but I wanted to say I'm sorry. For what you went through and for what I said. If I'd known..." His face darkened in self-reproach. "It doesn't matter. It was a shitty thing for me to do. I feel like a total A-hole."

"You don't have to feel like an A-hole." Something he said pinched up in my brain. "If you'd known what?"

"All the stuff you guys were dealing with at the annex. That guy Luke Renfield stalking people on the website. I shouldn't have made you feel bad about the situation you were in."

I took some time processing that. Ashok got antsy.

"Now I'm probably making things worse by bringing it up. I'll leave you alone. I just wanted to say, Ethan, you're an amazing person. You were always amazing, and I should've been there for you instead of making you feel bad about the choices you made."

My insides warmed. "You're not making things worse. That means a lot. Y'know, none of us know how to deal with this." I glanced away. "People act like I need to be handled with care. Or they just stare at me like I'm some kind of superhero. Really what I want is to be treated like a normal person so I can start feeling normal again, but none of this is normal, so I can't really blame anyone."

Ashok grinned. "You kinda are a superhero. I don't think I would've been so brave. You saved people's lives. That guy Luke Renfield wanted to kill everyone at Tau."

"I didn't really have a choice. I bet you would've done the same thing."

"*I* think you're really brave. And y'know, I think instead of everyone walking on eggshells at this goodbye party, we should be celebrating you. The news headlines should be: Ethan Leavitt Saved New Jersey State's First LGBTQ+ Frat."

I scoffed. Guys had come up to me to pump me up for what I'd done. They'd been quiet about it, but there were reasons for that. Anyway, I didn't feel like I deserved all kinds of praise.

"It's complicated. I mean, two of our brothers died. And the frat's disbanding. People don't want to be associated with it anymore."

"I get that," Ashok said. "But I don't think it's fair. What Luke Renfield did was a hate crime against all queer people. Tau was a good place. I probably sounded down about it sometimes, but the truth is, it helped me a lot. We shouldn't all be running off like we're ashamed of having been part of it."

I hadn't thought of it that way, but deep down, I'd been feeling it. He was so right. None of us deserved to be terrorized by some crazy homophobe. In a way, it was like he'd won, destroying the fraternity. I think that was a big part of my grief. I made a mental note to talk to my counselor about that. On top of losing friends and losing my sense of safety, I was losing my sense of pride now that the place that had accepted me was shutting down.

"I hope that was okay to say."

"It was totally okay to say." I was suddenly feeling drained, which happened two or three times a day. I sat back down on the couch and invited Ashok to sit next to me. I didn't have many friends I could really talk to about how I was feeling, and I really appreciated him.

Though it took me time to say what was on my mind. "I'm just so angry and so tired all the time."

"Do you want a back scratch?" he asked.

I smiled so hard, a tear formed in my eye. "I'd love a back scratch."

He sat up sideways and got both his hands lightly scratching my shoulders. My body melted from the sensation. I hadn't had so much relief from all the tension I was holding in weeks.

"You should be the next president of Tau."

I smirked. "I don't think I'm president material. And there's no frat to be president of anymore."

"You didn't hear? A group of us put in an application to form a new fraternity next year. We did some research. If we have new officers and bylaws, we can get rechartered by national. Nine guys from our pledge class signed on, and we're pulling in some other people."

"You're coming back next year?"

"Yeah. My parents aren't thrilled about it, especially my dad, but I told them it's what I want to do. Then my sisters laid into them. They said it was hypocritical to make me move back home and transfer to a local college when they'd raised all of us to be proud of who we are. Anyway, they paid my housing deposit just yesterday."

I desperately hoped my parents would do the same thing. It suddenly felt like things were coming into focus. I needed to be at New Jersey State. I didn't belong anywhere else. I wanted my chance to get off academic probation. I'd grown up a lot since the fall semester, and I had a ton of reasons to do better, including proving to that psychopath Luke Renfield that he hadn't destroyed me or any of the brothers.

"I'll sign on to the new frat," I told him. "I mean, there's a good chance my parents won't let me come back, but if you need another supporter, I'll help."

Ashok stopped scratching and held my shoulders. "That would be great. Is it okay if I hugged you?"

I nodded. Ashok embraced me from the back with his arms crossed around my middle. It was warm and snug, and then Ashok sniffled and hiccupped tears while he held me.

"I'm sorry," he said. "I've been emotional the past few weeks."

I clasped his arm. "It's okay. I've been emotional too."

He rested his chin on my shoulder. "I'm so glad you're okay."

We sat tucked up together while a lot of things streamed through my head. I could ask my counselor how to talk to my parents about returning to school next year. She'd said she agreed that keeping up with things that meant a lot to me was important. Through all my experiences that year, I was feeling like I wanted to learn about organizations and politics, and we'd talked about me changing majors if I came back in the fall. I could do it. I'd work all summer to save money and show my parents I was responsible. They had to let me come back. What happened with the frat was terrible, but I needed to stand strong and continue with college to get past it.

I'd come back next year, live in the dorms, and work really hard in my classes. I'd have my friends Ashok and Oliver, and hopefully Jayson too. I didn't know which other brothers Ashok was talking about, but we'd have our posse and maybe we could start Tau over again. I know it's corny, but I thought about a phoenix rising from the ashes. Too often, when I'd been knocked down, I just gave up and withdrew into myself. I wasn't going to do that anymore. This time felt even more important. I was going to show myself and show the world I was a fearless, proud gay man. Not just for me. For everyone like me. I smiled to myself. If I put it like that, how could my mom and dad say no?

About the author

Romeo Preminger has been called the master of the romantic thriller. He's the author of over a dozen books including the Southern Gothic Arizona series, the branded romantic thriller series Guilty Pleasures Editions, some naughty shorts called Storybook Editions, and two erotic romance standalones.

Romeo lives on the East Coast with his husband. Beyond writing, some of his favorite jobs on his resume are a brief stint as a zookeeper, an even briefer stint as a hot dog vendor, and a more substantial career as a counselor and advocate for LGBTQ+ youth. For more about Romeo, visit: https://romeopreminger.com or connect with him on Twitter at https://twitter.com/ PremingerRomeo.

Sign up for his mailing list at: http://eepurl.com/g5f64b

Don't miss out!

Visit the website below and you can sign up to receive emails whenever Romeo Preminger publishes a new book. There's no charge and no obligation.

https://books2read.com/r/B-A-KOQJB-ZTBFD

BOOKS 2 READ

Connecting independent readers to independent writers.

Also by Romeo Preminger

Guilty Pleasures Editions
Campus Call Boy
The Manny
Bad Stepfather
Killer Twins
Frat House Secrets

Storybook Editions
Wolf and the Three Little Pigs
Goldie and the Three Bears
Jaleel and His Three Suitors
The Three Idiot Brothers

The Arizona series
Sins of Yesterday
Daddy's Boy
Ties That Bind
Promises We Keep
When Fallen Angels Fly

Standalone
Thiago
Vegas

Watch for more at https://romeopreminger.com/.